Fragmented Fates

(Fragmented Fates Duology, #1)

Nancy Foster

Text copyright © 2024 by Nancy Foster. Mexico
Cover: Opм Twitter @armd_39

ISBN-13: 978-607-29-5551-6

NOTE TO ALL MY READERS

Thank you for reading my work, which was an effort that took nearly 2 years to complete. I hope to reach more readers and know their thoughts about my work without preference or bias. Love it or hate it, I'd love to read reviews and valuable ideas which will help me become a much better writer!

Visit the official website of the series in:
http://anominousbook.blogspot.com

CONTENTS

ACKNOWLEDGMENTS

I once again thank the people that have given me valuable advice on this book. Thank you Memo for your valid suggestions that made Talgel a far more intriguing character. I am also so deeply appreciative of my cover artist Armd for the fabulous work and hope to work with you again for the sequel of this duology.

CHAPTER 1 ♦ JAMARNID

(THE PAST)

"We execute Äimite guards for five reasons. Do you recall them?"

"Y…es, my Master." Jamarnid stopped scribbling on the sheet of paper and lifted his head to stare at the elegantly dressed elf whose face was beautiful and malefic. Salman had been waiting for this moment for the past few months. It seemed like he wanted to prolong the condemned black-haired elf's humiliation until the bitter end. Jamarnid set the quiver on the silver scroll and stared at the cursive Elvish script letters of his unfinished will. It was strange for him to wear white cotton robes, which only prolonged his lingering feeling of defeat. This is just another reminder that he was no longer considered a guard before being condemned to death today.

Salman soon grew impatient from Jamarnid's indecision. His manicured nails tapped the armrest of his throne on the grand patio with voracious impatience. "Have the guards been torturing you so much during your stay in Eurfouyr Prison that you forgot how to speak when your Master and owner asked you a simple question? Now, answer me!"

Jamarnid shuddered the instant Salman's clenched fist pounded against the armrest. Part of him felt guilty that he couldn't stand up and place an ointment on the fresh bruise Salman had on his hand to numb the pain. Despite the dire situation he ended up in, he appreciated the ruling Elf King and would always remain loyal to him. He spoke in a soft yet audible voice. "The five capital crimes of the Äimite Guard are: desertion, murder of the commander of the guard without justification, purposeful injuries of the Master or their offspring, impregnation with the Master or any of the officially recognized blood heirs, and…." His voice jittered from the shame.

Instead of showing insult, Salman rubbed his injured hand and grinned. "You were a well-behaved guard ever since you proclaimed your oath and never suffered from a flogging for any infractions. I still can't believe you would fall for such a vile-looking whore."

Laughter invaded the patio from every direction. Jamarnid caught a brief glimpse of Lord Serumo, the current ruler of the Grey Clan, and his distant cousin at the same time. The blond elf adorned in grey silk robes and a small hat sighed, showing no other emotion. The constant and almost imperceptible shifting of his feet implied the only hint of his true thoughts. Was he nervous about being labeled the mockery of the kingdom because of his imprudence, or did he have to show a small modicum of respect?

"You worthless bastard! Damn you and your debauchery!" A tall blond elf wearing grey silk robes pointed his finger at Jamarnid.

It did not surprise Jamarnid his nephew Hormandra would exert such a blatant display of impoliteness. Serumo was meanwhile drumming his fingers with increased ferocity than before.

Seeing Jamarnid was unwilling to continue speaking, a medium-height elf with unruly medium-length brown hair stood forward. As commander of the guard, Lord Ferhyr wore the Äimite Guard's most elegant ceremonial uniform, and a velvet half cape that covered his black leather armor with a silver chain. He spoke in a stern and condescending tone of voice. "You forgot to add the rule where we also execute our kind if they breed with someone who isn't an elf."

The laughter and jeers only grew louder as Jamarnid closed his dark green eyes because they condemned him for this very reason. He hunched his back and tears fell from his eyes.

Joviality embraced Salman today. "I can't believe it! Why did you throw away a promising career as one of my prized servants to sleep with a pitiful peasant? Ooh, but before you dare speak your mind, I wish to further stress to our beloved guests that you didn't fall in love with an elf. A pity because there are plenty of delightful women in our civilized nation."

Hormandra's laughter echoed the loudest among the public, prompting Serumo to tug his oldest son's sleeve in the hopes he'd stop embarrassing him.

Salman gloated even more. "I might have even felt a small pang of respect if you had slept with a human instead. Humans don't allure me, but Lord Yureha's fiancée Selina was suitable enough to merit my explicit blessing for their upcoming marriage next year. Foolish love-struck Jamarnid of the Grey Clan. You just had to stoop to the lowest denominator possible and impregnate a filthy harlequin!"

Discreetly, Jamarnid's eyes fluttered upon hearing this statement. He never expected Chandrice to possess demonic ancestry. On all accounts, save for her hazel eyes that sometimes glowed in the sun and darker skin, she looked like an ordinary human.

Ferhyr's restlessness increased as the sun lowered on the horizon and lifted his arm. The patio fell silent. Unlike Salman, he avoided revealing anything that resembled mockery and felt more of a tint of utter disdain for the condemned elf. "Lord Jamarnid, I bet you wonder why your captors let you suffer in your metallic prison cell for so long. The autumn foliage is proof we are on the 8th day of the Chartreuse month. In the common human calendar, today is the 15th of November."

Silence permeated the patio while Ferhyr granted Jamarnid sufficient time to understand why they left him agonizing until that moment. He closed his eyes and tried to recall the fated day he found out Chandrice was pregnant. She should have been killed when she confessed the truth. If only he had done it! He could have claimed her death was in self-defense or some other viable excuse. Jamarnid was certain he saw a dagger hidden beneath Chandrice's clothes. Love and wistful thinking prevailed, and he tried to smuggle her through the border.

It would have been cruel to cause undue suffering to the future mother of an unwanted hybrid elf in hostile lands. This was also his only choice. Chandrice could not give birth to a hybrid elf in the kingdom as a foreigner without eliciting unwanted attention from border agents.

Disaster met his good intentions when their attempts to flee the country failed because of a scrupulous ranger. Customs agents recognized the black stone ring adorning his right hand that marked him as a guard. Like a fool, Jamarnid claimed Chandrice was a petty criminal, and he was only smuggling her across the border out of pity. It was a bold move, but pointless because she didn't have an arrest warrant. They quenched his hopes of avoiding the death penalty on the day of his trial. Dragged into Salman's throne room like a caged animal, his heart sunk at the sight of Chandrice's protruding belly which guaranteed his sentence.

Jamarnid lifted his head and stared at Salman's cold blue eyes. "They left me alive until the child was born. Am I correct?"

Salman nodded with a sinister grin. "Like Ferhyr said, you are clever, but hopelessly foolish. I even had a few bets with some guards. Whoever guessed the date of your child's birth would earn the honor of being your two executioners."

Two guards stood forward. The guard standing to the right was a rare red-haired elf with countless freckles and a perfectly groomed mustache. Solid proof of the guard's human ancestry, which made him mortal.

It didn't take Jamarnid very long to recognize the second executioner. Tall, muscular and wearing his blond hair in a ponytail. His commanding presence complemented a handsome but hardened face that screamed for respect. "This is going to be real fun. Been ages since I last executed one of my kin."

Jamarnid shivered when he heard Froylan's baritone voice. There was no doubt Froylan was going to enjoy every minute of his execution. This observation prompted Jamarnid to examine him further, and a small gasp escaped his lips. For some unexplained reason, Froylan wasn't wearing his short cape like usual.

Another two guards soon arrived and gave the lucky executioners polished black masks with devilish horns. After fastening the masks, now all Jamarnid could see were their eyes that stared at him with equal revulsion.

Salman spoke once again. "In case you are wondering, the child was not born in my palace. Even though I had a vested interest in confirming its lineage, polluting these sacred grounds with its existence would be unacceptable. I had qualified medics tending to your lover to ensure she remained alive at all costs during her incarceration in Lord Serumo's palace. Given you were once a member of the nobility class of his clan, your lover should feel glad she spent her house arrest in relative comfort. Well, until we confirmed the child's identity and issued your long-awaited death warrant," a snicker escaped his lips.

Jamarnid sighed with a strange sense of relief. Even though he would have loved to see his child and Chandrice one last time, perhaps it was better that she didn't see him die. After glimpsing his will, he initially wanted to apologize to his clan for bringing them shame by straying from the oath he proudly took.

Pleased with the brief apology, Jamarnid hoped Lord Serumo treated Chandrice well during her ordeal. Most likely the poor child would end up as a social pariah. At least Serumo would provide some help until the infant died from old age.

A tint of determination prompted Jamarnid to write one last request on his will on Chandrice's behalf. Jamarnid finished writing and placed it on the table. Even though he wished he could delay his death, stalling his execution would entice Commander Ferhyr to rip his will apart in retribution.

Feeling convinced everyone had stopped wasting time, Ferhyr turned towards Salman. "Shall we begin, Master Lord Salman?"

It didn't even take Salman a second before he rested on the chair and nodded in agreement. "You may proceed."

Ferhyr then lifted his arm. "Begin the execution!"

Several guards took the small wooden table away, and guards ripped away Jamarnid's white execution tunic, revealing a skimpy white cotton loincloth. Jamarnid shivered from the icy wind caressing his exposed skin.

With acute dexterity, Lord Einman's phantom beast that was placed inside Jamarnid's body dug into the recesses of his mind to control his body's movements. The elf gritted his teeth at the mental strain of the invisible force that burned alien thoughts into his mind.

Jamarnid felt huge respect for Einman's immense talent in manipulating his body as he knelt before a granite stone tablet and offered his hands. Saliva gurgled into his throat.

As the two masked executioners approached him while carrying a pair of hammers, only one thought entered his mind. Anyone in his dire situation would presume he was afraid of the impending pain or sadness of shaming their family.

No, the only thing occupying Jamarnid's mind was the relentless tapping of Serumo's feet. Was his distant cousin afraid of watching him suffer? That was a logical possibility, which Jamarnid couldn't care much about. He would be dead in a few minutes, so it no longer mattered.

Ferhyr's dreaded voice boomed in every direction. "First, we must smash the convict's fingers who wielded his sword against his oath!"

Jamarnid shut his eyes and felt the small pair of hammers crush his fingers. He expected the pain and screeched as silently as possible to avoid giving Froylan the increased joy of hearing his complaints. Out of a morbid sense of curiosity, he opened his eyes to see the damage done. Instead of severing his fingers like Jamarnid expected, the executioners were careful to maim his hands without detaching them.

Before Jamarnid processed the pain, Ferhyr spoke once again.

"Second, we must smash the convict's feet who must not feel the earth of our land that his actions tainted!"

Jamarnid's shoulder trembled when he felt both guards aiming their small hammers for his feet. On this occasion, they were more forceful, and he collapsed to the ground from the sheer brutality of the blow.

"Why aren't you begging for mercy, Jamarnid? Do you want us to maim your limbs in disorder? Been a long time since a guard was last executed by the Puppet Man Method. There are always ways to move things around a bit."

Jamarnid bit his tongue and vowed to avoid falling for Froylan's taunt. Let him enjoy depriving him of that one tidbit of fulfillment. Froylan wasn't the commander, so he had few moral qualms about ignoring him.

Salman chuckled when he heard that. "No wonder you are my favorite, Froylan dearest. As long as he suffers in agony from his limbs being crushed into pieces while we still have some sunlight, I see no qualms to… move things around a little."

Ferhyr instantly gasped. "My Master! I don't care if you have a preference towards one of my men over me. We shouldn't be wasting any more time! You know fully well Jamarnid must die before it is nightfall!"

The warning only inflated Salman's ego as a cunning grin invaded his face. "What blatant nonsense you say! I know his death warrant will become voided the second the sun vanishes. And then I would have to let him scamper off for that crime. I also know nothing stops me from writing an edict to have him decapitated whenever I feel like it. Froylan, I give you the right to smash his limbs; however, you see fit."

Froylan chuckled because Salman had just given him his blessing.

Jamarnid couldn't believe it. Being executed by the Puppet Man Method was not objectionable because he accepted his guilt. Even more so because with his ruined body, he was good as dead anyway. Perhaps a talented medic could save his hands, but not his feet. Jamarnid shut his eyes and hoped Froylan would purposely choose his hip so he could die of hemorrhagic shock as soon as possible.

Froylan strode to the table which held several pairs of increasingly large hammers. His hands had a hard time choosing which of them he should select. Froylan garnered a sick eagerness reminiscent of a child about to squish an ant.

The second executioner growled at once and grabbed the second smallest hammer to abide by tradition. "Senior Lord Froylan, what in the hell are you thinking?"

"I thought I had garnered more respect since the Master promoted me to a senior position. Seems like I need to take you under my wing. I need to snap that sense of disobedience from your system, Lord Barmor."

Barmor stared at the hordes of elves gossiping in the distance. It was hard to discern what the guests were saying because of the relentless pounding of ceremonial drums. It only heightened his desire to stick to the original plan. "The Master told you to crush him however you see fit, but I will follow the tradition of the guard. My Master condemned Lord Jamarnid, not you. Upon his death, Jamarnid will be pardoned and buried dressed in his uniform like any other guard."

Mocking laughter escaped Froylan's lips. "Look at you! Huffing like a puffer fish while you parrot complete nonsense in front of me! It sure looks like I will need to assign you to serve under me once this is over."

Barmor seemed unfazed by the threat and stood even taller than before. "Whatever Serumo's clan does after Lord Jamarnid dies is not our concern." With those words said, Barmor aimed the second hammer at Jamarnid's wrists.

While Barmor wasted time arguing with Froylan, the assistant guards had already turned Jamarnid around and placed his four limbs on top of clean slabs of stone.

Froylan opted to aim for Jamarnid's left shin. It only infuriated Barmor even more that Froylan selected a medium-sized hammer instead of a larger one out of spite. Given Salman gave Froylan his verbal blessing to alter the tradition, Barmor preferred to focus on his gruesome task.

Ferhyr smirked as he spoke again while trying to ignore Froylan's blatant disobedience. "Third, we must smash the convict's wrists who will never punch the air again!"

Whereas Barmor followed Ferhyr's command, Froylan viciously aimed for the shin to guarantee the scream he wanted so much from Jamarnid. It was bad enough that Jamarnid felt his right wrist crumble into pieces. Worse, Froylan was so demeaning in the angle of his swing that Jamarnid couldn't take it anymore and yelped.

Froylan laughed hysterically at once. "My little plan to make you suffer worked pretty well." Without bothering to wait for the order, Froylan smashed Jamarnid's remaining wrist with the same weapon and rushed off to get the next hammer.

Both guards soon returned. Before Ferhyr ushered his command, Froylan smashed both of Jamarnid's kneecaps. The unfortunate guard stammered an inaudible insult as he gasped at the pain.

A crash of metal soon ensued when Barmor dropped his hammer to the ground and stood forward to protest. "Why are you insulting everyone like this?"

Froylan couldn't care less about Barmor's complaints. "We must fulfill the execution before the sun sets. Unlike you, I would prefer that Jamarnid dies from blood loss over decapitation. Go write a letter to a senior guard to complain, not that I care too much."

As Jamarnid tried to fathom the pain and sorrow he felt, two last strokes on his ankles severed his feet apart. To hell with his pride at this point. Jamarnid screamed as loud as he could. The pounding of both drums stopped, and the patio fell silent.

"Please show mercy for his lordship!"

After Jamarnid recovered from the initial surge of pain, he turned his head around. Serumo was standing while he trembled nonstop when he realized what he had just done.

Froylan was not in the least pleased. "Begging for a condemned elf's life, Serumo? Want to join him? Or are you only buying some more time?"

Serumo's jitteriness only increased without wishing to address the commander.

Serumo's charade did not convince Salman. "You care about your kin. Too late to save him, I am afraid. Would you prefer to switch places and have Jamarnid live the rest of his days as a clan leader? Oh wait, I forgot! A permanently maimed clan leader!"

Jamarnid's consciousness evaded him. While everyone wasted their time arguing, the injury to his legs was causing significant blood loss. Soon he will pass out, and none of this will matter anymore.

"You're wrong!" A determined Hormandra stood dangerously close to the protective barrier field. With a circular motion of his arm, mana invaded his body. White feathery appendages appeared on Hormandra's forearm, which extended and clashed against the silvery barrier field, causing white electrical sparks to shoot in the ground.

The guards nearby gasped at once. "That nobleelf has found a weakness in the barrier field!"

Ferhyr's voice sounded distant but more desperate than before. "Arrest that traitor and continue with the execution before it's too late!"

Jamarnid tried to focus, but it was increasingly difficult because of his injuries. He heard yelling, the summoning of countless phantom beasts, screams, and yells.

Froylan couldn't resist the temptation to fight with more opponents and charged ahead while he summoned fire magic.

The more sensible Barmor stood forward with the giant hammer aiming at Jamarnid's face. Tear droplets fell from the bottom of the mask. "Forgive me for skipping to the end, but they have left me with no other choice."

Jamarnid hoped Serumo and Hormandra didn't end up being decapitated for stalling his execution because he felt ready to go.

Instead of having the guard smash his skull to death, something else happened. The hammer crashed against the ground, and Barmor fell right in front of him. Shards of the porcelain mask broke in half upon Barmor's fall and revealed an inert expression on the guard's face.

Blood spewed on the ground, and Jamarnid soon realized something: Barmor was dead, and it looked like Serumo sent someone to rescue him. But who just killed his executioner, and for what purpose?

"Sorry that we are late, my Lord! My name is Garlas, and I have arrived to rescue you from your horrible fate!" The stranger fastened something on Jamarnid's legs that awakened him even further.

Jamarnid attempted to speak with difficulty. "A tourniquet? Leave me to die and flee while you still can, dear elf."

Garlas covered his body with a wool coat and picked him up. "Eat this. It is a potion that will buy you time." As if on cue, the mysterious man shoved something pasty and bitter into Jamarnid's mouth that he reluctantly chewed to speak. He then felt a jolt into the air, accompanied by a chilly breeze. Jamarnid's green eyes opened wide when he realized the paste was helping him recover consciousness somehow.

It did little to numb the agonizing pain in Jamarnid's body. There was something wrong with his anonymous rescuer. They were flying in the sky towards the looming night, yet Jamarnid couldn't feel any mana.

That was when reality hit: Garlas not only flew in the air without using a phantom beast, there was something odd about his rescuer.

While the darkness and blood loss made it difficult to see the man's face, his eyes glowed a bright pink hue. It was then when Jamarnid realized something: Garlas was most likely a harlequin, and he came to the Elf Kingdom to save his life at all costs.

CHAPTER 2 ♦ TALGEL

Talgel was an elf of exquisite beauty intermixed with an allure of mystery. As the seer of Almjarhad, it was her duty to foresee any adverse events and prevent them from happening at all costs. She was a mortal elf with harlequin ancestry, colloquially known as a halfling.

Just like most halflings, her skin had a medium sepia tone, glossy grey hair, which she wore in an assortment of hairstyles, and a penchant for wearing salient jewelry.

What always draws people's attention when they see her is nothing above. Whether a person saw her in the street or from far off, the masquerade mask only revealed a sinister grin on her crimson lips and the twitches of her pointy nose. Was the mask gold with gems? Or did it have feathers? Neither option would matter; each person let their imagination fill in the blanks.

Why would anyone care whether the mask had a doo-daw or a knick-knack? The only actual embellishment that mattered was in Talgel's eyes. At one time, they were a deep red that glittered flickers in the sun.

Whenever an observant was paying any proper attention, they'd realize there was no figment of a soul in that vacant expression. Her eyes never moved sideways nor vertically. They stared straight ahead with an impassive glare. Some people even believe Talgel never blinked, but the adornments of the mask made it difficult to discern whether this rumor was true.

On this day, Talgel was on a secret mission. Forfeiting an armed escort or delegating this task to anyone else went against common sense. Despite the dangers, Talgel would visit the neighboring nomadic settlement today alone.

"Don't do it!"

Talgel shook her head as her unreadable masqueraded face stared absentmindedly at the busy dirt streets while red dust particles gusted everywhere. That was not her conscience; it was just another echo of Jarahad's gruff voice. Sorrow imbued deep inside for hurting his feelings. Talgel will find a way to apologize later because she needed to perform this task alone. Such were her odd quirks. Not even Talgel could appreciate why her right hand clasped the dagger

Jarahad gifted her just the other day. Only that a nagging feeling deep inside implied it would come in handy.

She fastened a sachet containing simple travel supplies on her back and a leather pouch with coins on her hip. Talgel passed through the endless bustle of the still primitive-looking town of Almjarhad, wearing her first-month grey rayon dress that flowed with the roaring wind and relentless summer heat.

"Lady Talgel, would you fancy a shawl?"

"Going on an errand to his lordship's palace?"

With a polite nod, Talgel dismissed the good intentions of the villagers and scampered off. Her lithe figure drew the attention of some elves and even the rare harlequin daring to venture outside before the midday heat became too oppressive. Talgel soon reached the final tent on the outskirts. A vast cliff was looming ahead.

Talgel retrieved a crude walking stick from her belt with a heavy sigh. *"Seems like I will need this."*

Her youth overcame weariness and pain as she ascended the mighty cliff that protected her doomed homeland. She will forever feel glad for her people's magic because they maintained the dirt road flat.

"And to think he would have had a fit if he knew I went alone."

It was apparent what Talgel was referring to... or more precisely, who was in her thoughts. With a sigh, she tried to lock those pleasant thoughts away into the deepest recesses of her mind. This was no time for lamenting a romance with no future. She only knew she must travel this route on this exact date, and time was of the most critical essence. It mattered little whether her kin believed she was mad for embarking on a rather pointless journey. She had to do it at all costs.

With the constant taps of the walking stick, Talgel's ascent meshed with the sound of wood clashing against the stone. This effort became intertwined with the blithering wind hitting her face and the heat, which worsened with each minute.

Soon enough, exhaustion forced Talgel to retrieve her water canister and sip its contents. The road eventually flattened as the hours passed with no sight of other merchants passing by. The temptation to sit down and rest was alluring, but Talgel heeded those nagging thoughts and ventured on.

"No time to waste. I must go."

A blasting wind replaced the coastal humidity with its dryness and cold. It didn't take long for Talgel to mumble in annoyance as she felt compelled to fasten her locks into a simple ponytail, and she continued pacing without rest.

When the path steadied into the thanklessly dead valleys ahead, Talgel hurried her pace even more. Even though she was careful not to suffer any falls, she never rested her weathered body while sweat fell from her temples. As the hours passed, Talgel counted each turn on the road. She heaved in stark relief when she reached the fourteenth turn on the right.

"I did it!"

Featured in this turn was a small pagoda with a stone table and some stools alongside the path. Wind continued bellowing in every direction. The simple structure had a ceiling of thatched sticks that shielded her from the rays above.

This time, Talgel placed the walking stick aside and hungrily feasted on her waterskin.

"Why, hello there, fellow traveler! Going to barter with the nomads?!"

A grin invaded Talgel's mouth, and she perked from the source. Standing in front was a human with unremarkable features, filthy skin, sweaty rags, and a menacing face partially covered by a scarf.

"Good afternoon to you, too. The things I do are none of your concern, human traveler. What brings you to the brinks of Almjarhad?"

A sputter of saliva collided on the ground and hissed upon impact. The man jeered as he admired the delicate features of her body with a wicked grin. "You mutt skins sure love to take what is not yours. Invaded my ancestor's lands so recently, and you have already given a name to your shantytown of refugees?"

Talgel straightened her back and grinned in defiance. "You spew hatred against the elves and harlequins that have lived in peace. And yet your short-term memory has forfeited something important. Your kind, who could not grow crops in the desert or flatten the rocks in the bay to dock ships, left these unforgiving lands abandoned. Likewise, if any tribes need to address their qualms regarding our theft of worthless lands, they are free to visit his lordship's palace hall and barter an agreement."

"Cut off the lies, you skank, and give me your money!" With a dagger drawn, Talgel surmised from the beginning this wanderer was up to no good. Just another pathetic bandit out of his luck.

Talgel remained seated and stared in his direction, her unusually glossy eyes reflecting the sunlight with an unnaturalness that was beyond distracting. "Guard your weapon and let me be. You still have a chance."

"Like hell, you won't! I'm gonna cut off those ruby eyes and feed them to the dogs!" With lightning speed, the man charged toward the unnerved elf with his dagger aimed at her right eye. Talgel remained immobile without flinching as the edge skidded from the surface and slid off her right cheek harmlessly.

Expecting to see a gash of blood spewing, the shock of being unable to harm the woman at all awed the man. "Impossible!" Without waiting for any explanations, his hand clutched the hilt and dared slash her left eye to the same effect. Talgel remained rather bored from the pitiful display. It irritated the man when her impassive face never blinked even once under the shielded mask from either attack.

"You realize that by attacking me, you have sealed your fate. There are no longer any paths you can follow except for the one of your prompt demise," Talgel snarled.

The man observed his blade and soon laughed after confirming it remained as sharp as ever. "You may have some tricks under your sleeves, but I will kill you!"

"And yet you haven't been able to steal my eyes."

This taunt proved all too much. Instead of attacking Talgel's crimson eyes that continued shining among the brief glimpses of sunlight offered by the pavilion's roof, the bandit hurled his weapon instead at her forehead in the hopes of a swift kill. Unlike the past two offenses, Talgel tilted her back upon impact in a perfectly timed reflex reaction.

Instead of the crunching of Talgel's skull, both parties heard a distinct sound instead: the cracking of fractured ceramic.

"What?"

With a grin that seemed almost unnatural, Talgel took the annoyance of standing upright and stepped forward. She purposely tilted her face to reveal two odd-looking eyes. They were indeed crimson, like most of her race, with white sclera and pupils reminiscent of cat eyes. But the better view afforded by the lifted eyelids offered the man a terrifying sight. Nestled on her forehead where the dagger hit its mark was a thin ceramic mask beneath the masquerade decoration while cracks splintered the mask into two. It ultimately fell to the ground with a loud thud.

A pool of blood intertwined with splinters lodged into her skin littered Talgel's forehead from the impact, along with the eyes…

"Those are not eyes!"

"Given you have ruined the face that an artisan friend of mine gifted me, I guess you can feast on the truth you had ignored the whole time we have been enjoying this fruitless endeavor."

Without haste, Talgel removed the damaged parts of the mask that still clung to her face. Ceramic with mesh wiring crashed to the ground into pieces, followed by two glass eyeballs.

Standing before the man was an elf who had revealed her true self: a face unhindered by a meticulously crafted mask to hide her maimed appearance, aged far beyond the expected youth of her body, along with a pair of empty eye sockets.

The macabre discovery caused the man to toss the dagger to the ground and step backward. "You blood-sucking demons! So it is true your kind remove your eyes to eat them!"

It was only now that Talgel stood to her full height and her hand played with an ivory dagger hilt adorned with emeralds. Deviousness imbued a cruel grin onto Talgel's bloodied face. "For a long time, I had a vision where I had to visit this place to meet a fool. The idiot brought shame to his tribe when he had his way with a teenage slave. A wealthy merchant brought her during an important visit. You became a man of no worth who was honor-bound to live his days in exile and become another pitiful thief to make ends meet. I have seen your life. I lived through the pain you did to that girl and how she felt so hopeless because fighting the tribe leader's son would have garnered the death penalty."

"Impossible! I never told this to anyone!"

Cruelty etched upon Talgel's bloodied face. "Yes, I saw it. And I know what happened afterward. Perhaps you never found out, but the girl became pregnant with your child. As a token to appease the insulted tribe, your people liberated her. She ended up as your father's newest wife. Her child is now occupying the place you lost. While relations with that tribe inevitably soured, there are hopes they might make amends someday. She didn't get the life she expected, but your father has treated her well. You are suffering from the scabbing disease. How long has it been since you have last seen your face in a mirror, Yawad?"

The man gasped. A scarf hid part of his face that he pulled aside and felt the wound on his cheek. "How could you know all of this?"

"I have lost my eyes and gained something more. I may not always understand why I see the future of some individuals and not others. But I have answered my doubts regarding yours today. The only interesting thing about all of this is the fact you will be the first person who dies by my hand."

"What?!" Before Yawad could flee or defend himself, Talgel rushed forward with a speed that seemed impossible and pressed her dagger against his heart. As life seeped through his wound, she twisted the dagger to spew even more blood and sped up his bitter end.

With his strength all but gone, Yawad collapsed on the sand and stared at her hollow eyes with welling tears. "How did you know?"

Talgel felt a pang of regret for not telling him why she knew she had to embark on this voyage on this specific day to kill a stranger. Seeing futures that offered better outcomes vanish from her target always caused a nasty aftertaste. It was one thing she never enjoyed about her unique gift.

Before Talgel could answer, Yawad was already dead. Talgel's body movements soon became disjointed and forceful. Her hands rummaged on the ground and touched the round glass of one of her artificial eyes. She felt a layer of cracked shards on the entire surface.

"Darn, he is going to be pissed off. I ruined them."

If there were any hints that Talgel was in a rush to visit the nomad market, her reluctance to get off the stool as she stared into the unremarkable landscape that afternoon was proof her trip was a sham from the very beginning. As nightfall was about to arrive, Talgel turned her head and sighed.

Rushing in her direction was a familiar dark-skinned male elf adorned with leather armor fastened above elegant grey robes as he rode in her direction by horseback. "Talgel!" As expected, he was being followed closely by several guards that shrieked at the gruesome sight.

There was no need for introductions. Talgel was certain Jarahad had just found out about her escapade and arrived too late to act as her hero in shining armor. She didn't offer any resistance to his firm embrace as tears swelled from his eyes. All she could feel was the pounding of her heart.

"You are wounded!"

Talgel shoved him away with indifference. "Thank you for the dagger. It has proven to be useful."

"Why didn't you ask for an armed escort if you planned to visit the merchants today? I would have gladly come with you!"

It was the answer Talgel knew from the start would happen, but she had to do this alone. She averted his gaze and sighed. "There are a lot of events I will have to do that you and the others may not understand. Sometimes I will explain them to you. On other occasions, I must wait a very long time for them to happen on their own. I knew this day would arrive several years ago. I hoped to change the future so that you would suffer less heartache over my well-being. Please send my apologies to Daedoman. I believe I ruined the mask he crafted for me."

Before she knew it, Jarahad didn't waste a second lifting her into his embrace as they began the long voyage home by horseback. From the silence, it was undeniable proof she hurt Jarahad's feelings, which only caused Talgel to feel a deep sense of dread. As much as she wanted to kiss his lips and tell him everything would be all right, she knew she couldn't return his feelings. Knowing this harsh truth was far more painful than becoming blind.

Talgel's actions warranted a chain reaction of consequences. It was something she expected, given her arrival with a bloodied face while in Jarahad's company. The extent of his overreaction was still irritating to her.

Upon their first arrival, Almjarhad was a desolate bay with gold sand, a few palm trees, cacti, clay soil, and rugged dark stone. Deemed to be uninhabitable by humans because no potable water sources existed and the sea was impassable, the newcomers worked tirelessly to survive.

Twelve years had passed since their arrival. Instead of starvation, Almjarhad was now a dotted landscape of sloping hillsides with dozens of leather tents. Palm tree saplings had grown tall enough to offer coconuts while the constant stampedes well-trod the dirt roads. Further away from the slanted town center were rectangular stone water reservoirs with interconnecting tubes that reached the ocean. In the distance, citizens were bustling in the fields, growing various crops while livestock such as sheep and goats grazed.

At this time of year, there weren't a lot of edible plants for the poor animals except for meddlesome thorny bushes. Deemed to be useless even as lumber, Talgel discovered long ago its flowers had a pleasant smell. Along with the goats, she was probably the only person who didn't hate them.

As the only permanent building in the city so far, Almjarhad Palace was still in its early stages of construction. A planned domed roof atop the throne room remained exposed to the outdoor elements. The dry season was the best time of the year to construct the metallic skeleton. To shelter builders from the oppressive summer heat meant they had to work in the afternoon and early evening. As a result, a cacophony of pounding and metal invaded Talgel's surroundings. Even though Talgel wished the pureblood harlequins could be more useful in building more durable structures, she didn't mind her spartan living accommodations.

Jarahad brought her directly inside his unfinished stone palace. He rushed past the main entrance, where Talgel's battered face prompted hushed murmurs from security guards. They entered a luxurious bedroom with colorful curtains rustling against the soothing wind. He then placed her on a low-rise stone bed covered in animal furs.

A smile invaded Talgel's face as Jarahad caressed her forehead while she enjoyed the smell of his sweaty body. Lavender and mint permeated the air, and her hands touched a soft blanket made of a bear pelt. This brought back pleasant memories of her childhood when she lived in their last harlequin enclave. "You brought these belongings on purpose, so I can live here indefinitely."

Jarahad's voice trembled with doubt. "I would have never given this room to anyone else. A medic should arrive shortly to treat your wound, and you shall rest here for tonight."

Jarahad stood up and walked away. Feeling lingering remorse, Talgel grasped his wrist, prompting him to turn around. His hand felt clammy in her weak grip. "I… I am sorry for hurting your feelings today, Jarahad. I just want you to know this."

"Then why do you reject me?! I know you still harbor feelings for me!"

Talgel averted her gaze and sighed. She released her hand, and Jarahad turned around to stare at her. "I…"

"Stay away from my son, you mutt!"

A commanding and bitter voice beckoned both elves to stare at the entrance. Even though Talgel couldn't see the newcomer, there was no need for introductions. A fair-skinned elf with long black hair had interrupted their moment of solitude. Pureblood elves were few among her people, but most lived in tents as ordinary peasants. The newcomer wore black sleeping robes that didn't resemble the fashion style of the city's mixed-blood inhabitants. He sat in a wheelchair with his lap covered by a thin cotton blanket while a servant pushed it around. His maimed fingers twitched in an unnatural direction.

Jarahad spoke in a colder tone of voice than before. "Why are you up so late, father?"

"Stop treating me like a child! I demand respect!"

Talgel hissed at once. "You're the reason the kingdom exiled us, Jamarnid."

It didn't take long before Jarahad felt compelled to stand between his father and the woman who had just taunted him. With a tensed face, Jarahad bowed to the disabled elf immediately. "Please pardon Talgel's blight. A criminal attacked her earlier today, and she became injured."

Jamarnid grumbled and averted his penetrating gaze to focus on Jarahad. "Control the halflings of the clan if you wish to continue ruling it. I never asked to be saved, and you know it!"

As a servant ushered Jamarnid's wheelchair away, Jarahad sighed in relief.

Talgel wasn't convinced. "He isn't the true ruler of our people."

"Technically, nor am I," Jarahad replied with dryness.

"Then if you are against the agreement, why doesn't Sharad…."

"You know he has not opted to take my place, even though it is his birthright."

"I understand. Perhaps it is for the best that the elf remains neutral. I just wished Jamarnid…."

"He could have ordered for your execution just a minute ago. Don't continue pushing your luck any further by inciting his wrath. I know you don't like him much, but he is the clan ruler."

"That is a lot of nonsense! We are no longer ruled by the laws of the kingdom that abandoned us to our fate."

"Perhaps. However, I still have faith in the customs of our ancestors."

"But why? By living here, we have attained freedom never seen before in the history of our kind!" Talgel hollered.

Before Jarahad left the room, he stopped for a brief instant. "It's the only thing that separates us from them."

As Jarahad left her alone, Talgel knew he was referring to the harlequins.

Talgel tossed and turned relentlessly from agonizing dreams she could not remember. With a respite, she sat up with a startled face.

"How are you doing?"

Talgel turned toward a sickly sweet voice. The voice beckoning her attention was female and sufficiently grave to make her suspect it didn't belong to a teenage elf. "Good morning. Are you a harlequin, by any chance?"

"Oh, my! Lord Jarahad told me you were witty. I just can't believe you could have discovered my identity so soon. I tried my earnest not to make any noise with my wings."

"Don't feel surprised. I can discover things much more easily than most, miss… Henrietta."

Talgel couldn't see her visitor, but she knew Henrietta had a handsome face for a pureblood harlequin. Her umber skin was free of any blemishes or wrinkles. A pair of pink eyes glared in the dimly lit room as the sun peeked through the horizon in the distance. Despite being currently bald, Henrietta's beauty would have enticed more than one head to turn around if she had walked across the street. Henrietta wore a bright red dress that only highlighted her medium build and average height. Like all harlequins, she had a pair of tucked-up bat-like wings on her back, granting her the illusion she was wearing a long cape. The woman giggled at once. "Jarahad warned me about you being sharp. I am still very impressed you guessed my name so easily."

Talgel sat up and stretched her arms. "Jarahad sent you to keep a watch on me?"

"He knows you will abandon the palace now that it is sunrise. I am aware your residence is quaint, am I correct?"

Talgel sighed with annoyance. "You're going to be my roommate, are you?"

"I guess you can say that, and I don't wish to be rude. Jarahad believes that because of your handicap and what happened yesterday.…"

"Typical! He doesn't trust that I can care for myself because I am blind."

Henrietta shifted her legs, rubbing the stiff fabric with a crunching noise in the room's desolateness. "I will try to respect your peculiar lifestyle and only lend a hand regarding things like household chores." She then approached a wall to admire the bloodied dress Talgel left hanging on top of a basket last night. "Charming fabric. Jarahad told me you will probably wear the same motif for the rest of the year. I will wash it and guarantee that no stains remain."

"Well, I guess your help could come to good use. Pardon my bluntness. Have you lived in Almjarhad for long?"

"I cannot answer that."

"Huh? So you're not part of Hurrujat's clan?"

"Jarahad ordered me to be discreet regarding my personal affairs and your own. I will not divulge your secrets that don't hinder the clan's wellbeing. I hope you can abide by the same courtesy so our working relationship can run smoothly."

Henrietta's comments were disconcerting. Talgel was unsurprised Jarahad would end up assigning an assistant of some sort, but the fact he chose a harlequin over a hybrid elf was inciting her curiosity. Little did she know, Henrietta placed a cup of warm tea in her hands.

"Please drink up. It will help with the wound on your forehead."

Talgel complied, and her lips pursed as she organized her thoughts. Is this woman's presence in her life a test from Jarahad? To earn her love? That was a ridiculous possibility because she had never stopped loving him. To move into the palace? Indeed, Almjarhad Castle had perks such as servants and security guards, but living there was out of the question. She and Jamarnid shared a tepid relationship with the possibility they would inevitably fight each other to the death at the most minimal provocation. Talgel respected Jarahad and believed he was doing a suitable job, considering what little the clan had. However, Jarahad was more of a vassal ruler who couldn't disobey his father's whims. Choosing an outsider over an elf to tend to her needs was a rather odd move from Jarahad, something Talgel would research further if she had the chance. After a few sips, she settled the cup on a nearby cupboard and cleared her throat. "Has Jarahad informed you about what I do for a living?"

"I have not seen it with my eyes, but I know you are a seer."

The wheels in Talgel's head turned a notch. It was apparent her misguided former lover informed this stranger well. To what degree, she would have to find out. "You will soon discover a few things about me. We are not friends, I will only put up with you because your eyes could come in handy when I am alone, and you will never interrupt me when I perform a scrying session with my people."

If there was a second thing that surprised Talgel, it was the speed Henrietta shook her hand in effusing agreement. "I appreciate your kindness, my ladyship, and I promise I will never fail you!"

Scorching sun, soul-crushing heat, and the sound of countless pickaxes pounding the soil. Dozens of halflings were busy separating the superficial crust of stone on the surrounding slopes along the company of pureblood harlequins that flapped their wings in the air.

Among the hordes of halflings working tirelessly that day was a child with tousled grey hair, perky ears, and bright bi-colored eyes. Tioja always caused plenty of stares because of his reddish-green eyes since he was born. Just like usual, he had grown accustomed to smiling at his admirers as he continued pounding the land with a tiny shovel. It was a menial effort compared to the adults, but he didn't mind. Standing in front of him was a fellow hybrid male elf with a slight similarity to his face and short grey hair in a warrior's knot. The young teenager swiped some sweat from his brow and looked over his shoulder.

One harlequin landed and offered a bucket of ice-cold water to the workers in the distance. "Those guys sure get it easy."

Tioja continued digging in a knelt position without showing insult. "It is the summer, my dear uncle Nurran. Their skin rots if they stay outside for too long. And I believe it is most unfair that you say such vile things. While we sleep, the clan's remaining water mages purify ocean water, and the harlequins take our place building farms."

Nurran rested his head on the edge of his shovel and grumbled while he rubbed the sweat from his brow. "I still think they get it easy. How come our leader Jarahad helps with the hard labor on his assigned community service days while Hurrujat remains idle?"

"Leader Hurrujat is old and weary. You should use your energies more fruitfully, my son."

Both young elves jolted to the side to see the source of the grave voice. Standing beside them stood a pureblood male elf of medium height dressed in elvish brown peasant robes.

Tioja rushed to his side and hugged him. "Grampa Jamen!"

Jamen returned the gesture and sat on a nearby boulder. He retrieved a small leather canister. "Both of you are doing a fine job, even though community service is still voluntary for underage elves."

Whereas Tioja accepted the offer, Nurran crossed his arms. "Oh, save me from the lecture, dad! The village needs every hand we can get!"

"And does that include the harlequins?" Jamen lifted one of his thin eyebrows as he studied Nurran's heartfelt red eyes.

"Well, pardon my intrusion as an underage clan member. We are all tilling the land, building wells, and fortifying the city in the worst weather imaginable while they get to loiter."

Tioja smirked at once after he finished the waterskin's contents. "I already told you they work at night!"

Jamen sighed at once and crossed his arms as he watched the halflings working tirelessly in the distance without complaint. "Both of you have valid complaints." A tinge of regret intertwined with scant revulsion filtered through the wise elf's brown eyes as he recalled a painful memory from his past. "I never considered myself an elf of violence. I lived peacefully, obeyed the law, and respected the guard like my peers. There are things I am not proud of during the purge, and Svetlana helped me find my way during those dark times when we first fled the kingdom with our lives and nothing else. Maybe you feel resentment, Nurran, because you believe they should assist us with these grueling activities. Don't forget our clan would not be alive had it not been for the harlequins."

"But they should help us!"

"It seems like the young have short memories. Humans decimated their clan during the second purge, and they ended up with the same fate as us. Most of their mages were murdered as well. We barely hang on by the thinnest thread."

Whereas Nurran opted to kick a nearby boulder with his foot to vent his frustration, the comment saddened Tioja's face.

"You miss the kingdom and your previous life, don't you?" Tioja asked.

Jamen sighed. "I would be lying if I didn't. I was never rich or highly regarded among the noble caste. Still, my home was in a beautiful forest, with mountains that became covered by snow in the winter and maple trees that offered a stunning change of foliage in the autumn." Jamen focused his attention on the nearby bay. While the beach offered a beautiful hue of light blue on the unforgiving rock, he felt it proved to be a poor replacement for the home he had lost. "I have spoken to Sargegef about the possibility of using my earth sorcery to remove that dratted rock. Such a shame you can't enjoy swimming in those waters when it is so hot."

Nurran chuckled at the comment. "Someone in this town knows what our priorities are. Ouch!"

Tioja nudged him on the rib with a scowl. "We need fresh water to drink!"

"And a time to relax and enjoy life while it lasts." Jamen stared into the ocean's distance as the waves crashed over the rocky shoreline.

Nurran took advantage of his father's receptiveness today. "Hey pop, why did you guys choose this horrible place? While I don't mind the roasty toasty heat as much as you pale elves do, you should have chosen a better place to settle down."

"We were driven out by angry humans a few years before you were born. Hurrujat presumed another human king had allied with Master Salman to purge us for a third and final time. We soon quenched these concerns when we realized we were only overstepping a depopulated province because of an epidemic or some malady of the sort. I know it seems unfair to the second and third generation, but lessons learned from those unpleasant experiences dictated we would have to establish our new home in a swath of land nobody else wanted."

"We barely have enough to eat!" Nurran growled.

"One thing separates us from the human communities that failed to conquer these lands."

Tioja and Nurran stared at each other. "And what would that be?"

Jamen grinned for the first time that day, and mana invaded his body. A humanoid phantom beast resembling more a cutout paper human effigy than a typical earth beast appeared in the soil. With a flicker of Jamen's hand, it dug underground and shot itself in a straight line to the end of the field, leaving behind a perfectly distributed gap in the soil. Cheers erupted as Jamen closed his eyes and focused. The gelatinous green effigy finished tilling over fifty rows of soil within seconds and then vanished. Jamen completed the planned community service tasks for the day, and the hordes of workers began packing their belongings to return to the village. After removing some sweat from his forehead, Jamen smiled at the two children. "Some of us can use magic. Together, we will do the impossible and conquer these lands!"

CHAPTER 5 ♦ JARAHAD

Being the somewhat official clan leader of a group of starving refugees in an inhospitable land meant there were priorities. Perhaps it was because of the uncomfortable situation of his unwarranted birth or because his father was once an Äimite guard. Jarahad knew he couldn't sit in a palace wearing expensive robes while his people suffered. They needed him, and he would pave the way to save both clans from extinction at all costs.

"Stand still while we perform the ceremony!"

Even if it meant getting his hands dirty, Jarahad had to become stronger. Spiritually, he viewed himself as an elf just like his father. But every time he saw his reflection in the mirror, his hopes would never come true.

Indeed, Jarahad inherited the elliptical pupils and long ears as the common denominator of his elvish ancestry. Still, his medium-dark skin, red eyes, and grey hair he wore in a warrior knot were a constant and permanent reminder he would never be welcome in the kingdom.

There were more important things in his thoughts. The ruinous fall of Orsenmuray over fifteen years ago was proof he could not depend on his nascent harlequin sorcery. Despite being a capable earth mage in his own right, what stood Jarahad apart were the rare moments he could feel a fuzzy connection to mana hidden deep inside. His unique training helped to develop this rare ability.

He soon felt a crippling pain in his right arm, which he suppressed by biting the wooden stick in his mouth. An elderly harlequin was busy tattooing him with a strange silvery substance while he chanted in the forbidden harlequin tongue. Jarahad was certain he heard an incantation spell.

This was the fourth time Charon had done this, and the agony was the same every time. The mage's left hand glowed while the right traced a series of eloquent lines as he filled the glass pen with the silvery liquid. The needle prickled into Jarahad's skin at precise intervals.

Jarahad decided to focus instead on the face of someone he appreciated. Her soft dark skin, the curves of her body, the pale grey hair she adorned in a series of incoherently complicated hairstyles that seemed to look more bizarre with each passing year. And then he focused on the face. There was a time when Talgel had beautiful crimson eyes that radiated life in her flawless face despite the darkness of the harlequin city caves where he spent his difficult childhood. She then obtained magic and lost her eyesight. As the mage continued injecting the fluid into his right forearm, Jarahad tried to recall those final days before she summoned her beast for the first time. It was culminated by the kiss that sealed his fate and made him wish he could marry her. If he had to wait a hundred years for her to get used to her handicap and accept his love, he would continue fighting until the very end. Talgel was and always will be worth fighting for.

The pain receded as the harlequin mage chanted a different prayer, and the ink seeped into his skin. Jarahad sighed in relief as a cool sensation replaced the agonizing pain. He tossed the wooden gag from his mouth on the floor and touched his bloodied skin. It felt slightly numb to the touch.

The harlequin bent to the floor and placed the pen in a huge leather bag filled with other odd tools. "Most impressive, my Lord. Very few apprentices remain so silent during the monthly rituals."

"This is only the fourth vantage point you have placed on my body. How many are left?"

"Patience, young child of the immortals. I must perform twelve bridges connecting to the thirteen points I partially placed during the first test. You are not even halfway through."

"I'm worried the kingdom will send another army to attack us. Can't the process be sped up somehow?"

The old harlequin sighed and flapped his demonic wings when he heard that. "I respect you, but I dare say you are most impertinent. There is a reason my people developed this ritual. If you believe you have it rough, consider what the sword's soul resting on your belt had to endure when he was still alive."

Jarahad fell silent and stared at the new medium-length sword that rested by his side. A part of him felt disgusted at owning such a device, and the other half tried to ignore the haunting memory when he discovered how the sword was forged. "I apologize for my rudeness, Sword Master Charon."

Charon rubbed his beaten back and sat on a stool to relax. He was still most adept, and his wisdom was unparalleled by almost none.

It was a shame he had arrived on the eve of his life, and he would not perform this painstakingly tedious ritual on an apprentice ever again. "I was hesitant to initiate you, Jarahad, because your father caused our misfortune. He knew he would get punished for siring a cursed child. Instead of accepting his death, he fled his homeland and dragged us into the mess we are now in."

"I swear they coerced my father to escape! He had no intention of asking Hurrujat to stall the execution!"

Charon grumbled at once. "You should recall those human armies murdered my wife, children, and cherished students. Whereas Jamarnid gets to see you grow into a man, I had to bury my entire family!"

Jarahad bit his tongue and bowed very low, without even thinking. "Please forgive me for my impertinence. I…"

"I know why you want to finish the ritual. And I can guarantee it isn't because you wish to serve the clan."

"But!"

Charon grinned, revealing a mouth with scant sharp teeth that were rotting. "She will never love you… she knows."

Jarahad's eyes widened at the vagueness of his comment. "I…"

"Keep on wasting your time trying to regain the seer's attention; she knows everything about the sword."

Anguish filled Jarahad's heart. They forced him to remain secret about his training. How could Talgel know something that not even his father knew?

Charon seemed amused by Jarahad's reaction more than anything. "Talgel would have been a worthy student as well. Too bad most of the material I needed to forge more harlequin steel became destroyed when those human hordes conquered Orsenmuray. I do sense a lot of budding talent in both of you. Talgel has mastered her beast. When are you going to summon yours?"

The question felt like a sword pierced Jarahad's heart, and he almost collapsed on the floor of the nondescript room. "I can't summon a phantom beast! I've tried everything!"

"No, you have not. Talgel is living proof a harlequin elf can summon a phantom beast and help us save what we have left of our clans. As my last student, overcome your weaknesses and see that the impossible can be done. I felt mana in you while practicing the vantage point spells the other day. You are just too lovesick to fulfill your training. But you still have plenty of time. With each vantage point that my spells connect, energy will flow more easily within your body. Perhaps you will make a name for yourself: Lord Jarahad, the savior over Lord Jarahad, son of the coward." Charon rudely chuckled to himself.

It always hurt Jarahad when someone was being spiteful about his infirm father. There was little Jarahad could do on this issue to talk his way out of it. Jamarnid was technically the leader of the Grey Clan, but he was incapable of ruling in his current state.

The only reason the harlequins had put up with Jamarnid for so long was because of Hurrujat's softness and that almost nobody could summon phantom beasts. To have fallen from being one of the kingdom's elite soldiers into a disabled mana donor because of his poor decisions was humiliating. And Jarahad had to put with the jeers from the harlequins because it was their way of coping with their loss. He had no other choice but to take it in stride to maintain the peace. After it looked like Charon had rested enough, he soon stood up.

Jarahad didn't even think twice before offering him his tool case. "Please rest, Master Charon. I deeply appreciate you taking time off from your well-deserved retirement to assist me. Perhaps I cannot remedy the loss of your home and family or return my father to health. But someday, I will use the magic from my completed training will for the benefit of our clans."

"It better be. Don't leave me disappointed. I do not wish to waste the last slab of steel on a coward too blinded by love to reach his full potential. Keep on doing those exercises and think about why you haven't summoned your beast. As long as I stay alive, I shall return on the same day in a month."

The following day, Talgel rejected yet another marriage proposal from her ill-fated former lover. And so, she left Almjarhad Palace alongside her new assistant, the mysterious harlequin Henrietta. It was still early that morning, and few elves were busy walking in the streets. To avoid unwanted attention, Talgel covered her empty eye sockets with a silk blindfold. All the better for her because the fabric partially covered the bandages on her forehead.

"Good morning, Talgel! You're injured! Are you all right?"

Talgel sighed because it didn't take long at all for the first uncomfortable encounter. She just hoped things would get back to normal within a few days, and she could get on with her life.

Henrietta interjected at once. "Please do not feel concerned for her ladyship's wellbeing. The medic treated her wound, and she is feeling wonderful. Lord Jarahad would appreciate it if you could spread the good news and help patrol the outer perimeters from criminals for Talgel's peace of mind."

"Oh, um… I apologize. Have a good day!"

Even though Talgel didn't like Henrietta that much, the woman was talented at ordering people around with both firmness and a tint of forced politeness. Her curiosity was getting piqued with each passing minute.

"All right, my ladyship Talgel, the coast is clear! Once we settle down in your residence, I would be more than glad to tell everyone the good news to avoid overburdening you."

"Duly noted, Henrietta. Let's first make a brief visit. I am certain you know where I need to go."

Henrietta stood still and began shifting her weight. It was clear she seemed nervous. "Are you sure you wish to confront the artisan early in the day? I don't think he will feel happy to see you."

"That is why I must see Daedoman immediately so that I can get it over with and have a new face."

"Well, I am not sure why you prefer to wear a ceramic mask instead of just putting on a pair of glass eyes in your sockets, but you are the boss!"

Both women continued pacing around. After a few more encounters with concerned elves and harlequins that were dodged by

Henrietta's slick words of encouragement, they reached a nondescript tent that looked identical to the rest of the village.

Talgel drew a deep breath and spoke with uncertainty in her voice. "Daedoman, are you awake?"

"Come in, you brute. I have a few words I need to tell you!"

Daedoman's residence was teeming with ceramic dolls staring at their visitors with a glare that prompted Henrietta to screech more than once. Elf dolls, humans, and harlequins with beady glass eyes of an array of colors and robes from the blend of cultures were stored in simple stone shelves from bottom to top. A low rise semi-translucent beige ceiling only perpetuated the creepiness of their surroundings.

Daedoman was another one of the scant pureblood elves to inhabit the village. Unlike most of his peers, his short stature made everyone assume he was a child, along with a thick brow that only enhanced the severity of his tanned face. He had one beady grey eye, a black eyepatch and a scar adorning a considerable portion of his right temple and cheek. His stocky upright nose, prominent chin, and stubby hands made him resemble a miniature human instead of an elf. He was sewing a dress for yet another one of his disturbing dolls that only caused Henrietta's heart to pound ever more firmly, much to Talgel's amusement.

"With so much work to do in the village, I still cannot understand why you continue the unusual profession you had in the kingdom instead of bringing Almjarhad to life," Talgel said.

"And let me remind you, sweetie pie, to mind your business. I have not forgotten you caused the death of my son Egiel during the second purge." Daedoman snapped.

Henrietta gasped at once. "How terrible! Is this true?"

Talgel remained ambivalent to a certain degree. "I am conscious of that. While I lament Egiel's death because he protected me, I could never change his fate."

"Poppycock! You can summon a strange invisible phantom beast that allegedly lets you see future events. But so far, they always seem ridiculous. Oh, I've heard those stories when I go to the market to sell my wares," He began stitching the fabric with increased fury, while the only sound was the shifting of soil from a sand clock standing nearby. "Nasty harlequins marrying who knows who, adventurers finding hidden treasures from crashed vessels in the sea, gossip, and more nonsense. Most worthless magic indeed. The only reason Jarahad tolerates your company is because you can donate mana to the harlequins so they can use their magic. But I will not be one of them!"

Henrietta found the elf's attitude beyond condescending and had the urge to step forward. Despite the expected rebuttal, Talgel firmly held onto her forearm. "Why are you stopping me? He's a racist old loon!"

"Didn't you promise me you would try to avoid getting involved in my personal affairs when they involved my sorcery?" Talgel rebutted.

"Huh?"

Talgel stepped forward and bowed at the elf. "I know you feel angry about what happened to your family and believe being rude to me will somehow bring Egiel back to life. Most of you think my sorcery is a gift from the gods. In more ways than one, I only see it as a curse. Some things will happen, terrible ones and good. Sometimes I can tell them beforehand. Others would only cause great heartache for both parties. You will remarry someday. I can guarantee it."

"Ha! What a joke! I'd rather drop dead than marry a harlequin or a bloodthirsty halfling like yourself!" Daedoman replied.

"Neither one of those scenarios is in your future."

Instead of feeling touched, Daedoman set the doll down, opened his arms, and turned in every direction. "Look everywhere in this cursed wasteland! The only true elves you will see in these parts are men! As far as we know, not one woman survived the first purge. And I am not interested in betrothing my fellow male countrymen either!"

Talgel smirked, but she tried to remain ambivalent. "You will end up marrying a human."

Wild laughter invaded the small tent. "I haven't been able to speak the local dialect of these strange humans with customs that are unappealing, and you state I will marry one someday? Hilarious! Not even his lordship would bother to do that."

Henrietta growled at once. "Lord Jarahad has no intentions to marry, and Leader Jamarnid has stayed firm with his oath of celibacy."

This prompted Daedoman to cackle. "Stupid foreigner, you haven't heard? Neither one of those brutes is the legitimate leader of our people."

"Huh?"

Talgel cleared her throat. "As much as I enjoy bickering with you, please try to be polite to my new assistant, Henrietta. She doesn't know about the clan's situation, so her ignorance about his lordship is fully justified."

Daedoman grumbled from her well-warranted defense and resumed his tasks. "Silly chap! Sharad is an adult with a full right to reclaim his title, yet he prefers to mope around all day. Given you are new to this village, Henrietta, one word of advice: don't get too involved in other people's business. If Jarahad chose you to babysit this ungrateful twerp who ruined the lovely mask I made for her, just stick to being Talgel's caregiver and don't mess with me. I already agreed with Jarahad that I didn't have to engage in community service if I spent a few nights each month converting that ocean over yonder into potable water under the condition it was to be used by the elves and not your kind. Both of you are extending your welcome in my shop. I will finish your new mask in a few weeks. Now bug off."

As they exited the tent, Talgel's knees trembled from the uncomfortable encounter, and she collapsed on the ground.

"Your ladyship! Are you all right?"

"I… I wish to return home."

Happiness marked most of Tioja's childhood. He often played with the other children, spent time with Jamen and Nurran, and tried his best to build his birth city.

There was one thing he enjoyed the most in this world, and it would have to be…

"Now huff and puff and blow, son!"

Tioja placed a hollow wooden paddle into a bucket of soapy water and perked his cheeks. With a decisive blow, a bubble floated into the air. Tioja chuckled at once. "Look, mommy! It's so big!"

Hamara was beautiful, even for the standards of elves. She seemed to inherit the perfect softness of her harlequin mother's skin and the almond-shaped eyes of her elf father. Her red eyes glowed with a slight pink hue, and her sand-colored skin was lighter than expected for a halfling. Her wavy grey hair was medium length and rustled in the sky as she watched the bubbles float above.

Standing beside them was Tioja's pureblood elf father, Jamad. Despite having a similar sounding name to his maternal grandfather named Jamen, both elves swore they weren't relatives. Which caused a lot of awkward situations because harlequins would occasionally mix them up from time to time. As if to further confuse everyone, they had the same hair and eye color, albeit Jamad was taller with thicker eyebrows. He had spent most of that day pounding nails on a series of white fabric screens piled in the corner of their modest tent.

Hamara turned around with a slight frown. "My love?"

"Hrm?" Jamad was too busy to even bother lifting his head, but Tioja knew he was always paying attention.

"The village is in such dire need of actual houses, and you are busy assembling painting screens. Shouldn't you use your carpentry skills to help them?"

"When the summer ends, and before the rainy season begins, I will be more than happy to build a dignifying home for both of you. I'm fed up with living in a tent. Unlike some of you, I am not used to this horrible weather and suffer from heatstroke. Go ask the medics the last time I woke up under their care when I tilled the land in the outskirts of town."

Hamara frowned, but Jamad made a valid point. It still bothered her he would do something that neither improved the comfort of their living arrangements nor made a lot of money. Tioja was making more bubbles while listening absentmindedly. "What do you plan to do with them?"

"Well, I was just thinking. Almjarhad is growing in population, and we have so many children. As a pureblood elf, I find it strange to see them. Most cities in the kingdom only have a handful of children at a time."

"Okay, so you are not used to dealing with children. What does that have to do with this activity?"

"I believe these kids could use a bit of direction. I heard stories from the mortal Red Clan of the way they educated their young in Gilmirah City by housing them in buildings called schools. Like most of my kin, our family homeschooled us, and richer elves had private tutors that would stop by every day and teach them. I thought the children could paint on these things."

Hamara lifted her eyebrow at the oddness of his comment. "You want to teach Tioja and the other children how to paint? You draw horribly!"

"Nah, I'm just volunteering to make some frames for the kids, and Yerta and a few harlequins will teach them. I also think it is time for Tio to learn how to write our sacred Elvish script and get some history lessons from his nation."

"What is the point in teaching them that? As long as Salman lives, Tioja may never set foot in those lands. Humans don't bother engaging with so many antiquated cultural rules. Teach them how to hunt or Harlequin script instead!"

"No! We are not carnivores, and I will not let you teach my son how to read and write that cursed language!"

"You have a problem with Tioja learning about his ancestry? Look at him and tell me what he is!"

Jamad set his tools down and frowned. Tioja perked his ears and turned around to listen. "He is an elf, just like yourself. I tolerate seeing the halflings speak that pidgin language that combines elements of Elvish, Harlequin, and the assortment of local human tongues to communicate more easily. But Tioja will not learn a language that only causes misfortune or, worse: death. The way I see it, Tioja will be better off speaking proper Elvish when he is at home and use the common meshed tongue when dealing with others."

Hamara tensed her fists from the blight. "It is my mother's birth language. You want him to forget the other half of his ancestry?"

"You're technically half harlequin, so I tolerate hearing you speak to Svetlana in it. However, Tioja will not learn the tongue while he lives in my home. The decision is final."

Hamara marched off and grabbed Tioja's wrist.

"Ouch! Where are you taking me? Dad is angry!"

"I believe it is time for a bath."

Little did Tioja know, this would only be the first of many fights between his parents.

The two women remained silent as they reached a colorful tent with assorted red triangles on the bottom and gaudy blue squares on the roof.

Henrietta gawked at the odd sight. "Who would ruin those animal hides by painting this?"

"While I didn't paint them, I asked artisans from the village for their help. You don't like my home?"

"Well, I was expecting something a little more… normal. Perhaps even rustic, given you live here instead of in the palace."

"Come inside." Talgel lifted the carp, and it bombarded Henrietta with literal overstimulation from colorful shelves stocked with clothes, racks of necklaces, other assorted jewelry, and even a handful of wigs. Every crook and cranny of the small enclosure had perfectly organized belongings. It was nerve-wrenching.

"You have quite a place, Talgel. It's like you want to play the mad traveling fortune teller stereotype. The outside of the tent looks rather bare. Why would you bother painting all this if you can't see anything?"

Talgel grunted and sat on a cushion. "I knew you wouldn't understand. If you spend enough time with me, you will realize I am not as blind as you think." Before long, mana appeared within the woman's body.

Henrietta gasped at once. "Impossible! I thought only pureblood elves can summon phantom beasts!"

By then, Talgel was no longer paying any attention. Her mind became enveloped by a shadow, and it transported her to a dark void. Her eyes were once again full as she stared in every direction.

It didn't take long for a familiar voice to manifest. "A nice servant you have there, Talgel. A slave, perhaps?"

"Do I always have to put up with your annoying presence when I summon my beast?"

Before long, the voice materialized into a semi-translucent humanoid being with reptilian blue skin and hollowed black eyes that shimmered with white color pupils. The being was nude with a long tail, clawed appendages, and large bat-like ears. Otherwise, it sort of resembled a man. A shrill hissing voice that annoyed Talgel to no end echoed in every direction. "You chose this power, remember? I just feel glad I gained some liberty when you first summoned me. I can see you met Yawad's demise."

"No help to you! I wished I could have known the exact moment future events would occur."

The demonic being floated around with a huge grin on its face. It felt amused that Talgel wore the same dress as yesterday and prepped her grey hair in another elaborate hairstyle. "I believe you have found an unusual but helpful way to circumvent one of my power's many defects to give you a rough time estimate for your advantage. How are things going with Jarahad? Still making him suffer?"

"His dealings are none of your concern."

"Well, either tell him the truth behind your aloofness now, or wait until the future you saw happens on its own. I only care about events that affect me."

"What's the point of your taunts? It's not like you can escape this place."

"For now."

"Will you let me choose to view the future of a person, or will you send me the knowledge in a convoluted mess, like usual?"

"I like your bitterness, but you know my powers have limits. After using this gift for the past thirty-five years and discovering its secrets, you realize that most of the events you see are only possibilities, and they won't come true. Be thankful I have given you the mental acuity to memorize these separate paths to pinpoint which of these futures will happen. Or you would have gone mad long ago. Perhaps I have been sending you to observe events of little importance in the greater scheme of things. As a token of my goodwill, today will be different."

As soon as the demon finished speaking, he melted away in a cloud of smoke. The fumes invaded Talgel and she was teleported to a place covered in palm trees and the brilliant ocean. Talgel marveled as she studied her surroundings and could even spot a few pureblood elves standing on the beach. The place was both familiar and different. Talgel walked within the hordes of spectators, including some children that were now grown up. Almjarhad had changed a lot in this future, and it filled her heart with pride and joy to see her efforts helped give everyone an actual city to call their home.

Dwellings had replaced the simple tents. While the streets were still littered with red dust, a suitable sewage system was already functional.

A beautiful beige castle with a gold-domed roof was visible in the distance. Talgel could pace around and that bothered her. Usually, her visions were static, and she was only a spectator from the target's point of view. Intrigued by the liberty of this vision, Talgel ignored the beach and headed towards Almjarhad Palace. She rushed past a few guards who ignored her presence and raced up a circular ramp with large windows offering stunning views of the growing city. She reached a room with two arguing elves: Jarahad and his father, Jamarnid. They hadn't changed at all, which didn't hint the exact moment this vision would happen or its ulterior purpose. Jamarnid's unpleasant face was full of wrath, like usual.

Jarahad stood forward. "Why don't you want to accept this deal? It could mean the clan's salvation!"

"I did not consent to your private dealings with those nomads. Now that most of the filthy harlequins have gone forever, we can try to learn how to be self-sufficient for once. Forge alliances with the human savages for mana, but cancel your dealings with those people!"

"You don't understand! They can help us master our magic!"

"Magic? The elemental sorcery that I can't sense? You are the son of an Äimite guard. Try to act with dignity and focus your energies on mastering that strange phantom beast instead!"

Jarahad walked around in circles, ushering insults to himself in a low voice while Jamarnid stared out the window. Talgel was growing impatient over the mundane activities of this vision and crossed her arms. She thought to herself. "The harlequins have left Almjarhad? Little surprise, they have wanted to decapitate that useless elf Jamarnid for ages in retribution for losing their city. Kind of nice to know Jarahad can summon a phantom beast. I'd love to know what it does." A nasty smirk full of envy filled Talgel's face. Jarahad looked the same as always, albeit now he wore fancier robes than the usual beige cotton ones. It wasn't surprising that Almjarhad was economically doing well, which granted nobleelves the chance to wear robes more akin to their social position. But that was a menial matter. Jarahad's body looked complete, with no remarkable changes. His mind also seemed sharp, like usual. It soon hit Talgel's pride, causing her to clench her fists in frustration. "You bastard! While I ended up handicapped forever, you get to enjoy your health and your beast. I thought we all ended up maimed when we summoned our cursed phantom beasts!"

The demon soon appeared and floated next to Talgel. His black claws grasped her shoulder, and he watched Jarahad continue arguing with his father. "Yes, Talgel. Many hybrid elves will soon master their sorcery and summon demonic beasts. Their beasts always possess a serious drawback. It will be hard to find a teacher capable of understanding their special needs, but you will be the only one with a major physical handicap. Jealous of Jarahad's good fortune?"

Talgel marched outside rather curtly. She found an open doorway in the hallways and went inside. The room was luxurious and unfamiliar. It was less utilitarian than what she had grown to expect from Jarahad and more filled with lavish décor, books piled in disarray on the floor, chests with an assortment of jewelry, and a refined rug covered with a few carpentry tools and sawdust. Right in the middle was a peculiar medium-height pureblood adult elf as he was sawing off a slab of wood. There was an unfinished birdhouse resting on a nearby stone table. Talgel smirked at the oddness of the sight and approached him. The elf lifted his head and smiled. "Talgel! Welcome!"

"Huh?" Talgel turned around and saw her reflection in the mirror. She realized it was the first time she was the target. A new masquerade mask adorned her face, prompting her to sigh in nervous relief. At least it looked like Daedoman had forgiven her and replaced the one she broke. She wore a raffish red dress along with countless jewelry and a silver tiara on her short, grey hair. This would prove useful in pinpointing the year of this vision. For unexplained reasons, even though Talgel remained blind, this wasn't an impediment to watch her vision.

"I was waiting for your arrival!"

It was the first time Talgel had seen someone interacting with her in one of her visions. Despite feeling uncertain of herself, she opted to approach the blond elf dressed in royal blue silk robes. She acted like herself while feigning ignorance. "What in the hell are you doing, Sharad? Why have you moved into the palace?"

"You told me you would say that."

"Huh?"

Sharad finished sawing off the edge, and a wood block fell on the floor. He then knelt to pick it up and tossed it into a wastebasket. "Well, it is awful strange for me to be speaking to you like this. You might wonder why everyone has ignored you. Well, strange as it may seem, you are not going crazy. You have seen the future of this day play out in so many ways that you pinpointed the date and opened up to me about it."

Talgel's confusion increased as the elf grabbed some sandpaper to soften the rough edges of the slab of wood he was working on. "Jarahad and Jamarnid can see me?"

"Well yes. You told me this always happened when you experienced a rare vision affecting your future. You could use your body and interact with others like in real life. The palace guards are used to your visits, so they never bat an eye. I bet Jarahad is too busy arguing with daddy smearfest to have seen you. But I can see you loud and clear, and it feels odd because you told me we would have this same conversation and said it word by word several years ago."

Assuming she had not gone insane from her demonic beast, Talgel chose her words. "Did I tell you to move into the palace? When we arrived to Almjarhad, you didn't know what to do. That is why you wandered around the human lands for ages."

Sharad chuckled at once. "Yup, you said those same words when you urged me to visit your weird tent the day before you moved into your new home. You opted to wait until you saw the other event before you could warn me."

"Warn you? About what?"

"It is hard to explain. You saw a critically important event way into the future and might alter it. I don't know what will happen, but I will play a pivotal role." Sharad placed another block of wood on the table and smiled at her. His freckled face lacked any tint of malice and revealed a wholesome sweetness that had fallen under some difficult times. "You are wondering why this is important. After you helped convince the harlequins to leave the city, things have reached a new sense of normalcy. The first batches of children born in this city are almost grown, and Jarahad can summon his phantom beast, which dons some nifty abilities I have never seen before."

"What is so special about this day?"

"Seems like you ran straight for the palace to see Jarahad instead of staying on the beach."

"The beach? What is so important about that place?"

A cruel grin invaded Sharad's face as his blue eyes shimmered with excitement. "The Cursed One will summon a demonic beast that will spell doom for the clan."

"Your ladyship! Please wake up!"

Darkness soon replaced Sharad's face. Henrietta was shaking her body, and Talgel shook her head. "I am fine. When I use my beast, I enter a trance-like state that to you might have lasted just an instant, but to me, it could last for ages."

Henrietta sighed in relief and stood up. "You could have given me a little warning beforehand. Lord Jarahad instructed me to help you in every way I could. I want us to become friends, or at the very least, trusted business associates. I never expected you to scream in pain like that."

"Screaming in pain? What pain? I never say a word when I am in meditation."

"Well, looks like this time was different. You were hollering about a cursed one or something. I'm surprised a horde of elves haven't stormed the tent by now because it was so offsetting."

And then it hit Talgel hard. The vision was strange because she could interact with Lord Sharad, who was roaming the human lands with no set return date. Upon hearing Henrietta's odd remark, Talgel was sure she had not gone mad. The vision was most likely real, which meant she had to pinpoint the Cursed One's identity to save the clan.

CHAPTER 9 ♦ JAMARNID

(THE PAST)

"You miserable fools!"

"Goodness gracious! He's drenched in a pool of blood!"

"Tell the medics to prepare an operation ward!"

"What are you saying?" After discovering Garlas was holding his body while they flew towards an unknown destination, Jamarnid's mind wandered in and out of consciousness. He hardly even noticed being placed on an examination bed while bright lights illuminated his mangled body. Alertness shook his body upon hearing hordes of voices shouting in every direction.

The next thing Jamarnid knew, someone flashed a light in his eyes that irritated him. He attempted to move his shoulder while several firm hands pinned him on the bed.

"Lord Jamarnid sounds disorientated, but he's somewhat awake. Maybe we can still save him."

"Let me die, please!"

Jamarnid couldn't continue protesting. The medics placed magically enhanced needles into his forehead, and they soon knocked him unconscious. Time settled into a blur, only that his mind was sharper than before. With a few grunts, Jamarnid opened his eyes and saw a mosaic stone ceiling with an array of tasteful red and grey tiles alternated with painted circles of varying grey tones. The room was brightly lit, and he could see a bottle of transparent liquid dangling from a hook on the ceiling. They connected this vial to a rubber tube, which ended in a painful needle that was fastened to his neck. His bandaged neck made it annoying to turn his head and get a good view of his surroundings.

There was a loud voice on the side of his bed. "Jamarnid! You're awake! Bless the heavens!"

Jamarnid knew that voice and a flurry of emotions soon engulfed him, causing tears to fall from his eyes. "Chandrice!"

The woman soon pulled a stool, prompting a dragging sound of wood against the stone floor, and was now visible from his restricted field of vision. Bronze skin and glowing hazel eyes, Chandrice's black hair was almost unnaturally straight and silky to the touch. Jamarnid resisted the urge to giggle when a long strand of hair tickled his cheeks. It gave him pleasant memories from kinder times. Jamarnid lifted his left arm, only to have his hopes quenched because he could feel a terrible bout of pain followed by a heavy cast that further limited any arcs of movement.

Chandrice caressed his biceps to stop him from forcing himself. "Please, I urge you to relax. You were wounded."

Reality soon hit. Even though seeing Chandrice one last time filled Jamarnid with a joy he hadn't experienced since his arrest, concern about Serumo's fate caused his eyes to well in tears. "Why didn't you tell me you were a harlequin?"

Upon hearing the accusation, Chandrice's eyelids fluttered as she averted her gaze.

Jamarnid soon heard a pair of footsteps approaching his bed.

The voice was both familiar and exhausted. "I hope it was worth it, you pathetic prick. If I had been Serumo, I would have selected a suitable plot of land on the remotest mountain of our lands after the shameful thing you did."

"So, your mockery of my ill fortune was not an act. Right, Hormandra?" Skepticism etched on Jamarnid's face. One of the last memories before being scuttled away by Garlas was Hormandra summoning his phantom beast and destroying the barrier field that isolated him from any rescuers. A part of him felt glad his relative was still alive.

Hormandra grunted at once. "Believe me, those feelings were genuine, and I was not acting. Serumo knew how disgusted I felt during the trial when Master Lord Salman ordered your death last summer on the very eve of the Elvish new year. Serumo could have invited plenty of supportive family members to the execution. Still, he chose me to deflect even the remotest signs of disloyalty because it risked his plans to save you."

"It was Serumo who came up with this plan. Why would he do this? I accepted my guilt long ago and didn't oppose being executed! Please, I beg you to tell him I will surrender to the Master so that he pardons you."

"That is pointless now." Hormandra shook his head and grunted.

Something soon piqued Jamarnid's interest. Hormandra's beautiful face was filthy and covered in grime after their desperate escape. It mildly surprised him the elf was still wearing the same ceremonial grey robes from the execution, albeit they were now in tatters and covered in blood. Hormandra crossed his bruised arms with tensed muscles. A grey stone ring was now adorning the middle finger of his nephew's right hand. "Serumo is dead, and you inherited the leadership of the clan!"

"My father didn't even survive long enough to give a decent fight. Senior Lord Froylan went straight for him and smashed his head with a hammer. I had some hopes he survived the blow when the body fell and jolted for a few moments. Until I realized during the frantic battle, the movements were just muscular spasms. I believe Froylan did it on purpose out of spite."

Jamarnid sighed when he heard that. Hormandra's tone of voice intonated a sense of dread combined with resignation. It somewhat disgusted Jamarnid that Hormandra wasn't sad about his father's unfortunate passing. Realizing the clan's sacrifice for his life, he quenched his curiosity. "Did you take the ring?"

"You seriously believe I would waste my time rescuing a ring while battling one of the strongest Äimite guards in a duel? Unlike my deceased father, I value my life and the responsibility that comes with my cursed inheritance."

"Cursed inheritance?"

"Ha! While you were fighting for your life, I had difficulty deflecting Froylan's hammer with a magically infused pipe that I miraculously smuggled into the patio during your execution. Meanwhile, one of Chandrice's harlequin friends knocked Froylan into the air with strange earth sorcery and found the time to steal the ring that now rests on my hand."

"So, it was true. Garlas is a harlequin."

Chandrice whimpered as she stared at Jamarnid. "Garlas is the treasured bodyguard of Lord Hurrujat, a very talented mage and the bravest harlequin you will ever meet. He offered to be the one who would bring you to safety while the others caused a diversion. The survivors said it was complete bloodshed. They killed hundreds of Äimite guards and nobleelves in the crossfire. I… if only I hadn't begged help from my grandfather, Lord Hurrujat…."

"You're a noblewoman of a harlequin tribe?!"

Chandrice sobbed even more and covered her face with her hands. Jamarnid lifted his left hand to console her, only to pant from another jolt of pain. And then he realized something. His torso and abdomen were unharmed, while something else numbed the pain in his legs. Ignoring Chandrice for a moment, Jamarnid mustered the willpower to push his elbows as best as the cast permitted and sat up. Loss filled the embattled elf with despair. Even though he knew the executioners injured his body, the sight of severed legs above the knees was something even a hardened guard would have a hard time overcoming. His cousin Serumo was dead along with countless innocent bystanders, and all for what? Plenty of handicapped nobleelves can find other fulfilling duties to make themselves feel beneficial to society. Still, the severe loss caused him to collapse into a wave of despair. He didn't moan or complain, but nothing stopped him from feeling one small tear falling from his eyelid as he tried to understand everything.

Hormandra growled at the sight. "Serumo was hoping the harlequins would arrive so that they could extract you and scamper off to exile. He thought entering the capital would be easy, but they stupidly brought a few harlequins who couldn't use magic. They wasted precious minutes arguing because the non-mages only saw an endless forest because of the barrier field. The sheer amount of guards that outnumbered the scant harlequin mages only hindered the poor planning of the rescue. Most of them barely caused any damage before they died."

Silence ensued for quite a long time while Chandrice sobbed, and Hormandra stared outside the window. Acrid smoke in the air further prompted Jamarnid to set aside his victimization and continue to speak. "I wanted to die. I was ready for it. And to know my hands are now stained with the blood of innocent bystanders and fellow guards because Serumo believed I deserved to live… it's inconceivable! Please, Hormandra! Write an edict to the Master offering mercy because Serumo forced you to follow his plan. I will be glad to surrender!"

Hormandra grunted. "I have to monitor you while I try to sort amends with the Master. I will probably end up arrested, but they pinned me to a wall from the very beginning. Serumo abused his political power to make me join his cause, and the Master would have punished me if I had tried to sabotage Serumo's plans. If we are lucky, the messenger will arrive with the Master's response. We can travel to the capital together on my phantom beast and get executed in exchange for the clan."

"Clan?! What do you mean?! Why would you feel worried about our people?"

A knock on the door soon interrupted the heated argument. Hormandra rushed to the door and opened it.

"A package for the Grey Clan Leader Lord Hormandra and an edict from Master Lord Salman."

"Odd. Why would the Master give me a box?" Hormandra shook his head and placed both items on a nearby table.

"What is in that box?"

Hormandra ignored Jamarnid's insolence and broke the gold wax seal of Salman's signet ring. It was rather odd the Elf King himself would seal a mysterious box for no apparent reason, but he needed to know the answer before things got worse. His eager hands ripped the fabric covering and revealed an ordinary-looking wooden box. He opened the lid and shrieked.

"Please tell me what's inside the box!"

Anxious, Hormandra broke the edict's gold twin griffin wax seal and read it. The elf threw the box against the wall. Jamarnid turned his head and shrieked at the sight of an elf's severed head. "Is that the messenger?"

Hormandra's breathing deepened, and he stared at his relative with wrath combined with defeat. He collapsed against the wall and laughed, despite the absurdity of it all.

Chandrice turned around. "What is going on? A dead elf head!"

Jamarnid closed his eyes and understood why Hormandra seemed so nervous. "The edict... the Master wants something more than our heads, doesn't he?"

Disturbing laughter invaded the room while tears fell from Hormandra's eyes. After trying to understand their predicament, he spoke between nervous laughs. "Master Lord Salman has declared war on the entire Grey Clan, and the Äimite Guard is coming for us tomorrow afternoon to exterminate us!"

CHAPTER 10 ♦ JARAHAD

Things were going relatively normal in Jarahad's life after Talgel's scare. He continued spending his days training his mind and body for the next session with the sword mage, obeying Jamarnid's orders, and helping the peasants tilling the land before the autumn rains arrived. With everyone's efforts, they could enjoy a better harvest and be less reliant on bartering with the human nomads.

Only one thing bothered him, and he paced around his bare office in circles. The blacksmiths worked tirelessly every evening to continue building the domed roof. Jarahad believed the last remnants of Hurrujat's gold should help the clan in other ways.

Still, Jamarnid and Hurrujat accorded with the deal as a token of goodwill after Jamarnid saved his life during the second purge with his phantom beast. The gold panels were close to completion, and the masons were already placing the exoskeleton above the open space that would end up as the throne room.

Jarahad always wondered what the ancient Elf Kingdom castles looked like from the inside. In all effects, Almjarhad Palace didn't have the straw flooring from Jamarnid's stories or sliding doors. It made little sense to build such things when wood was in short supply. He stared at his feet and sighed. "Elves are supposed to have standards. And here I am, wearing boots inside my home. I must look like a savage."

"You're not one, Lord Jarahad."

Jarahad lifted his head and smiled when sweet Henrietta entered the room.

She wore a blindingly bright royal blue dress while her medium-length sword dangled on a belt. Her black hair had grown, albeit its shortness offered contrasting masculinity to an otherwise feminine body. Henrietta observed the scant surroundings of the office and realized it only had a hastily built stone desk, some stools, and a few stacked boxes with books. She smiled at the sight and sat down.

Jarahad sat on the other stool and fiddled with his fingers for a few moments. "Please pardon the unkempt appearance of this room. The masons finished building it the other day. There isn't even a door yet, but I helped them sweep the floor as best as possible. When nightfall arrives, I'll ask a water mage to help me clean it."

"I don't mind that at all. I am impressed with the speed the artisans are finishing your palace."

Jarahad grumbled at the thought. "I'm not the clan leader; I am just following Jamarnid's orders as his servant."

"And you are doing a fabulous job, my Lord. I know you feel frustrated everyone is prioritizing the castle over homes for your people, but you have to understand a ruler must demand respect. The human enclaves were always respectful of Hurrujat's old city."

"Until they sided with King Salman and helped the Eirmite guards slaughter everyone. They most likely traded our lives for gold. Seeing that blatant display of wealth on the roof disgusts me."

Henrietta sighed. "You will see things differently when your mind is no longer clouded with worries because your people are struggling right now."

"I realize you have a warped view because…."

Henrietta placed an index finger on her lips. "Please, my Lord, we have agreed not to speak about my true identity. Your office doesn't have enough privacy for such sensitive matters."

"Very well, we shall avoid that topic. How are things going with Talgel? Is she treating you well?"

"Sort of. You warned me about Talgel's rudeness, but I think my eyes and reliability have appeased her. She helped me move some crates so I could put my bed."

"How about her visions? Anything important?"

"This is the second reason I'm here. I swore to Talgel that I would reveal nothing regarding her sorcery, and I believe it would be disrespectful if you abused your power to force the truth out of me. I told her I would visit you after you invited me earlier today and asked her permission to reveal what had been going on."

"Has she granted you permission to speak, or will I have to visit her?"

"She has been using her sorcery every three days."

"What?! She suffers from the same blood disease I do, and using sorcery wears her out! Why is she risking herself so much?!"

"Please, Jarahad, you must calm down. She never suffers from an attack because I have been very helpful. She needs to revisit a vision at all costs. So far, she has been unsuccessful because most of her visions are rather menial. Maybe you can help her get back on track."

"I'll be happy to help!"

"Talgel wants to talk to a certain wandering elf that doesn't want to be found."

Jarahad soon understood Henrietta's warning and slumped on the stool in defeat. "Please tell Talgel I would move heaven and earth for her, but I can't force him to return!"

"Oh, Talgel already knew you would say that. She saw this exact conversation during one of her visions. Your father will say yes if you speak to him. Shall we proceed?"

Resigned, Jarahad learned long ago that Talgel's visions never failed. If she believes bringing the true lord of this castle back home just to speak to him was necessary for a future event, then he must abide by her request. Jarahad walked alone to the first floor and stood in front of a room. He digged a key from his pocket and went inside.

Ending up disabled posed an enormous set of problems for the proud Jamarnid, who was once an elite soldier. To be demoted to the ruined shell of his former self felt worse because of the shameful things Jamarnid needed from others to survive. Losing his legs would have been mildly tolerable if only he could use his hands.

Jamarnid was currently nude, seated on a stool with a headrest to lean on while a servant was brushing his glossy hair that touched the ground. Jamarnid once told him being forced to cut his long hair was one thing he hated about being an Äimite guard. Growing it so long was likely a coping mechanism for everything he lost because of his poor decisions. Another servant was scrubbing his chest with a sponge while his eyes remained closed.

The instant Jarahad's footsteps were audible on the stone floor, Jamarnid's hyper-awareness of his surroundings jolted him awake and prompted him to turn around. "Who goes there?!"

"It is me, your son Jarahad. I apologize for this intrusion."

Jamarnid smirked and turned away while the servants resumed their tasks. "Enjoying watching your humiliated father being bathed in the privacy of his home?"

"Far from it. Nothing would give me greater joy than to see you healthy once again, and I swear upon my tainted blood that I am being honest."

"Well, you couldn't wait a while for me to look presentable. This must be important."

"A servant assisting Talgel's daily activities has relayed a message. I believe you should know it before I decide."

"Go on, I am listening."

"Talgel had a vision that might affect the clan, and she urgently needs to speak to Lord Sharad."

"Nonsense! His lordship must be still suffering from the trauma of seeing his family perish, his home burned to the ground, and the violence of the second purge when he was barely an adult. He suffered too much from a young age and wasn't ready to rule his clan."

"I am aware of that, and I am grateful I was just an infant when we fled the kingdom. However, even though we are just a couple hundred people, we are still his subjects and have sworn our oath to him. He deserves to know the events that directly affect him."

"What do you want me for? I already permitted you to rule the clan while I act as your advisor."

"You are my father and the official ruler of the clan in Sharad's absence. Without your explicit blessing, I would never do important things such as contacting his lordship."

"Fair enough, and I permit you to leave the city to search for him, given you have such a vested interest in the seer's personal affairs. Ask Soremin to suspend any community service tasks while you are gone. I want him to cover for you."

"I appreciate your generosity, and I'll locate him immediately."

Now that he had attained Jamarnid's permission, the issue was locating Sharad. He had fled the city and wandered around for the past ten years in the human lands. Jarahad would occasionally send a messenger to relay information about his wellbeing. Still, this time he had proven to be elusive, and nobody had heard any word of him for at least three years.

Given Henrietta was his bridge to Talgel, she could provide a helpful clue so that he didn't have to waste several months searching for him.

As if on cue, Jarahad's blessings were counted when he saw Talgel in his office seated on a stool alongside Henrietta. Her back was relaxed, and she seemed in a rather jolly mood. He knelt at once and kissed her hand. "My dear, you never cease to surprise me with your unannounced visits."

"Hogwash, I knew you would visit me, and time is of the essence. I want you to leave at dawn with a small group of soldiers. Sharad is in a bit of a bind, and he could use some help."

"What?! His lordship is in danger?! Then I must depart now!"

"Um… The danger hasn't happened yet. Go south to Tranquility Bay and ask around for a blond elf. You'll find him. I order you to wait until dawn. Do not, under any circumstance, leave before."

The vagueness in Talgel's warning was disconcerting, but Jarahad had grown somewhat used to it by now. She saw the future of many people, and trying to alter fortunes could prove dangerous. Sometimes Talgel would give an entire string of information to avoid an adverse event. Other times, she had to let a terrible event happen because there was no other better alternative. Knowing she never joked or messed around regarding her visions, Jarahad sucked his pride and bowed before her. "I swear I will do as you ask and feel glad Sharad has hidden in a nearby area. I was worried he would visit a pirate haven or something like that."

Talgel abruptly stood up and approached the door while Henrietta chased after her. "Bring him to my tent the second you return to the city. Give him this letter I wrote. I hope he doesn't mind my handwriting. It is difficult to write when you are blind."

The cryptic request will make sense when the time comes. Jarahad placed the letter without reading its content into his pocket and bowed as the seer and her assistant left. The tricky part came: convincing Sharad to return to his new home.

CHAPTER 11 ◆ JARAHAD

Time was of the essence. Before Jarahad could organize a small group of soldiers to depart at the specified time, he needed to locate a certain elf. It did not surprise him that Jamarnid would request a pureblood elf for this task. Even less, it would be Soremin, of all people.

After passing the patio filled with blacksmiths and then the dusty streets as twilight covered the sky with a brilliant array of colors, Jarahad ascended a cliff that granted a pleasant view of the bay and located a small wooden temple. Even though wood was a priceless commodity that couldn't be wasted even for the palace, Jamarnid insisted their people couldn't lose the religious customs of the kingdom at all costs. Jarahad didn't fuss when human nomads sold the required building materials for a hefty fee because it brought a smile to his father's face.

Despite the miniature size, the handful of pagodas with handrails and tiled roofs connected by a series of wooden hallways starkly contrasted with the rest of Almjarhad. Whereas the harlequins found the style displeasing, Jarahad felt a sense of inner peace every time he visited it.

Adorning the ground was a series of perfectly manicured gardens with cactuses and other hardy succulent plants that could resist the heat. Elves believed it was somewhat unorthodox to have a garden filled with palm trees. Still, Soremin was unusually pleased when human nomads sold them a few sago palm saplings for a steep price because they were commonplace in the more temperate regions of the Elf Kingdom.

Despite their current size, Soremin guaranteed the sagos would grow to an impressive height and had them planted far away from any permanent structures. For now, they had ample space to grow, which granted the garden a rather bare appearance. The only thing Soremin lamented for their absence were pools with koi, and he had to settle with white gravel stone gardens between the buildings. Visitors frequently spotted Soremin raking the gravel into a series of spirals. It always amazed Jarahad how the pureblood elves would spend their endlessly long lives doing rather senseless tasks like that, and it only filled him with envy because he was born a mortal.

Prioritizing the urgency to rescue Sharad, Jarahad ascended a wooden staircase that creaked incessantly and removed his boots. He soon located a pair of indoor slippers and then reached a pagoda where the murmurings of prayers were audible. Despite being familiar with the sacred Elvish tongue because of Jamarnid's vigorous upbringing, he was still incapable of understanding the poetic meaning of the prayers.

Jamarnid highly regarded Soremin as the head priest of the clan. And apparently, he was also one of the oldest surviving elves in the whole world. Being an ally of one of the oldest surviving immortals who could teach others about past events from millennia ago was always something Jarahad struggled to grasp because of his youth.

Living a long time after seeing so much violence also took a toll on Soremin. He was, however, a mind of reason and always welcome as Jamarnid's advisor. Soremin strived to show mercy for arrested criminals during his verdicts and usually forced the condemned to train as his student over imprisonment or corporal punishment.

As it seemed, the desperation that enticed halflings and harlequins to commit petty crimes was a profitable endeavor for the elf. Jarahad couldn't deny the priest was both cunning and merciful. Seizing the opportunity to recruit criminals filled him with many promising students to pass on his knowledge. Anyone who broke specific laws and didn't abide by his verdicts became expelled from the city. There was a reason Almjarhad had scant criminals serving time in prison.

Jarahad would have wanted to let Soremin continue praying for a while longer, but he was in a rush. He cleared his throat and spoke in a low voice. "Master Soremin?"

The room fell silent, and Soremin opened his sea-green eyes to stare at his visitor. He nodded in acknowledgment. "Lord Jarahad, is there a problem?"

"I am deeply sorry to have interrupted your activities. I need to leave the city immediately because of an urgent errand. Lord Jamarnid would appreciate it if you could stay in the palace and cover me during my absence."

The smile soon vanished from Soremin's face, and he became pensive. It didn't take long for him to stand up and stretch his muscles. "The tone of voice proves you have spoken the truth, and I will abide by his Lord's desire. However, leave your malignant sword behind the next time you visit these sacred grounds. I find it very disrespectful of you to bring it here."

Jarahad swallowed saliva when he realized Soremin could sense the evil magic imbued into his prized weapon. He bowed immediately to avoid aggravating the priest. "I am very sorry for this, and I promise it won't happen again."

Soremin nodded in agreement. "I hope you will not break your promise. Or else I will have another able-bodied student who will spend some time wearing a white apprentice robe. You could end up begging on the streets of human villages for charity donations, like some of my less obedient students. Maybe suffering from a blood attack will teach you how to appreciate the things you have. Unlike that student over yonder who continues to defy my teachings."

After realizing Soremin was encouraging Jarahad to turn around to prove a point, he saw a rather pitiful sight. Kneeled on a patio was a nude female halfling who was praying relentlessly as her thin body cowered. Halflings tolerated sunlight rather well, but the traces of sunburn proved she had spent at least a day in that painful position. Another student struck her back the second she momentarily slouched her shoulders.

The sound of the wooden stick hitting her back only interrupted the eery praying, which was now covered in painful bruises. She continued her prayers without interruption while a small tear was visible in her eye. Her body trembled nonstop, and it didn't take Jarahad a long time to realize the reason. "Do you even let her rest? How long has she been there?"

The students offered Soremin space to cross the room while the priests continued caning the woman from afar. "She has been there for five days and will continue to pray in that position until she collapses. My students feed her enough sweet water to survive, but she will continue to be deprived of other nourishment or rest until I determine she has learned her lesson."

"But… This is cruel!"

Soremin shook his head and sighed. "Jamarnid knew about my methods and agreed with them. Most priests from the kingdom never did these things. But these are desperate times where citizens need to help the clan, like you have, despite your social position. She tried to relieve herself this morning until students placed an ointment on her burned skin so that she could focus on the pain over anything else. Once she recovers, I will order her to serve Jamarnid's personal needs until we both determine she can resume her training."

This confession felt concerning. Unsurprisingly, nobody paid the apprentices that cleaned Jamarnid's body and fed him. They also had to eat austere diets of bitter root soups and water. Jamarnid was challenging to deal with during the best times, and Jarahad envied no one who had to tend to his most intimate needs. It was a somewhat effective way to entice a criminal to remain obedient and even thankful for Soremin's training to become the future priests of the clan. There was little doubt that Jamarnid was passing some of his personal experiences as a guard to keep his people submissive. While Jarahad disagreed with these cruel methods, he had little power to change anything.

Knowing he had far more pressing matters over discovering Soremin was ironically a spiritual sadist, Jarahad bowed at the priest. He rushed off before he gave his father some ideas to make him join Soremin's flock.

Uniting the group of soldiers was easy enough. He only had to mention they were going to rescue Sharad from a dangerous situation, and he soon had twenty volunteers preparing their horses for the impending ride. Even a few pureblood elves volunteered, but Jarahad declined the offer because of safety concerns.

The refugees learned one lesson from the second purge; they had to protect the pureblood members at all costs. Jarahad felt ecstatic that he would bring Sharad home because living beyond the city's limits could mean a death sentence if a mercenary discovered he belonged to the condemned clan.

One halfling finished buckling the saddle and stared at him in the open-air stables. "Can't we depart immediately?"

"Talgel strictly warned us not to leave the city until it was dawn," Jarahad replied.

"Has she told you why?"

"You know she keeps information if she believes we will act in haste. I don't know what kind of danger Sharad was in, but she seemed confident we would arrive on time. Go to sleep, and we shall depart at daybreak."

As promised, the group departed the city at Talgel's specified time and had an uneventful trip. Halfway on their voyage, they reached a grassy field with a dirt road covered in fresh tracks.

One volunteer descended, studied the tracks for a few minutes, and stared at Jarahad, who wore bare leather armor above his peasant robes. "I think I now know why Talgel ordered us to depart at sunrise, my Lord: a group of riders on purebred steeds were here several hours ago."

"Could they have passed last night?"

"It is likely. None of them were drawing carriages. No track marks from vehicles to be seen anywhere. Horses were also adults and traveled fast in the same direction we were going. The horseshoes tacked on their feet also have some strange symbols, but I find them hard to discern."

Jarahad bit his thumb at the sheer thought. Jamarnid spent countless hours teaching him many of the inner workings of the guard that very few civilians knew. "Get on your horse, Hadire. I think I know these people, and they plan to murder Sharad."

During the trip, the strange track marks detoured in another direction. If Jarahad's suspicions were correct, the group of assassins had the wrong information and was heading for another city. Spies might have spotted Sharad purchasing something and assumed he lived there. It wasn't proof they were going to make it to Tranquility Bay on time, but Talgel seemed confident about the success of their mission.

Thicker vegetation and hordes of palm trees eventually replaced the grassy fields; the soil was rich red clay that covered everyone with dust. Almjarhad had similar ground, except for being blended with coarse rock and dark sand. They arrived at Tranquility Bay just after sunrise the following day with a group of exhausted horses and weary riders. The beach was absurdly flat and stretched into the sea for miles, making it a pleasant place to swim but inconvenient for trading vessels or pirates. A few peaceful human communities had settled here, and most worked in art trades. Jarahad felt baffled Sharad would prefer to live here of all places instead of Almjarhad.

The group soon reached the village and asked around.

"Oh yes, you are looking for good ole Shaddy? Everyone knows where he lives!"

Jarahad swallowed saliva upon realizing the first human they encountered knew his whereabouts so quickly. "Shaddy? That is his name?"

"Well, he claims it isn't his birth name. The children call him that way, and it sort of stuck. I don't even know what the real one is. Crazy young chap, always a joy to spend time with!"

The elves stared at each other and shrugged their shoulders. Sharad was a quirky elf, so using a nickname was probably one reason he was so hard to find. The problem was this sense of anonymity meant little if Äimite guards asked civilians if they came upon a blond elf. He would not allow the truthful leader of his people to be murdered during a raid.

Jarahad spoke with urgency in his voice. "Can you tell us where he is? I need to see him immediately. I am his friend."

The woman pointed to a mine on the outskirts of town. "Crazy ole Shaddy bought that property when he heard stories ghosts haunted it. Most humans would never venture into such a place, but he is brave! Claims to be digging for treasure or something!"

This was not good news. Talgel was unspecific regarding the danger he was in.

An elf spoke to Jarahad in Elvish to avoid alerting the human. "Could it be that Talgel's vision was a premonition he ended up buried alive in a mining accident?"

The instant the halfling finished his sentence, a poof of air was visible from the exit, prompting the group to ride in that direction. They soon reached the place and hollered in every direction. "Shaddy? Are you here?"

"Yup! I uh… this is embarrassing!"

Jarahad recognized the elf's cheery voice immediately and sighed in relief. "Maybe Talgel was right, and his life wasn't in peril." He then stared at his friends. "All of you that are earth mages: please help me fix the collapsed wall!"

Twelve halflings, including Jarahad, dismounted and touched the ground with their hands. They soon located a ventilation shaft that collapsed on their friend and mentally ordered the earth to solidify. As if on cue, the ground rumbled for a second, and then a cloud of air exited the mine, followed by Sharad, wearing some odd human trousers with buckles connected in the front and a folded paper hat on his head.

Sharad was carrying a pickaxe and was coughing nonstop until he sat on the ground. Few people could ever believe this nincompoop was the true leader of the Grey Clan as he removed his ridiculous hat and brushed soot from his messy, long hair. "Yeesh! Talk about good timing! I never knew humans could clear up rubble so fast!"

"I forget pureblood elves can't sense harlequin sorcery."

Sharad's dirty face suddenly became blank, followed by a sharp squeak. "Eek! It's you guys! How did you find me?"

While the other elves chuckled at his sense of humor, Jarahad shook his head and crossed his arms. "Talgel told me to save you from yourself."

"Wow! I knew she was good at seeing the spooky ookies like ghosts and stuff, but damn!" Sharad began murmuring eerie sounds and flapping his arms like they were floating ghost lights, which only irritated Jarahad even more.

"Quit playing around, my Lord. This is serious! We suspect your life is in danger, and you are only risking yourself… umm… I do not know what you are doing here or why you purchased this mound of land."

"Well, for starters, the place is haunted, according to the humans nearby. I just had to see for myself. When I discovered a skeleton deep inside but nothing that resembled sorcery, I became convinced the tale was less fantastic and more the tragic story of my good friend Bradley."

"Bradley? Huh?" Jarahad was becoming convinced Sharad was utterly insane. It was little wonder why he had voluntarily left the safety of Almjarhad to pursue his strange endeavors.

"Oh, he is a splendid chap, that Bradley! I had plenty of conversations with him about life and stuff. He's always silent, never responds, still indecisive if I should give him a real burial or if the shaft he died in is better. Great times, great indeed!"

Jarahad shook his head and realized that reasoning with Sharad was pointless. "Okay, so you spent a lot of money to, uh… be a friend to a skeleton."

Sharad twitched his index finger. "Nope, nope, and nope! I bought a dirt-cheap abandoned mine inhabited by a dead guy I named Stanley!"

"Bradley."

"Oh yeah, I uh… he sometimes likes to switch names, quite a character that Murray."

Jarahad rolled his eyes. "Whatever. How in the hell did you support yourself all these years?"

"Well, maybe because I found these things right after I bought Hanky's home!" Sharad yanked a gorgeous glistening jewel from the front pocket of his trousers and proudly showed it to Jarahad.

Jarahad grabbed the unpolished greenstone and gasped when he realized what it was. "Is this a precious jewel?"

"Yeah, Harvey's home is filled with these things. The humans have no idea! I try to live frugally to avoid detection. You know, humans being humans and all. I have a contact further south in a major port where he cuts the jewels. In exchange, I let him keep some of them. But don't worry, I only give him the puny ones. The good ones are yours!"

Impressive indeed! Sharad was quite a character that did whatever he felt like, but he was clever in his unconventional way. Soon enough, a butterfly was flapping nearby, prompting Sharad to lose his despairingly short attention span and jump into the air. "Oh! A butterfly, blue and pretty! The best! Come to papa!"

"Wait, Sharad!"

Sharad stopped on his heels and turned around. "Huh?"

"This is very urgent. Please come with me to Almjarhad. If you wish to live here mining for jewels to support the clan, I will be glad to bring some bodyguards and invent a reasonably believable story to avoid drawing too much attention. But Talgel needs to speak to you immediately."

"I am not going! No way!" Sharad crossed his arms and sat in a lotus position on the dirty ground.

Jarahad covered his face with his left hand with annoyance.

One halfling approached him with a smirk on his face. "Yeesh, he is pouting as if he were a child. Jarahad, do something!"

"There isn't much I can do. He is our leader, and we must obey his commands even when they are incoherent." Jarahad then recalled Talgel's letter and retrieved it. He then offered it to Sharad. "My Lord, Talgel wrote this for you in the hopes you will be convinced. I promise I haven't read it."

"Okay, okay, let's see it!" Sharad instantly became jolly once again and grabbed the letter. Shock filled Sharad's blue eyes when he read its contents.

Greetings, Lord Sharad Shaddy, the best friend of the skeleton, Bradley the First of the Grey Clan. Lord Froylan is going to kill you if you stay there any longer. Return to Almjarhad immediately if you value your life.

Yours truly, Talgel, the haunted fortune teller.

PS: If you return alive, I will tell you some spooky stories! Come see me!

Instead of freaking out, Sharad stood up with a solemn demeanor. "Let me fetch my special jewels bag, and let's go!"

The instant he returned with a satchel of belongings, Jarahad offered him his horse. "Come with me, and we shall share my steed."

Sharad shook his head. "Two don't fit! I can ride my Artica instead!" Without thinking of the consequences, Sharad became infused with mana and summoned an elongated ethereal blue lizard phantom beast that he mounted.

Jarahad screeched in terror. "No! Don't use magic, you brute!"

"Why not?"

Sharad barely had enough time to turn his head when green energy blasted dangerously close to his head and ricocheted backward.

Sweat infused Jarahad's face when he saw a group of pureblood elves mounted on horses wearing an identical black uniform. He offered Sharad the reign to his horse. "Get on my steed, you bloke! Everyone! Return to the city! Protect his life!"

"Yes, my Lord!"

As Sharad mounted the horse and darted off along with the volunteers, most of the guards departed. This left Jarahad to face a blond male elf wearing a half cape and a second medium-height elf with straight brunette hair. Both guards stood next to a green anteater-shaped phantom beast Jarahad surmised was likely a Yerjaha.

Jarahad stood in a defensive stance and drew his special sword that ringed a song of death the second he released it from its sheath. "So, we meet at last, Eirmite guards. Surprised you have remained to fight me to the death."

The blond elf didn't feel even remotely worried and set his friend aside. "Stand back, Tameer. This one is mine."

Tameer grunted, and the green phantom beast dissipated into thin air. "Do you want me to follow them? Looks like they will risk their lives to save that condemned grey elf."

"Nah, the guys will finish them off with their phantom beasts. I am curious to know why they called this one a nobleelf."

Jarahad spat into the ground and growled. "I might be a mortal hybrid, but we have followed the tenets of the kingdom to this very day. We are not the savages you think we are."

The blond elf grinned at the comment. "Interesting indeed. I don't know who you are, but you should feel pleased to know you will be executed by Lord Froylan himself!" In an instant, Froylan drew his black sword and thrust a powerful right-angled blow that Jarahad had difficulty deflecting, so he took it straight on.

Jarahad's shoulders ringed with a spat of pain from the kinetic energy, and he closed his eyes. Something was wrong. Without giving him a chance to ponder, Froylan parried him again, and Jarahad was able to deflect it with incredible difficulty. Standing sideways, he drew a low angled swerve that Froylan quickly blocked, but it caused a ringing sound that made him lose focus. Jarahad took advantage of the moment of confusion and kicked Froylan's abdomen, forcing him to retreat.

"Lord Froylan!"

"Stand back, Tameer! This beast is mine!"

Froylan's constant attacks forced Jarahad to step back to avoid getting killed. Recalling his lessons from Jamarnid, every impact in fencing and hand-to-hand combat that didn't reach its target was more physically tiring than any connected hits. He could not outperform Froylan's superior technique and experience, but he wasn't a weakling or a fool.

Even though Charon hadn't finished Jarahad's training, he was halfway through and could feel the threads of mana in his body that were being sucked into the vantage points of his tattoos with each pressing blow from Froylan's sword. And a sensible revelation came; the vantage points were directing mana into the harlequin spells etched on his skin, granting his arms superior strength.

Fear versus determination, both thoughts battled in Jarahad's mind as he charged forward and thrust Froylan backward, causing the guard to fall on his back.

Jarahad heaved from exhaustion yet felt enthusiasm for outperforming a superb warrior with the help of the spells imprinted on his body. His legs, meanwhile, trembled in pain and fatigue. Charon stated those were the next portion of his body he had to work on, while they always left the head for last. That didn't matter now. The fact Charon infused sorcery into his arms meant he had the upper hand and just needed to wear out his enemy to deliver a death blow.

Froylan soon stood up and grinned. "You've got some talent. Too bad you are not a real elf. Would have considered inviting you over to my team if my Master allowed it."

Jarahad ignored the taunt. He knew better than to risk his life in such a foolish way. There was no way a halfling from the exiled clan would ever set foot in the kingdom. It was painful, but he had already accepted that harsh reality long ago.

The two elves continued sparring for what Jarahad felt like an eternity with the midday sun battering far above. How many hours had passed? Jarahad couldn't care less at this point. Every minute Froylan wasted fighting him meant Sharad was closer to his city. And yet, a nagging feeling tormented Jarahad's mind. Froylan was showing tints of exhaustion. While he didn't breathe heavily, Froylan's swings became sluggish and imprecise. No, Jarahad felt something else. "Harlequin steel?"

Froylan set his sword aside and frowned. "What in the hell are you blabbering, you impertinent fool?"

Tameer cleared his throat and spoke rather matter-of-factly. "Your enemy wonders whether your sword is made of harlequin steel."

Froylan chuckled as he stood in an attack pose. "During my long life in exile, I seldom saw harlequins. Seems like your kind multiplied like cockroaches after I joined the guard almost a thousand years ago. But I'm glad to meet someone with the talent to detect something unique about my sword. Given I am going to behead you, I might as well confer you that bit of satisfaction in knowing a mage of the seas blessed my sword a long time ago."

Froylan purposely placed the sword at an angle, revealing a brilliant hue of multiple colors that glistened like a pastel rainbow against the sun. "See the metal? It is special. Blessed with a magical pearl covering and touted to be indestructible. But you won't live much longer to enjoy it!" Froylan charged forward. Before Jarahad could react, he felt a small stab to his left thigh.

Jarahad's fast reflexes helped him avoid a more severe wound. But lacking any harlequin spells on his legs because of his incomplete training proved to be an unfortunate mistake. Jarahad bit his tongue and resisted the pain. Now that Froylan had confessed the secret of his sword, he knew he would never be capable of breaking it apart. No, he had to take advantage of the things he had that Froylan lacked.

Aiming his arms, Jarahad closed his eyes and said a harlequin prayer at a low volume. Mana invaded the tattoos, and his arms soon glowed with bright symbols on the inked skin. Froylan stopped to admire the strange markings on his body as Jarahad charged forward and stabbed him in the belly at an inhumanely fast speed.

As Froylan dropped his sword and collapsed to the ground, Jarahad aimed for Tameer, who drew his own weapon in the nick of time. Unlike Froylan's strange sword, Tameer's weapon was made of ordinary steel and became sliced apart with one swipe. Affected by the kinetic force of the blow on his chest armor, Tameer became tossed several feet away and fell unconscious. Froylan attempted to stand up, but the blood spewing from his body made him grunt in pain.

Jarahad grabbed the sword to admire it. "My father told me many stories about you. He sends you his kindest regards and will feel very pleased to know I defeated you in an honorable battle."

Instead of feeling insulted, Froylan grinned. "You are Jamarnid's son. He's still alive?"

"No thanks to you, I am afraid. We rule the clan together, and I will propose a truce because of my father's abetted loyalty to the kingdom. I will let you live and won't even steal your precious sword. In exchange, I want you to deliver a message to your king."

"Message? Do you want to barter? With what? Like every guard, I am replaceable."

"Perhaps, but my proposal is very generous. Master Lord Salman is always welcome in Almjarhad, and we shall treat him as an honored guest. Master Salman can also execute Lord Jamarnid anytime he wants. If you promise to remain disarmed within the confines of the city, you are welcome to be present. However, any hostility against my people will be met with equal violence, and my men are not as merciful as I am." Jarahad shoved the sword into the ground and summoned earth magic to envelop it in hardened stone. If Froylan wanted to retrieve his weapon, even his earth mage friend Tameer would have difficulty fetching it. It will give him something fun to do before he returns home.

"Come right back, you unwanted creature! I am not finished with you!"

As Jarahad mounted Tameer's horse and settled into the saddle, he stared at Froylan's face with indifference. "Oh, and one last thing. After getting treated for those wounds and saving your friend's life, ask the villagers to sell you a few body bags. Chances are all the guards you sent to kill my friend are dead."

"What?! Impossible! My men are the best warriors in the world!"

"I am lending this horse. Don't worry; I have no intention of keeping it. The animal's horseshoes and hide have the unique brand of the guard, and nobody would ever want to buy it. I'll pay a human to bring it to the border unharmed." Jarahad then unfastened the travel pouches and tossed them next to the wounded guard. "In an extra token of my kindness, I return your friend's belongings. It might take a month or more for the horse to be brought to the kingdom, and I hope you don't mind. Please send your message to the Elf King. We will welcome him with open arms to finish what Jamarnid always wanted from the start. Have a good day."

Ignoring Froylan's insults as he remained unable to even stand from his wounds, Jarahad rode back home. Halfway back to Almjarhad, he spotted several rotting corpses and the signs of a vicious battle. There weren't any murdered grey elves, prompting him to sigh in relief. After offering a brief prayer for the fallen guards that died because of Froylan's miscalculations, Jarahad continued riding until he returned home, where a horde of elves was awaiting him.

"Lord Jarahad! You're alive!"

"Are you infirm? Do you need a medic?"

Jarahad smiled and shook his head. After accepting a canister of water and washing his face, he offered the horse to a peasant. "This horse belongs to an Eirmite guard. Ensure the beast is rested and hire a human courier to return it to the Elf Kingdom."

"But my Lord, wouldn't you like us to keep this one along with the others we stole?"

"Someone marked those horses with the symbol of the guard, and they are worthless to us. Bring all those horses to the kingdom as soon as possible."

"Yes, I will!"

Jarahad soon reached Talgel's tent. Much to his surprise, she was telling funny stories to a rather jolly Sharad, who was unscathed from the battle. Much to his disappointment, Sharad wore the same dirty trousers and paper hat from the other day. Old habits die hard for this elf, it seemed. "May I join you?"

Henrietta shook her head as she continued to serve both elves some tea. "This is a personal matter with my ladyship and his lordship. I hope you don't mind."

Jarahad frowned, but he couldn't feel any offense. Talgel had rather unconventional ways of doing things, but she helped him save Sharad from certain death. After waving everyone goodbye, he passed through the streets and saluted the hordes of curious citizens until he reached the palace. The gold dome was almost fully assembled, and it was only a matter of days before he would use sorcery to place it in its new home.

A huge smile invaded Jarahad's face when he finally processed the day's events. He no longer felt like a refugee suffering under poor circumstances. Defeating Froylan filled him with a sense of pride. He stormed upstairs and smiled at the sight. Jamarnid was dressed like usual in his black robes while anxiously staring outside the window. The weariness on his face proved he hadn't slept after his departure. Seeing a vulnerable side to the elf for a change was rather pleasant.

Soremin was also in the room, and he bowed at him with vehement respect. "Welcome home, Lord Jarahad."

After patting the priest's shoulders, Jarahad smiled at his father. "I am home and brought Sharad safe and sound."

Jamarnid's hands tried to caress his son's face, and tears fell from his eyes. "I worried about you when I found out the others returned with stolen horses. Who ambushed you?"

And then Jarahad's eyes widened when he realized nobody wanted to tell his father that Äimite guards attacked them. If Jamarnid knew the truth, he could flee the city and surrender to the guard.

Knowing the implications, Jarahad told a white lie for everyone's peace of mind. "Human pirates attacked Sharad. They discovered he visited other villages to barter jewels he mined in lands he stupidly bought, and they went after his treasure. I defeated the ringleader while my men killed the rest. Hopefully, they will learn their lesson, and Sharad will stay within the city's limits."

"Then all is good in the world. I am so thankful you are home safe. I don't know what I would have done if you had died. Please, hug me so that I know it is you!"

A tear fell from Jarahad's eye as he hugged his father with all his might. Soremin was frowning because he knew Jarahad was lying. Maybe if he understood Jarahad's point of view, the brute wouldn't strip him naked and force him to pray on a patio all day as punishment. He made a little mental note to offer a rather generous donation to the temple during his next visit.

A few days passed after Sharad's desperate rescue and safe return to Almjarhad. As expected, welcoming the true ruler of the clan was a cause for celebration. Talgel stood on a magically built stage made of stone in front of the palace. The cacophony in every direction meant almost every city inhabitant was present for this joyous event. Between the battering sun and noise, Talgel focused her ears and estimated there must be around 300 people cheering for her.

It was during times like these she felt glad she was wearing a ceramic mask, or else everyone would notice her flushed cheeks from the inherent shyness of stage fright. A soft hand grasped her, prompting her to turn around. Sharad wore silk ceremonial robes and a small pair of emerald studs on his ears. His long golden blond hair was being blown in every direction from the late summer wind. A tinge of humidity was palpable in the air because of the upcoming wet season. Talgel knew the eccentric elf was on her side.

As expected, among the entire group of volunteers was an unusually jolly Jarahad, who opted to wear regal light green robes and a vest. He could no longer hide his leg injury and had a thick bandage wrapped around it while he ambled around on a pair of crutches. Even though decent medical facilities were unavailable in the city and he could risk losing his leg, this celebration was too worthwhile to rest on a bed. Because of the festive nature of the event, Jarahad let his shoulder-length grey hair loose instead of donning its accustomed warrior knot.

Jamarnid was again wearing black robes, albeit rather elegant silk ones, with a half cape dragging on the ground. On this rare occasion, he was wearing a silver tiara on his forehead that seemed all too reminiscent of the type of ceremonial jewels he once wore as a guard during important festivities.

Sharad quietly whispered in Talgel's ear. "Jamarnid looks happy for once."

Talgel smirked. "He can smile? I thought the Eirmite took everything away from him."

Sharad shrugged his shoulders as he kept on saluting the crowds. "I guess he is happy to see me after so long. He is my uncle, albeit a distant one."

Talgel shook her head. Sharad was miles better than Jamarnid in every way, and she hoped he would stay within the city's safe confines. Knowing him, it would only be a matter of time before he felt imprisoned within the city walls and would once again run off to continue living a life of leisure and adventure.

Henrietta was noted for her stark absence. Because she had no participation in Sharad's rescue, all parties agreed she would watch the event alongside the eager crowds. Standing in her place was the leader of the harlequin clan, an elderly man named Hurrujat. Talgel had known him her entire life when she was born in his ruined underground city, Orsenmuray. He was a harlequin of very short stature and hunched back with thick bushy white eyebrows that reached his shoulders, which garnered a stark contrast to the sparseness of hair elsewhere. He was physically repulsive, with a sharp and crooked nose. A bulging wart had grown on his nose over the years, and it was shedding bloody scabs.

Talgel and the other halflings could tolerate the heat and sunlight very well. Whereas the pureblood harlequins seldom left their tents during midday because of the risk of severe burns. It was only a matter of time before Hurrujat died of natural causes, leaving no heirs. Despite the humiliating losses he suffered during his life, a smile usually invaded his loathsome face, and he never seemed glum or disappointed regarding his situation. Talgel found him occasionally overbearing because of his relentless positivity, but she was incapable of truly hating him. Jarahad was lucky to have earned Hurrujat's blessing to be initiated in the harlequin combat arts as a token of trust between both clans.

After it seemed like the crowds were calming down, Jarahad lifted his arms to speak. "Dear citizens of Almjarhad, we are all gathered today for a significant occasion! After nearly thirty years, our city welcomes home a truly extraordinary guest: the one and true heir to the leadership of the Grey Clan. Let me proudly present to you, Lord Sharad!"

Talgel could hear clothing rumbling rather abruptly. It was apparent everyone greeted Sharad with a polite bow. She was not obliged to perform elaborate salutes, but she still placed her free hand on her chest and quickly nodded her head out of politeness.

Sharad grasped her hand more firmly for a brief instant, released it, and then stood forward. "It has been quite a long time!

Wow, guys, you are doing a fabulous job. Almjarhad is going to become a great place to live. I have traveled from the tip of the northwest peninsula on foot to the dangerous pirate enclaves of Yurtoda Bay. Oh, don't look at me like that, Jamarnid. It is important to meet many kinds of folk even if you disagree with them. I also rode a boat to a different continent! Maybe I will sound disrespectful to my friends born in the kingdom, but there is an enormous world for you to explore. I know everyone wants to improve Almjarhad. Trust me, I was present when we first set foot in these barren wastelands and pondered if we would survive our first winter. So, with little ado, I hope all of you can finish building this city and make it self-sustaining so that you can take a world tour. You won't regret it!"

Half of the crowd remained silent without knowing what to make out of Sharad's odd speech. The rest assumed he wasn't being serious and laughed. A sudden rumble of a small object near Sharad's foot made Talgel surmise one of the city's bitterest residents threw either a pebble or a peanut on the floor. She was curious to know if the offended party was a harlequin or a pureblood elf and whether Jamarnid would punish the culprit.

Jarahad's crutches stomped on the ground, and he spoke to Sharad's ear in a low voice. "I think it is time to settle down, my Lord. As you can see, we have worked very hard to improve the city's potable water problems. Once the castle is completed, we will continue building houses for some of our more affluent citizens. We have done this for you, expecting your imminent return to power."

Jamarnid's snappish baritone voice became audible further away. "Please come forth, my child."

Sharad strutted towards Jamarnid. "Hey there, old fella." Jamarnid's wrists fumbled with some kind of object on his lap. The sound was hard to discern at first, which made Talgel queasy regarding the brutish elf's intentions.

At some point, Sharad snatched it, and a metal latch was unlocked. The younger elf gasped at once. "Impossible!"

Talgel wondered what was going on, but Jamarnid soon quenched her curiosity as he spoke. "Lord Hormandra kept that precious ring in the power of our people during his brief rule, and I have been safeguarding it ever since. I feel guilty I didn't return it to you the instant you became of age, but Orsenmuray was already under siege from human invaders. We prioritized defending it and ultimately fleeing when all hopes were lost. For the following three years, we wandered on a trek that none of you would ever want to remember. It was difficult, and we lost several good friends along the way until we established ourselves in this city. I understand why you fled the first time I offered you the keys to your new domain, and perhaps I was rushing things too much. You might have been an adult, but you still had the mind and body of a teenager with too much energy to spend. I am glad you found your way back home, and I hope you will feel satisfied with everything I did to bring Almjarhad to life. If Master Lord Salman wishes to collect my head, I will offer it with a sense of peace in my heart. Welcome home, Lord Sharad!"

"Long live Lord Sharad!"

Even Talgel bowed with vehement politeness after Jamarnid's speech. She felt he purposely sugarcoated the story to make himself look better than what happened, but it didn't matter.

Sharad, meanwhile, fiddled with what Talgel surmised was a small box for a few moments and grabbed the grey stone ring of his inheritance. The instant he tried it on his finger, the crowd applauded in a massive standing ovation.

"Sharad! Sharad! Sharad!"

"No, wait, everybody!" Once again, Sharad urged complete silence. "I… um… Okay, here is the thing: yes, I am Serumo's youngest child and the nobleelf with the strongest claim to the title of my clan. According to the laws of the Elf Kingdom, I am supposed to be your boss, and it sounds fun at first. The problem is that, well, I am not good with the sword or with politics. All the attacks stalled my education too many times. My uncle Jamarnid and cousin Jarahad have been doing a good job. I would never get things so well organized or build a castle, and wow, this castle looks great! It sure looks much better than the castle I left behind and will never see again."

Jarahad sighed. "You don't want to rule."

"Well, um… I guess you are right, Jarahad. Not that I don't care about everyone. I just think you can do everything better than me because you are so brave and organized and… Oh wow, is that a cicada?"

Talgel covered her masked face with her hand when she heard the ring fall on the ground while Sharad ran off to chase a bug for no apparent reason. If there was proof that Jarahad would continue being the somewhat official ruler of the clan, Sharad's irremediable hyperactivity was probably the primary culprit. If Sharad could bloody stay put in the city dawdling around or eating dirt for all she cared, it would guarantee the critical events of her vision would be fulfilled. Maybe he will someday grow up and rule. But in her limited experience dealing with immortals, their personalities and mannerisms become set in stone from a young age. It becomes pretty much impossible to make them change their minds.

After a servant retrieved the ring and awkwardly returned it to a somewhat dumbfounded Jamarnid, Jarahad stood forward. "Please accept my apologies for his lordship's behavior. I pledge my allegiance to Lord Sharad and will be glad to continue fulfilling the arduous task of ruling the clan until he feels prepared to claim his birthright. I hope all of you can continue offering him the same loyalty as always. And without further delays, let us perform the dome placement ceremony!" Jarahad then directed his voice toward Jamarnid. "Father, will you help us do the honors?"

Jamarnid spoke in a chipper voice. "Certainly! I always enjoy feeling useful for a change." Jamarnid, several pureblood elves, and the only remaining pureblood harlequin earth mage named Sargegef became focused. The elves summoned an array of phantom beasts of the four elemental colors: white, red, blue, and green, while Sargegef's invisible harlequin sorcery caused the ground beneath the inverted gold dome to tremble and then elevate it into the air with absurd ease. Jamarnid closed his own eyes, and mana invaded his body. A quadruped earth beast with the body of a wolf, a humanoid face, and a spiky back emerged from the soil. Its eyes glowed a bright green, meaning Jamarnid was completely in meditation. Humans and pureblood elves that awakened their magic could summon a specific type of familiar devoid of intelligence known as a phantom beast. Once you summoned it, you could not summon a distinct form or change your birth element. Even though Talgel never liked Jamarnid, she felt a pang of envy that his mind could fuse with his gelatinous beast and roam the lands when he entered meditation.

The crowds were cheering relentlessly as the phantom beasts grabbed a series of ropes while the halfling earth mages lifted the soil to elevate the enormous domed roof into the air. With perfect synchronicity, everyone's beast coordinated marvelously as the dome flipped over the prepared metal skeleton, and welders began fastening the parts together. They placed the structure on its new home with such softness that it barely made more than a small thud.

Talgel felt someone hugging her and grumbled. It was Jarahad who seemed to beam in joy. "We now inaugurate Almjarhad Palace!"

The celebration continued well into the night. Even though Jarahad seldom drank alcohol because of his harsh upbringing, this occasion was a sufficient excuse to consume enough fruit liquor to shift his weight on both legs while trying not to fall on the ground. He sat on some hastily created stone benches around a campfire alongside the city's most important inhabitants.

Even Jamarnid was unusually jolly while servants fed him small amounts of liquor. It was unthinkable for an Äimite guard to drink alcohol in public because of the risk of being castigated. Talgel continuously wondered what kind of training Jamarnid had endured to garner that amount of self-restraint.

And then came the singing. The horrible, atonal voice of a very inebriated Sharad while he once again wore his ridiculous paper hat. His fingers were scratching a metallic dish scrubber on a handheld chalkboard. Of all the things he had to snatch from Talgel's home when he visited her tent that night, it was something that made the most grating noise imaginable. Nobody found Sharad's behavior to be annoying. It was among the many perks only a clan leader could enjoy from his subjects.

Talgel crossed her legs the other way after they started feeling numb. The bonfire was burning, which imbued the camp with an acrid smell and warmth from the plummeting outdoor temperatures. She could hear thunder in the distance, meaning it was only a matter of hours before the monsoon began for the next few months.

"Hey, your ladyship? Would you like me to fill your cup?" Henrietta's voice was even more cheerful than when she was sober, which felt too sickly sweet for Talgel's taste.

"Not really. Taking advantage of the occasion, I think these past few weeks have been more than sufficient time for you to quit evading my questions and tell me why Jarahad sent you to help me. I have already asked Lord Hurrujat, and he claims you are not a member of his people."

"Oh, you have poked your nose into Jarahad's personal affairs. Unfortunately, the only person you can pressure for those answers is Jarahad. Given that it seems like he will continue covering for Lord Sharad, you won't be able to threaten anyone to discover the truth."

Talgel sneered in response. "Perhaps you are right. Jamarnid would never help me with personal matters, and Sharad is unreliable. But I still have my methods."

Henrietta chuckled at the threat at once. "The phantom beast that offers you fantastic knowledge about the bowel movements of the city's inhabitants? Or how about the barking dog that made a guy fall from his bed?"

"I get it. Just because most of my visions are inherently worthless doesn't mean you will keep your secret away from me. And once I find out, I will make you suffer for trying to lie to me. You shall see!"

Talgel grabbed her walking stick and rushed off. Most of the city's inebriated inhabitants were lying on the dirt streets, making it hard for Talgel to cross the city without stepping on anyone. She reached an alley, collapsed against a tent, and whimpered from sadness while tears filled her empty sockets. And then something felt different, enticing even. Without realizing it, Talgel filled herself with mana and encountered the demon, who grinned in return.

"We meet again, my dear."

"I summoned my demonic beast? Why?"

"It doesn't matter. But it seems like you got into a heated argument before you came. Touching."

Talgel rubbed her cheek and felt the tear. She then recalled she fought with her roommate without even knowing why.

Not that the demon could care. "She is nice, that woman."

"Will you tell me who she is?"

"Perhaps, all in due time. But that will not speed up my plans."

"Plans?"

Before Talgel could continue arguing, the demon vanished, and a vision enveloped her. It was a dark room, a tent perhaps? Sticky heat was everywhere, along with the aroma of ecstasy from two bodies making love. Like most visions, Talgel could feel the sensations and emotions of her unwilling target. The person she was living through was panting laboriously while being filled with satisfaction from the upcoming culmination of an orgasm. She clutched her chest and trembled from the pleasing electric jolt of energy felt by the subject. It was too dark to know who this was, but there must have been a purpose.

"My love, it was beautiful!"

"Patience, I need to rest. I am not young anymore."

Talgel gasped the instant she recognized the scraggy voice. "This is Hurrujat's future!"

Things got clearer. After a brief inspection, she was currently in Hurrujat's tent. It was indeed bizarre. Jarahad stated a while ago that he planned on building residences for the city's highest-ranked citizens. The first dwelling he wanted to construct was one for Hurrujat, hoping it might improve the skin rot that deeply afflicted him. As the lovers continued talking without revealing any valuable clues, Talgel recalled the vision where Sharad informed her she would drive the harlequins out.

"Could it be I encouraged Hurrujat to fall in love with someone?" That sounded plausible but by itself not a sufficient reason for him to leave the city. There must have been something more sinister, and Hurrujat's lover was a crucial piece in the puzzle. Then, as if by sheer luck, the visitor ignited a candle with a match, and Talgel caught a brief glimpse of her beautiful face. "Who is that?"

Every time a vision ended, Talgel became tossed into the same void while gold leylines branched off into future events she could freely observe. When Talgel entered mundane visions, the branches where the future was still possible to alter usually had ordinary resolutions. For example, the vision where she was the elf having a hard time sleeping because of a barking dog. Every vision had him falling on the floor from his bed, but one leyline showed him chasing the dog away with a broom. In another, he might sleep in another tent altogether. The demon did something to her so she could visit each possible future event in seconds without going mad. This future was different. Anything related to Hurrujat's new lover and his future away from Almjarhad was likely critically vital as it stretched forever.

Talgel floated into the potential futures and soon became increasingly convinced she had seen this woman before. She was not a friend of the woman but recalled seeing her once or twice as a background character during a vision. Plenty of leylines died off, usually meaning Hurrujat died before he could perform something meaningful for future events. In every one of these failed futures, Hurrujat either remained in Almjarhad or didn't leave with his lover. She wasn't sure right now why this was important. When she saw repetitive patterns, it meant she had to do her best efforts to ensure the future happened at all costs.

Curious, Talgel floated into the future and reached a dark city. Standing before her was a medium-height harlequin. He possessed a fierce face, brilliant glowing reddish-pink eyes, and impossibly long grey hair in a braid. "Since when can harlequins have long hair?"

Talgel shook her head and focused. The stranger was an adult; she was sure of that and had never seen him before. It potentially meant this man was not alive yet. Hurrujat was nowhere to be seen. "Huh? That makes little sense!"

And then Talgel froze. Leylines usually ended by her target's death, unless it came to actions that led to them having children. Talgel collapsed on her knees when she realized something: Hurrujat had to leave Almjarhad with a new wife to have a son. She desperately wanted to find out more, but she was running out of mana. A burning sensation that began in her throat expanded to the rest of her body, and her limbs seared in agonizing pain.

"My ladyship? Are you all right?"

Talgel was panting nonstop while her hands trembled from the pain and agony. The area was colder than before, meaning it was still nighttime.

Henrietta was standing nearby and grabbed her immediately. She flapped her demonic wings, and Talgel could feel the chilly wind blasting her face. They soon reached Talgel's tent with its telltale incense scent, and her assistant stuffed a cup of wine into her hands. "Please drink up. It is the beverage I had been telling you about. You will feel better."

Talgel tasted a sweet red wine with an exotic coppery aftertaste. Henrietta shoved the whole cup into her mouth until she finished its contents. Talgel then gasped as the pain receded and her strength returned. "What is this drink?"

"An experimental beverage that helps control your attacks while being able to store the blood you need to survive for long periods. It is still in the early development stages, but it might solve one of the most pressing problems for your people. If you like it, I would be more than glad to bring some more!"

The woman was a never-ending story of enigmas. It only piqued Talgel's curiousness even more. And while it seemed like her friend showed no resentment towards her selfish behavior, she still wanted to know her true identity and Jarahad's plans that never seemed to appear in her visions. For now, she had a critical mission and only had a few weeks to set the wheels in motion while Hurrujat remained in his tent. If she didn't make him fall in love with his mysterious lover immediately, he would stay in Almjarhad until he died of natural causes. Talgel furrowed her brow and stared at her assistant. "Both of us have a mission, Henrietta. We must locate a woman at all costs so I can speak to her privately."

CHAPTER 13 ♦ TIOJA

The fights between his parents only became worse. What initially began as minor quarrels because of Hamara's insistence he learns his grandmother's birth language soon became constant fights over many issues. In his childish mind, Tioja thought it was his fault.

After witnessing another fight that morning, prompting Jamad to rush off in haste, Tioja ran outside. He passed the endless dusty dirt roads, and eventually reached a desolate alley between two tents. As he heaved air into his lungs and felt crippling pain in his abdomen from the exertion, a sweet and high-pitched noise was vaguely audible.

"Mew!"

Tioja's eyes glistened, and he crept on his knees to dig around and locate the source.

"Mew! Mew!"

"A kitty? Don't worry, I'll rescue you!" While clutching on the ground, Tioja reached his arm beneath the side of a tent. His hand soon felt something warm and soft that was desperately attempting to escape from his clutch. "Please don't move. I'm here to help you!" While taking extreme care not to harm it, Tioja held onto a black kitten that attempted to escape. From its small size, Tioja surmised it must be between eight and ten weeks of age. His hands caressed the coarse, filthy fur lined with a few fleas, prompting the little creature to purr. "Where is your mommy? She doesn't love you?"

A disturbing thought came to him as he continued soothing the poor little creature. "I wonder if my mother loves me. My parents are angry, and I think I did something. I try to apologize, and it only worsens things. Maybe if I brought you home, they will feel happy again and forgive me. Wouldn't you like to come home with me and play? I'll take excellent care of you!"

"Mew!"

With increased bravado, Tioja wrapped the unfortunate thing in his filthy cotton robes and rushed back home. Hamara was sweeping the floor with a broom, invading the entrance air with the irascible red dust particles that seemed to sit in every unwanted piece of space in the city. "Ugh, useless Jamad. He always leaves me alone to clean the tent while he drinks with his stupid friends! And this dirt! It's everywhere! I'm so sick of living like this!"

"Mommy?"

Hamara lifted her head and blushed when she saw her distressed son. "Hi, sweet Tio. Is something wrong?"

"I um… I brought a new friend. Please, I want you to be happy."

The instant Hamara heard the shrill mewling of the kitten, her crimson eyes briefly shimmered and then squinted at the little creature struggling to be released from Tio's grasp. "Did you steal someone's belongings?"

"Not at all! This little kitty is skinny, and he's hungry. Can we keep him? I promise to feed him every day! Please say yes!"

Instead of showing anger, Hamara averted her gaze and sighed. She then set her broom to the side, taking care it didn't slide, and unfastened her apron. After hanging her robe in the tiny closet of their cramped living quarters, she stared at the kitten with a tint of disdain. The kitten briefly hissed at her and then sniffed her hand. Hamara petted it, prompting Tioja's hands to feel the familiar vibrating sensation of a purr. Tioja's hopes of convincing his mother to accept a new family member seemed to work, judging from the softness of Hamara's face as she caressed it in silence.

"Did you know my father owned a dog when we lived in Orsenmuray?"

"Wow! I never knew that! Was he big or tiny?"

"His pet was female. Called her Jian, like the wife he lost during the first purge."

Hearing anything related to the losses of his family stirred Tioja to whimper for a moment. "How sad. Grampa looks happy with Svetlana."

Hamara continued petting the little kitten while showing no anger or disappointment. "Jian was an ugly-looking thing. My father would have considered bringing the dog home, but Hurrujat forbade the refugee elves to own pets."

"How mean!"

Hamara chuckled when she thought about it. "I initially thought the rule was strange until life taught me to see beneath the surface, and I never took it as a personal offense against my father or his unfortunate friends. Jamen never really planned on owning a pet.

He would offer himself as a volunteer to visit nearby human enclaves for business transactions to get some sunlight whenever he could. On one such trip, he was eating a meal on the road and fed some scraps to a starving puppy. Little did he know, the animal started following him back home. Assuming the dog would scamper off, Jamen entered the city through a hidden doorway, leaving the dog to fend for itself in the forest. Much to his surprise, the dog was sleeping right where he left her the next time he went outside with one of my older brothers."

Tioja giggled when he thought of the look on his grandfather's face. "I would have enjoyed seeing that happen with my own eyes!"

"His kindness transfixed the poor dog and it became loyal beyond my imagination. Whenever Jamen left the city, Jian would always accompany him with an erect tail that wagged nonstop and barked at any person she deemed to be untrustworthy. I believe Jian saved my father from getting mugged at least once. She was quite a good watchdog."

"You say she was ugly! But she was a capable guardian!"

Hamara beamed even more. "There was nothing remarkable about old Jian. She wasn't all that big, and her fur was black. Oh, and she had a white spot on her hind paw."

"She wore a sock!"

"Yes, Tio, she sure did. Why don't you take off that shirt and put it in the washing basin? I don't want you to get covered in fleas. If they set foot in our home, it will be impossible to get rid of them."

"Can you wash the kitty, too?"

The smile on Hamara's face soon vanished. "Please, Tio. Do as I say before your father returns. He will get angry at you."

Tioja gave the kitten to Hamara and rushed to the other side of the small tent. He unfastened the dirty grey shirt with ease and tossed it into a bucket already half full of water. It seemed like Hamara planned on washing the laundry later that day anyway. He smelled his armpits and nodded. "I can skip my bath another day. We have to save water!" Flouncing his nose from the slightly uncomfortable odor of his sweat, Tioja grabbed a spare shirt from the closet, dressed, and turned around. "Hey, mommy? Is the kitty sad? I can't hear it purring."

While his mother was busy cutting something in the tiny kitchen, a familiar elf returned. Jamad was slightly drowsy and stumbled inside, reeking with a penetrating alcoholic odor as he burped at least once. "I'm home!"

Hamara didn't even bother to salute or acknowledge his return. "If you have any filthy robes, please deposit them in the basin. I will cook dinner in a while."

Tioja soon realized something was wrong. If Hamara didn't plan on cooking, then why was she holding onto a knife?

Before Tioja could find out, Jamad spewed the bad news. "What in the hell are you doing?! Defiling our sacred home with a filthy dead cat?!"

Absolute terror and a voiding sensation filled Tioja's stomach. "Mommy? Where is my kitty?"

Hamara then turned around with a sense of sorrow in her eyes. She set the bloodied knife to the side. "We are destitute and have to eat a rather unpleasant diet because of the endless droughts. There is only enough to feed all three of us."

Tioja's hands trembled, and he took a step backward. His little boot hit the basin filled with wet laundry. He had never felt so trapped as he listened to his mother's disturbing tale.

"Jian survived the second purge unharmed, and we brought her with us during the march. Do you remember, Jamad?" Hamara asked with indifference.

It was an uncomfortable truth that Jamad preferred to forget. He closed his eyes tight and clenched his hands. "I would prefer not to remember what Jamen did. It still gives me nightmares."

Hamara nodded in agreement. "I was around Tioja's age when I learned the hardships of life. To survive starvation, a parent must do the impossible to save their children because they are the world's hope. I know you had good intentions, and someday you will understand. We cannot feed any pets, and I did the only thing in my power to save that unwanted creature from a life of suffering." Hamara placed a small ceramic cup in Tioja's hands. "Drink."

Tioja then gasped when he saw what he held in his hands. Tears flowed from his eyelids as he tried to process why Hamara had given him a cup of fresh blood. "Why? Why are you so cruel?"

"I order you to drink!"

With a yelp, Tioja complied and gulped the coppery fluid in one gulp.

"Geesh Hamara, I thought the cat was a wild animal you found on the street. Did you just kill Tioja's pet? How dare you?!"

"What is wrong with you, Jamad? Tioja was born with a blood disease, and his affliction is far more serious than my own! If he doesn't drink it regularly, he could die! Is that what you want?"

Tioja couldn't take it anymore. Upon seeing the idle kitten and the upcoming fight between his parents, Tioja burst outside without thinking. "Why did I have to be so foolish?! I killed him!"

The following day, Tioja was in the kitchen of his grandparent's tent while his grandmother Svetlana was cooking a dish that inundated the room with the odor of meat. He knew harlequins were devout carnivores. Having their kind in the city benefitted both groups because the animals they raised for food provided the blood that kept the halflings alive.

As a pureblood harlequin, Svetlana was mortal. At over 100 years old, she had already outlived any human in existence. A graying tone had replaced part of her black hair while wrinkles invaded her face. Like all harlequins, she neatly folded her demonic wings like a cape while her hands swirled the stew with a spoon.

Several pureblood elves were against the very concept of marrying a harlequin. To a certain degree, everyone assumed Jamen only did it out of desperation because losing his family was particularly traumatizing. While Jamen initially had a flawed concept of the occasionally vicious inhabitants of Orsenmuray, Svetlana was different. She spoke human dialect absurdly well and tried to find accommodation for the elves so they didn't have to feel alienated. Despite being carnivorous, Svetlana found Elvish culture to be quite intriguing. While Svetlana allowed Jamen and the others to feed her vegan cuisine, which she miraculously tolerated, he didn't seem offended when she fed him a few of her dishes. From then on, they soon spent extended amounts of time together, even venturing into the open air for at least a few hours each day and exchanging stories about their people. It was only a matter of time before they realized how compatible they were. Even though several elves found Jamen's decision to betroth her to be beyond offensive, Jamarnid was supportive because it strengthened their alliance with Hurrujat. Conscious about Svetlana's age, Jamen insisted he wanted to have a large family as soon as possible. Therefore, Tioja had five uncles and aunts. The youngest child was his spunky uncle Nurran, who would likely be the last of Jamen's brood.

Tioja found the dish rather unappealing, but he opted to eat it out of desperation for the chance to stay away from his home for a change. As she broiled the food in the pot, Svetlana observed his face with her glowing pink eyes. "Tell me, young child. What is going on with your parents? The neighbors are worried."

"They... I don't know. My mother wants to teach me the secret tongue, and my father thinks I should learn how to read Elvish. I lied to them, saying I was taking language lessons from you and grandpa separately."

Svetlana frowned as she continued stirring. "It would be unwise to drag others into your family's conflicts. These are difficult times for my people."

"Your people?"

"As much as I find elves enjoyable and virtuous, the harlequins have been suffering. Your skin seems to enjoy the sun, and I never see the halflings sweat more than a few drops, even during the summer. While the heat is rather enjoyable, being held prisoner inside a tiny tent most of the day is miserable. Especially since the pureblood elves are too busy farming and building the city, and most hybrids are still children."

Svetlana's point of view didn't seem encouraging. She then filled some spoonfuls of soup, and Tioja grabbed his bowl with both hands. This was a sign of respect for the harlequin custom of showing gratitude and proving to others that you are unarmed. She then served herself, and her hands touched her forehead. Tioja imitated her without flinching. The elderly woman began reciting a prayer in the secret tongue. "I now bless this meal. For if it is my last, better to enjoy it with a friend than a foe."

Tioja replied in the language, one of a few phrases Hamara had taught him in secret that were important within their culture. "And peace is upon you for this token of friendship."

They both began eating. After a while, Tioja felt irritated about the silence and spoke. "What happened to Jamen and Nurran?"

"Your grandfather is working with an air mage to increase the soil fertility where he drags minerals hidden deep within the earth to the surface with his sorcery while his friend injects air particles to make the soil more porous. The season's first rainfall proved to help the saplings, but he wants them to grow bigger before the floods begin. He is hoping we will have a great harvest this year."

"And Nurran? Is he doing community service?"

Svetlana shook her head. "Lord Jarahad and Hurrujat had agreed to teach sorcery to every harlequin elf. It seems like your kind has an enormous facility to learn our special sorcery, even though it is still somewhat weaker than the magic from our pureblood mages. Nurran has begun the first stages of the training, and he will smoke the potion soon."

"My papa Jamad told me he learned sorcery after drinking something called söma."

"Priest Soremin knows how to make that beverage. While I have never savored it, my people have a different training method that works perfectly fine. Soremin stated a long time ago that he couldn't locate some plants to make söma in these regions and believed even if a human nomad sold him the seeds, they would not survive in this climate. Chances are they will summon you soon to train. Every mage is a blessing for the clan. Don't forget that, sweetie."

"I will, grandma."

The hours of peace with Svetlana were quelled when two bickering elves stood outside the tent. Tioja lifted the tarp and screeched. Jamad and Jamen were arguing with each other, and he knew the reason.

"If you were out in the fields using sorcery, then who has been teaching my son Elvish?"

"I swear I don't understand your words, Jamad! Tio visits my home very often, and I would have never assumed it was because he wanted to take language lessons. I can guarantee I heard no news of this."

"Tioja! I can see you hiding behind that tarp. Come out right now!"

"Uh… yes, papa Jamad." With trembling steps, he stood forward and bowed at his father while tears fell from his eyes. "I lied, I know! I am a foolish ungrateful son. If you want to punish me, do so. Please don't get grandpa and grandma involved! They are innocent!"

"Grandma? Have you been lying to Svetlana as well?"

Svetlana soon stood outside and crossed her arms. "That is correct. Hamara wants to teach him Harlequin, and you want to teach him how to read Elvish script. Both parents have a valid reason to infuse their cultural heritage to the next generation. Yet you should realize there are drawbacks to learning both tongues."

Jamen rubbed his weary eyes at once and stared at his wife. "Tio told you about this, my love?"

Svetlana nodded. "Oh yes, Tio told me everything during lunch. Both arguments are valid: Harlequin words can activate dangerous sorcery by accident or provoke unwanted hostility from my clan, and the halflings believe Elvish script is too cumbersome to learn. Nobody could salvage any books from the Elf Kingdom, and Almjarhad has more pressing problems than finding a place to print books. The poor child is only getting confused! I believe you should not use him as a bargaining chip because of your marital problems. Jamad, if you have a problem with your wife, ask us, and we will visit Lord Jarahad's throne room to offer a solution."

Jamad grabbed Tioja's hand with a sneer. "You're not my family, and you have no right to order me how to raise my son!"

The fighting only worsened that night. Previously, it was just differing opinions on how to raise their child. Now, their bickering strayed to other problems of marital life, such as Hamara's cooking and the incident with the cat from the other day. She would then accuse her husband of being a lazy slob who squandered his dowry on drinking with his friends over helping with house chores.

One day, Jarahad showed up unannounced. Standing alongside him were two young women. The female harlequin had cropped black hair fastened with a pin containing some pearls. With half of her face concealed under a gold masquerade mask, the accompanying halfling wore a striking grey dress with an array of necklaces and belts that made a lot of noise wherever she went.

The instant the three elves saw their visitors and recognized Jarahad's face, they knelt in his presence. Taking advantage of the limited immunity granted to underage elves, Tioja lifted his head before Jarahad permitted him to observe his angry face. He swallowed saliva at once.

Jarahad spoke in a stern tone of voice. "Word has been circulating all over the city for the past few weeks that you are constantly bickering. You don't have to give me any explanations. My assistants have been watching you and confirmed the stories."

Tioja stared at his perplexed parents that remained kneeling like statues.

The masked halfling with a vacant expression stood forward and softly held Jarahad's shoulder. She stared at Hamara. "Citizen of Almjarhad Hamara, please stand up."

Hamara obeyed without question. The twitch from her eyelids suggested she recognized the masked elf.

The woman remained impassive from Hamara's reaction. "It is possible there are still inhabitants in the city who are unfamiliar with my powers. My name is Talgel, and I am the clan's seer."

Tioja almost fell to the ground from a jolt when he heard that. The great Talgel was here to visit his mother? Why? He anxiously stared in her direction while she seemed almost as confused as him.

Talgel didn't bother to wait for an answer. "I summon you to my tent immediately. Come alone."

As the three women walked away to Talgel's colorful tent downtown, Jarahad remained stiff and unusually abrasive. "Just because Talgel only wants to speak to your wife doesn't mean I haven't forgotten about you, Jamad. As one of the pureblood elves of the clan, you enjoy a lot of privileges. I will be more than glad to listen to your complaints in the privacy of your home if you don't mind. If it is something I can fix, I will always be your closest ally. However, the repercussions could be severe if you cannot find common ground to keep the peace. I will let you explain your side of the story while Talgel is busy speaking to your wife. Do you understand?"

Jamad sighed while remaining knelt in front of Jarahad. "Yes, my Lord. I am your loyal subject and remain faithful to the laws of your people. I permit you to come inside."

With a grunt, Jarahad entered the tent without even staring at Tioja. It was rare to see the clan leader angry, and it only made the little elf even more curious to know more about him.

After describing the woman of the vision in vivid detail to Henrietta, the harlequin wandered around the city in search of an adult female halfling with wavy medium-length grey hair, a somewhat ample bosom, and delicate facial features. Henrietta eventually located a potential target that was Hamara. Talgel knew for sure the woman in her vision was critical to the safety of her clan, and she couldn't risk addressing this issue with the wrong person, or the correct future would not happen.

Henrietta brought Talgel to a secluded alley to eavesdrop on Hamara while she chatted amicably with a few harlequin hog breeders nearby. She stared at her boss with concern. "They are speaking in Upper Harlequin. Can you understand them?"

Talgel grinned with utter cruelty without bothering to answer. She was surprised Jarahad never warned Henrietta she was completely fluent in the forbidden tongue and would make a mental note to keep Henrietta ignorant out of spite. Henrietta's job was to be her eyes and housekeeper. Maybe she would open up to the friendly harlequin if she revealed tidbits about Jarahad's motives or the real reason she lived in Almjarhad. There was plenty of time to get to know Henrietta better. She only had a few weeks to have her target enamor Hurrujat before all hopes were lost.

The instant Talgel heard Hamara's lyrical voice, she felt relieved. With that settled, she briefly stared at her assistant. "Hamara is our target."

"Do you want to invite her to your tent immediately?"

Talgel shook her head. "When I lived in Orsenmuray, I spent most of my time with my deceased parents and Jarahad. We never spoke to each other growing up."

"I heard from the villagers you traveled across the desert together before you reached this city."

Talgel frowned at once. Henrietta still hadn't mastered the art of keeping her mouth shut. "According to the memories from that awful period of my life, I recall she was just a child. We are almost three hundred people, and I spent most of the endless trip in Jamarnid's carriage because we are handicapped. Believe me; I had no interest in engaging in small talk with rambunctious children when we were resting."

"Jamarnid, is that awful?"

"If you live here long enough, he will inevitably say something offensive about your race in your presence. He will be especially intolerant because you can't speak the sacred Elvish tongue. I am surprised he has treated you with even minimal decency."

Henrietta didn't fall for the ruse, and the monotone tone of voice hinted she would say nothing revealing about herself. "I have barely spoken to his lordship because my mission is to assist you by Lord Jarahad's command. Lord Jamarnid has not summoned me to his presence, and I believe it is because he doesn't care about me. As long as Lord Jarahad feels confident in my capabilities, I doubt I will be summoned to the palace. Is there something you want from me regarding this woman?"

"The fact I could not pinpoint the woman in my vision was Hamara is proof I know nothing about her. I can't summon her to my tent until I fully understand what I am facing. You could take advantage that she doesn't know you. Speak to her to learn more about her personal life and motives. Try to be discrete and avoid making her suspicious. If she knows I am involved at this stage, she could ruin everything by lying or running to Jarahad. Discover everything you can about her life and report to me. I will then figure out how to set my plan in motion."

It didn't take long for them to discover she was married to an average-looking brunette elf named Jamad, and they both had a rather odd-looking child with reddish-green eyes named Tioja. Despite Talgel's initial concerns that Hamara would be madly in love with her husband, it didn't take long for her to realize Hamara's constant complaints about her useless husband with his closed-minded views were practically a godsend.

The relentless vitriol spewing from Hamara's mouth regarding her husband whenever she visited her pureblood harlequin neighbors was only proof that Talgel's worries convincing her to become closer to Hurrujat might not be an impossible obstacle after all. Given the woman had grown up in his city, chances are he had seen her from time to time. Or at the very least, they could rekindle stories about their fallen homeland and discover they had a lot in common.

After fetching Hamara, the three women entered Talgel's gaudy-looking tent. Talgel unconsciously sat on her comfortable rug and crossed her legs, per the harlequin custom, to stir an unconscious reaction in Hamara. It seemed like Hamara didn't fall for her scrutiny and remained standing.

Henrietta sat on her modest bed and observed them from afar.

Talgel spoke without staring at Hamara's face. "Please sit on the rug, Hamara, and let me tell you something."

Hamara briefly bowed and followed her command. "I am all ears."

"Abandon your worthless husband at once."

Both Hamara and Henrietta screeched at the same time. "What?!"

Before Hamara could even process Talgel's insensitive words, Henrietta stood up to protest at once. "My ladyship, I thought you wanted to spy on this woman for the past few days to save their marriage, not further ruin it!"

Hamara grunted. "How dare you spy on me!"

Talgel continued without showing insult. "Sorry about hiding the reasons, Henrietta. Both of us know Hamara's marriage with that stupid elf is a lost cause. Better sever it immediately so she can find true happiness with another man."

"Are you insane?! I am not leaving Jamad just because you say so! I don't care that Jarahad is banging you every night!"

The blight prompted Talgel's lips to twitch for a brief instant. "That was low, Hamara. My dealings with the clan leader are my concern only. And yes, your personal life is my problem because I have seen your future, and Jamad does not appear in it."

"Huh?" A stutter escaped the enraged woman's lips when she heard that. She didn't like Talgel, but her predictions were a legend within the city. Nobody knew when or who would become invited to her tent to learn their future. Everyone knew Talgel's predictions never failed. When Hamara heard Talgel encouraging her to leave Jamad, it felt both baffling and insulting. Yet, it incited her curiosity more than everything else. "Are you saying Jamad is about to die?"

Talgel smirked as she thought about it. "I studied your future, and Jamad does not appear in it. I am uncertain what becomes of him. If you could at least listen to what I have to say and keep an open mind, your future will be filled with satisfaction and happiness you are not attaining for as long as you live here.”

Increasingly intrigued, Hamara relaxed her shoulders. She felt disgusted regarding the concept of abandoning her husband. Another side of her conceded Talgel had the answers she was desperately waiting for. “You have my attention. Even though I disagree with your ridiculous suggestion, I cannot deny I feel pleased I will be told my fortune ahead of time.”

“My sorcery doesn’t work that way. I can see future events up to a certain degree and how the future will be affected depending on several factors, but the person I see in a vision can still abide by their free will. In your case, if I hadn’t arrived to speak to you in private, Jarahad would have summoned you and Jamad to his throne room. He would have then forced you to remain miserably married while trying to pretend you are all one happy family. You won’t be allowed to say a word of Harlequin in the privacy of your home or savor any meat near Jamad’s presence. Jarahad might even force you to kiss Jamad without grimacing. He is steadfast in keeping the clan united at all costs.”

“Ha! Kissing him in the throne room? Jamad doesn’t even know he is a miserable lover in every way, and yet I have fooled him for ages.”

“Once again, I couldn’t care less about those things. You could continue hating your husband and pretend your marriage is doing fine. Jarahad is obsessive when he sets his mind on something that could cause inner conflict within the clan, but we can easily fool him. The problem will be Soremin. Lord Jamarnid worships that old bastard, and Soremin has methods of persuasion that can detect even the most minimal degrees of deceit.”

“I couldn’t care less if I lied to a priest. I don’t care about the religion of the pureblood elves.”

“Maybe you will care about this: You might be forced to swear an oath in Jarahad’s throne room where you will amend your marriage. If you cannot convince him, Soremin could force both of you to live in his temple indefinitely and receive counseling. If you thought you hated your husband now, imagine being forced to have a horde of priests eavesdropping on you during every waking minute of the day. Do you want to pray nonstop in penitence and have Soremin driving you mad until you commit suicide?”

Henrietta gasped at once. "Suicide? Seriously?"

Talgel nodded with a smirk on her face. "One of the possible futures was Hurrujat being present during your funeral while Jamad commits suicide. Every future in which this scenario happens always results from both of you living in Soremin's temple."

"I… will inevitably die if we swear to Jarahad we will try to salvage our marriage... and Hurrujat is present during the funeral? Why is that even relevant?"

The conversation had finally veered towards the place where Talgel wanted. It had all been too easy to lie to the foolish woman about the marriage counseling visions. In reality, she never saw that in her vision. Soremin would have probably reignited their love and made them forgive each other. Talgel didn't have any moral qualms in lying to her subjects to obtain the correct future. "Tell me, Hamara. What do you think about Hurrujat? You must have spoken to him growing up."

The strange comments took the woman by surprise. "What?! Hurrujat is too old-fashioned! With that disgusting scab growing on his face that never heals. We never even spoke to each other when I lived in his city."

"Those are just superficial differences. I have known Hurrujat my whole life. His heart is true and kind. He is a misunderstood visionary who has never felt shame about his ancestry and customs. While most people believe he was too soft because he gave the rest of his gold to decorate Jarahad's palace instead of building his own castle, I believe the man knows how to repay a debt far beyond the societal requirements of a good deed. Since when has Jamad ever done anything for anyone that isn't himself? Or complimented your kind mother? Why did he marry a hybrid elf with strong emotional ties to her harlequin ancestry when he could have married a human instead?"

The words sank into Hamara's mind. She had never realized those things until now. Hamara continued to feel offended by Talgel's intrusiveness, but something felt different. It was as if Talgel understood her actual needs better than she did herself. Her feud with Jamad was more of a symptom than the core of the problem. Living in Orsenmuray was bliss compared to a struggling tent city ruled by elves. It felt like a poor replacement for her happy childhood among her true people. She wasn't sure at this point why Talgel insisted she should get closer to Hurrujat and wanted to figure it out.

Talgel's grin only became more prominent as the minutes went by. "You know, there is a reason Hurrujat didn't want to live in Almjarhad Palace. Haven't you found that to be odd?"

"Odd? In what way? Why would a proud king become a servant in his enemy's castle?"

"Exactly! Hurrujat feels indebted to Jamarnid because he saved his life, but at the cost of being treated like a second-class citizen. If you speak to him privately, he will confess he desires to live in a wonderful underground cave without being locked inside a tiny tent all day. Imagine the frustration he must feel about spending over half of his day walking in circles without being able to go outside to relieve himself. To have lost his luxurious life and end up with a limited life in poverty. You could spend hours discussing your common problems and see you are meant for each other. Perhaps he isn't physically attractive, but his devotion and kindness make up for it tenfold. He wants to relive his glory days ruling a true harlequin city. Yet nobody has talked to him about these things. Your heart clamors for the same escape, and I assure you he will listen to your suggestion he should live the rest of his life with the happiness he deserves. Imagine how wonderful it must be to have a man truly pay attention to your words instead of the indifference of your husband." Talgel then drew a deep breath of air. Hamara's laborious breathing was a good sign she was thinking about abandoning Almjarhad to create a new harlequin city. When Talgel saw the vision where Sharad told her she drew the harlequins out in such a nonchalant way, she presumed he was mad. Now that she thought about it, the concept made perfect sense. And she didn't even have to get blamed for driving the harlequins away because Hamara would do it for her. She wasn't sure this was enough to attain the future she needed so desperately, but it was a good start. "Now that you have heard the words I have to say, I urge you to avoid speaking about it with your husband or with Jarahad."

Henrietta was unconvinced. "My ladyship, how do you plan to do this? Jamad could use emotional blackmail, and Jarahad can abuse his political power."

Talgel smiled once again. "Jarahad gives me ample freedom to speak to my subjects because he respects me. If either person causes Hamara any problems, she can claim I forbade her to speak to anyone. Jamad won't be able to do anything because Jarahad never demands me to reveal more than I need. You should think about these words and decide, Hamara. I cannot force you. I am merely the messenger."

After pondering for a few moments, Hamara felt tempted to speak, but she shut her mouth at the very last minute. The halfling merely bowed at both women and left without ushering a word. Talgel didn't feel proud she was going to sever a marriage and cause undue pain to her innocent child, but she knew it was for the best.

CHAPTER 15 ◆ TIOJA

Things were getting stranger with each passing minute. As the lowest-ranking member of the family, it was Tioja's duty to serve Jarahad in Jamad's tent with the highest quality of service.

Not that Tioja minded it all that much. He didn't know Jarahad very well, and it was amusing to have him eat lunch in his tiny home. The clan leader always presented himself as a serious and hard-working person. So, seeing him trying to lift Jamad's spirits with a bottle of hard liquor was a pleasant change of pace from the prior bickering he had endured for the past few months.

It didn't take Jamad long to get tipsy, and he was already shifting his weight to avoid falling while he sat in front of the tiny stove where Hamara had already started a hearty soup that bubbled into the enclosure.

Inebriation also affected Jarahad, but only enough to let Jamad keep his guard down and try to get to the root of the problem. "Tell me, good man. Are the rumors true you are having trouble in paradise?"

Jamad nodded as he gulped an entire cup, and tears fell from his eyes at the burning sensation of the beverage and his woes. "I love her, Jarahad. Somehow, she is running away from me with each passing day. Having a large family like Jamen was something that I had high hopes for. I love her as much as you adore Talgel."

Jarahad smirked at the response. "I wouldn't be the best person to give you romance advice. Everyone knows I have begged Talgel to marry me, and she outright refuses even though I have given her everything she has ever wanted. Maybe Hamara just didn't feel ready. You must understand she is barely forty years old and spent part of her childhood in Orsenmuray."

"That's one of my conflicts with her! She has spent most of her life in Almjarhad, yet she is obsessed with the life she lost in the second purge. I just don't understand her. Unlike us, Hamara was traveling with her family to the neighboring human villages to barter supplies. She never saw the bloodshed when the Outambilan army crushed the city. Her parents survived the purge completely unscathed."

"That may be true, but the voyage in the desert was a grueling ordeal. Not everyone survived the three-year march with their minds intact."

Jamad sighed. "We have all lost so much. I was courting a fine dame in the Elf Kingdom who was killed during the first purge, and I barely escaped with the clothes on my body. Maybe Hamara views my homeland as something malignant because the elves rejected us. I don't wish to return because Master Lord Salman has placed a price on my head, but Hamara could still see the wonders of the Elf Kingdom. Maybe if we find a way for the halflings to visit it without getting harmed, they would realize how wonderful our society truly is. Please agree with me."

Jarahad smiled even more warmly and served him another cup of liquor. "I was just a newborn infant when we fled, so I have no memories. From my father's stories, it was certainly a wonderful place. Now that Lord Sharad has returned, I may contact the kingdom and barter a deal."

"Gah! Master Salman wants to chop off Jamarnid's head and burn all of us alive. Lord Sharad has his reasons for fleeing this city when we first arrived, and it just makes me sad. He remembers the paradise he lost, whereas my wife wants to… speak that vile tongue and ingrain those ideas into our son!"

Tioja squeaked when he realized both elves were now staring at him. He was trying to seem marginally visible by quietly stirring the stew, hoping to hear the conversation without being an active participant. With a trembling hand, he dropped the wooden spoon into the pot. "Eek!"

"I'll get it." Jamad summoned a string of water magic that adhered to his hand and removed the spoon from the stew. He then returned it to Tioja. "Be more careful, son. I don't want you to get burned."

"Sorry, papa!"

Both elves chuckled when Tioja began bowing profusely until he got dizzy and sat on a cushion with a loud plop.

Jarahad smirked at the odd spectacle. "Are you drinking sufficient blood?"

Jamad growled at once. "Of course he does! I try to keep him healthy by feeding him blood from the goats the harlequins raise to eat, but Hamara keeps on finding stray pets to kill. She has traumatized our son on purpose!"

Jarahad shook his head. "You are one of my dear friends, Jamad, and I do not want to force things. But you must understand, I can't allow friction among the clan."

"Are you referring to Hurrujat?" Jamad asked.

"I have offered to let him live in Almjarhad Palace, and he outright refuses. I appreciate him very much and wish I could do more for him. Now that the crops are growing so well and the critical components of my castle are finished, we can start setting our eyes on the street planning of the city. I would love to grant Hurrujat the residence he deserves."

These words were inciting Tioja's interest even more. He didn't know Hurrujat very well, but he always seemed like a nice person. Seeing the stew was cooked, he scooped the servings into three bowls, rushed to Jarahad's side, and offered the bowl with both hands.

Whereas Jarahad took the dish and recited the harlequin prayer of gratitude without even blinking, Jamad was only angrier than before. He grabbed his bowl and started munching on his meal without waiting for Tioja. The little elf sighed and quietly ate his dinner with a furrowed brow.

Jarahad remained pensive as he picked his food. "You must let Hamara teach at least some harlequin customs to your son."

"I won't do that!" Jamad's clenched fist pounded the ground and accidentally spilled some soup on the fire that hissed.

Jarahad lifted his hand and redirected the flow of smoke into the air.

Whereas Jamad didn't think too intensely about what he just saw, it soon became clear to Tioja that their guest was doing something enviable. "Is that air magic? I thought you were an earth mage!"

Jarahad blinked for a moment and ultimately chuckled. "This child is so sweet! You didn't know halflings become attuned to two elements?"

Tioja's face became blank as he shook his head.

This amused Jarahad even more. "Your child is very young, Jamad."

"Should I take this as a compliment or an insult?"

"Neither of the two. We have been so busy trying to stay alive in these lands that it forced us to leave the children without formal instruction."

Jamad then spoke with an inquisitive look on his face. "So, have you located a person who sells the plants Soremin urgently needs to make the potion?"

Jarahad shook his head with a heavy sigh. "Some key plants need a cooler climate. I know Talgel summoned her phantom beast with the aid of the harlequin method after a grueling training when we lived in Orsenmuray. The first time I tried it, I felt inconsistent results. After a second attempt, my harlequin earth sorcery was awakened, and I soon started commanding the earth to do my bidding like it was the easiest feat in the world."

"Ah, the dangerously addictive potion you have to smoke and enter a dreamlike state. I don't think I want my son to risk himself like that."

"Another valid point, but we have little choice. I risked smoking the harlequin potion a third time and awakened my second element. I encouraged other halflings to emulate me, and all became dual mages."

"Amazing!" It was Jamad's time to gasp in awe, and he stared at little Tioja, who was scooping radishes into his mouth with a sense of enchantment from the conversation. "Dual mages are extremely rare among my people! Every single one of them ends up invited to the Äimite guard!"

Jarahad nodded in agreement. "And pureblood harlequin mages are only attuned to one element, just like humans. I think it has something to do with our mixed ancestry, and I have already started a program where the older halflings are being trained."

Tioja spoke with a trembling voice. "Such as my uncle Nurran?"

Jarahad chuckled. "There are so many halflings that I can't recall Nurran's face. I wouldn't be surprised if he awakens his first element soon. We urgently need earth and water mages."

It was Jamad's turn to nod in agreement. "We sure do, but I am worried about my son. Are you sure there is no other way? Wouldn't you prefer to give him söma instead? It is a safer method."

Jarahad sighed. "I already had this argument with Soremin and Jamarnid many times. Maybe we can ask a human from a northern country to smuggle the plants because they can't grow here. After what happened to Sharad recently, I believe traveling alone is far too dangerous. We don't even know if Tioja can summon a phantom beast."

"What about you? If Talgel can summon one, wouldn't you have the same ability?" Jamad asked.

Jarahad smirked. "Perhaps the mana I sometimes feel is just a fluke because of my human blood. Talgel has been very secretive regarding how she summoned her strange beast."

"By the way, it seems like the women are running late. Do you think Hamara will spend all afternoon spewing vitriol about me?"

Jarahad crossed his arms and thought. "Talgel told me we needed to visit you at once because she saw Hamara's future."

"Do you have any idea what she saw?"

"It must be important if she was so desperate to see her without notice. Maybe little Tio can help us. Hey Tioja!"

Tioja perked his ears and bowed at Jarahad with politeness. "Yes, my Lord?"

"It seems like we will not require your services. Maybe you can locate your mother and tell her we have finished speaking, and she can come back inside."

"Yes!" Feeling pleased because Jarahad improved Jamad's mood, the little halfling rushed outside, crossed several streets, and tried to locate Talgel's colorful tent. He soon stepped inside with a massive smile on his face. "Hello! Is my mom here?"

Talgel seemed somewhat ambivalent about Tioja's unannounced visit as she stitched together a new piece of gaudy stone jewelry. Henrietta was meanwhile sweeping the floor with a broom. "I have finished speaking to your mother and no longer have any business with her."

"Oh, that seems nice. Lord Jarahad has spoken to my father as well!"

A cunning grin invaded Talgel's cruel face. "Oh, did he? What did he want?"

"Well, he says my father should let me learn some Harlequin because not everything is bad and… oh, and I am going to learn how to use magic soon!"

Henrietta began clapping with overt enthusiasm. "Oh, how lovely! You will certainly become a great mage!"

The smile on Talgel's face only increased a notch. "You are destined for greatness, little child. Practice very hard every day, and you shall be rewarded. If you are searching for your mother, I am certain she will return home soon. Perhaps she went to the market to buy groceries or to think about what I said to her. Now, be a good little boy and go back home. Your father awaits your safe return."

"Well, that seems fine, thank you!"

As Tioja scampered off, he crossed several streets, hoping to see his mother in vain. Recalling Jarahad's words, he reached Hurrujat's nondescript tent that resembled everyone else's. Tioja didn't bother to go inside, but the air by the entrance smelled like Hamara's favorite perfume. Little did he know, far worse things were happening, and there was nothing he could do to stop it.

Jamarnid spent a good portion of his days recalling the life he left behind and whether he could get his long-awaited execution. Even so, Almjarhad Palace was a suitable replacement for the home they lost. The increasingly luxurious commodities of the circular-shaped dwelling were a pleasant respite from living inside a tent.

When engineers agreed upon the building's design, wheelchair accessibility was a significant concern. Exorbitant fees for wood and an impetus to make the harlequins feel more integrated meant elf architecture would be unfeasible. And so everyone agreed to construct the beige stone palace in an unusual circular shape.

Designers did this so that an intertwining staircase could be lodged between the rooms facing the windows and the central throne room. A ramp built alongside their mirror staircase would require crossing the entire hallway in the opposite direction to reach another level.

Being forced to always take a long detour to the opposite end of the building to change levels was a minor annoyance. But Jamarnid preferred this solution because this ensured the ramp inclination wasn't too pronounced. Staff soon became used to alternating between climbing stairs and the ramp on a given side. Jamarnid never found it too annoying to bump into someone taking a detour if they were polite enough to step to the side and ensure his wheelchair had priority.

And then the memories of her haunting face returned. Jamarnid should have killed Chandrice when he had the chance because her carelessness condemned the entire clan. He gave her coins to purchase potions to avoid pregnancy, and she stupidly squandered the money away on clothing. He just had to fall in love with a high-born harlequin-human hybrid who didn't want to settle for a peasant lifestyle! If only he had done things differently, he wouldn't feel the anguish of her loss as much.

A soft knock on the door was audible. Jamarnid stopped looking at the window, overseeing the urban sprawl, and nodded at a servant. "Open it."

"Yes, my Lord!" It was funny how Jamarnid could preserve the Elvish tongue within the palace, even though most of Almjarhad found it easier to communicate in a vulgar pidgin language that only menially resembled Elvish. The servants tending to his many needs today were pureblood harlequins. He didn't like their kind that much, but he grew accustomed to their company. They were just as reliable as the halflings and spoke formal Elvish in his presence at all times with shocking fluency.

Dressed in his customary white robes, Soremin barged past the servants that were dutifully kowtowing in his presence. He bowed at Jamarnid at once with a smile. "May I have the pleasure of sitting down?"

"Come join me, for I cannot stand up!"

Both elves chuckled, and another servant hiding in the shadows offered the priest a comfortable wooden chair. He was most impressed as his hands touched the intricate carvings. "This piece of furniture must have cost a fortune."

"My son Jarahad has been using his influences, and humans shipped these materials to the city. Lord Sharad learned how to become a carpenter, among other strange endeavors during his travels. Building things keeps his mind busy. I am intrigued by his talent, quite impressive indeed for a nobleelf."

Soremin nodded in agreement. "Does Jarahad do it on purpose just to keep him here?"

Jamarnid sighed. "This city is both a beacon of life and a crushing prison. I initially allowed Sharad to wander around because we heard no news from the Äimite guard after the second purge and assumed they would never travel so far away from the border."

"So you discovered the truth," Soremin smirked at once, and it looked like he would have a conversation with Jarahad about lying to his father in the future.

"It was Jarahad who finally confessed to me. He couldn't accept the guilt of hiding things from his father and only kept the information because he worried I would risk my life if I knew Froylan was nearby."

Soremin lifted one of his thin eyebrows with suspicion. "Senior Lord Froylan visited these lands? Could it be he plans to locate our city?"

"He probably had to cower back to the kingdom to lick his wounds and bury the small squadron Jarahad's men killed with ridiculous ease. Now that he knows Sharad is living in this area, it is only a matter of time before he pinpoints the location of our city."

"Yet you haven't written an edict forbidding the pureblood elves to leave this sanctuary."

"I may have to ask Jarahad to do it in the future. I can no longer write it."

"Will you ask Lord Jarahad to seal the edict with Sharad's signet ring?"

Jamarnid's hands caressed a velvet pouch dangling on his neck with sadness. "I would never do this to the true clan leader."

Soremin didn't feel convinced and pursed his lips. "The guard took away your Äimite ring, and it is likely a piece of decoration in Lord Ferhyr's office."

"I will think about a solution. Jarahad deserves to have his nobility ring. It might be the right time to give him one so he can truly act as a nobleelf. In the meantime, as long as Sharad keeps his mind busy and stays put in this city, we still have plenty of options. I know you have little interest in leaving Almjarhad and wish to focus your time on teaching your students, but several pureblood elves have wandered to the nearby cities alone."

"If you are worried about their lives, they should start wearing a disguise or travel with an armed escort." Soremin replied.

"About that. How are the students doing? Any new mages?"

"The harlequin priest Harselon uses a potion I find worrying because one of its key ingredients is highly addictive. Luckily, harlequins have the common sense of restricting the knowledge of making the potion to a select few individuals. As long as the halflings use it under supervision, they become attuned to at least one element with no problems. It is indeed quite miraculous. Just this week, we have three new water mages. I asked Sou to start intensive classes for these students. The summer has ended, so he doesn't have to worry about exerting too much."

It was good news, and Jamarnid's softer voice magnified it even more. "Good, very good. I would still prefer the halflings learned how to summon proper phantom beasts so they are less reliant on donated mana. The more mages we have in the city, the safer we will be if the guard attacks us."

"I agree. I feel like the halflings are cursed because they were born out of sin. It pains me that no matter how many purification ceremonies I do, they still need to drink blood to survive and suffer the change once every few years. It disappoints me because a lot of my students have exuded great promise."

Jamarnid felt somewhat ambivalent about that statement. His eyes focused on the window and spotted a familiar elf parading around the streets with her ever-present accomplice, Henrietta. He sneered at the sight.

Soremin instantly knew why. "You dislike Lady Talgel."

"She is a disgrace to our people and a bad influence on my son. I'm glad she has cruelly rejected his hand in marriage. I would have exiled Jarahad if he married her."

"I will not meddle in those personal affairs. I am, however, concerned about Talgel's behavior."

"What do you mean?" Jamarnid asked.

"She is hiding something. It simply isn't natural none of the halflings can summon a phantom beast. But she attained the ultimate gift without disclosing the technique she used. I find it to be selfish!"

"Jarahad claims she smoked the harlequin potion when we still lived in Orsenmuray, but she remains tight-lipped about her training. My son has tried to equal her. Once he achieves it, I am certain he will share the knowledge with everyone because he is a person of decency and goodwill."

"I concur, my Lord."

A servant soon arrived and offered a cup of warm tea to Soremin. A second servant offered a spoonful to Jamarnid to sip in silence.

Needing the help of servants to perform even the simplest activities was degrading to Jamarnid, but he had grown used to it. At least Soremin's pupils were always helpful, and they maintained his skin free from any pressure sores.

Soremin then stared at the distance. "You miss the kingdom and the guard you betrayed, don't you?"

"More than anything in the world."

Soremin's face became pensive as he stared outside. "If something bad happens to this city and we end up attacked, I promise to tell you how I got my scars."

"Ha! You never wanted to reveal your little secret for centuries. Why confess to me now?"

"I sense a change in the city. Something is pulling our people apart. I do not know what it is, but we shall know soon." He then stood up and bowed at Jamarnid with profuse politeness. "I just wanted to give you this piece of knowledge to be used as a last resort. Good day."

The farmers could now rest after an unusually successful harvest. There was a possibility they could terraform even more significant swaths of land with the help of the clan's new mages. While the rain brought a lot of benefits in that respect, it brought misery in another. Dozens of tents had to be dismantled because earth mages discovered underground basins that rendered the land prone to flooding after one persistently long storm.

Following Talgel's sensible suggestion, Jarahad waited a few months before building Hurrujat's home because of this problem. Luckily Almjarhad Palace was far away from the flooded areas, and the patio was currently the abode of at least a dozen families.

He did everything he could to make their stay more comfortable, but there was one essential person who was missing. The second he learned from a soldier that Talgel had just arrived at the palace soaking wet and carrying all of her meager possessions in a cart, he rushed to the entrance at once. It didn't take him very long to spot the halfling drenched in rainwater. "Just what in the hell are you doing, Talgel?!"

An equally drenched Henrietta guided the donkey up the path with her usual carefree attitude. "Isn't this water soothing? I love the temperature! Why can't it rain like this all year round?"

Jarahad shook his head and focused on the woman in a front-row seat.

Talgel remained unimpressed. "Someone stupidly placed my tent in one of the newly discovered flood-prone zones, and we had to leave. Luckily, my assistant hired a carriage. The neighbors helped me pack my belongings. I hope you don't mind my unannounced presence among the other refugees."

"Nonsense! Both of you are going to live in the palace! And don't snap at me with that menacing face of yours, Talgel. You will get a warm bath immediately before you end up infirm. Henrietta, you must accompany her."

"Yes, my Lord!" Henrietta nodded in agreement, whereas Talgel sighed with annoyance.

Talgel's rudeness annoyed Jarahad to no end, and sometimes he wondered whether it was a godsend they hadn't married yet. While his servants gave both women a blanket and accompanied them inside, Jarahad felt increasingly concerned. Jamad's tent was also stationed on his patio, yet he could never find the increasingly elusive Hamara. Even worse, none of the pureblood harlequins with flooded tents wanted to accept his invitation to live on the patio, preferring the small hill downtown where Hurrujat lived.

Focusing on more pressing issues, Jarahad offered to assist the soldiers. "Give me one of Talgel's boxes. I will help you guys set it up in her private room."

A while later, Jarahad became soaked after hauling Talgel's crates into her guestroom. She soon arrived with a confident poise after memorizing the palace's architecture, accompanied by an overly eager Henrietta cleaning her short black hair with a towel.

"The baths in this palace are sure nice, your ladyship! We should stay here indefinitely!" Henrietta cheered.

Jarahad agreed with Henrietta. "Ignore my father's demeaning comments. As long as you avoid angering him, you are welcome to stay. Sharad now lives here too, and you can spend time with him."

Talgel didn't show the same enthusiasm as her hands touched the individual crates for several minutes. "Fifteen boxes. Looks like you brought everything here." She approached Jarahad and pulled a few errant strands of hair from his messy warrior's knot. "You are wet as well. You did the tasks of a common servant for me?"

"Of course, I would! I am still patiently waiting for you to accept my hand in marriage. Nothing you have done has taken away my huge appreciation for you."

"I didn't need the bath. I could have dried myself up fairly easily."

"Huh?"

With an annoyed sigh, Talgel's right hand caressed Jarahad's cheek, and he felt a brief wave of harlequin sorcery. Little did he know, the warm sensation erupted all over his body, and steam evaporated from his skin until he dried up within seconds. Shock and awe left him speechless.

Henrietta giggled at once. "You never knew her ladyship can summon harlequin fire sorcery?"

"I thought Talgel could only summon her phantom beast. How is this possible? When did you learn?"

"I learned in Orsenmuray a few days before the purge, but I could never properly use it. Henrietta encouraged Harselon to give me the harlequin potion late at night. I always knew I felt some connection to fire sorcery, and it was only recently that I could fully use it. It sure comes in handy, even though I can't do much with it."

A blush emanated from Jarahad's cheeks because he felt an increased attraction toward her. "You are just one never-ending series of secrets, Talgel. But I believe you will feel more comfortable here."

A grin invaded Talgel's face from the offer. "Oh, I guess I can concede defeat for once. Staying inside for the next few weeks will be good for me."

Jarahad lifted an eyebrow. "You saw a future event, haven't you?"

Talgel nodded with indifference. She touched each crate, and steam invaded the containers until everything dried up. With Henrietta's help, she sat on the bed and stretched her aching muscles. "Something important is going to happen to the clan, and I don't want you to feel upset because nothing you will do can stop it."

Jarahad swallowed some saliva because he knew it wouldn't be pleasant. "What do you mean?"

"During the summer, I had a different vision. It revealed to me something important that you may disagree with, but it must happen at all costs. I have used my influence as the clan's seer to push things towards that goal. The other day, my beast revealed to me that the future has been written in stone. Nothing you will do can alter it at this point."

"Is it the death of someone I know?"

"Fortunately, not for now. But I can guarantee Jamad's marriage is finished."

A void filled with dread invaded Jarahad's chest, and he turned in both directions with a sense of panic. "Is this the reason I have not seen Hamara? Where is she? Is she okay?"

Talgel cruelly grinned when she thought of it. "Oh, she is doing very fine. She has never felt better in her whole life. She has found true love, and any attempts to separate her from her new lover will be pointless."

Jarahad's hand trembled at the dire thought. How foolish he was! He assumed Talgel wanted to speak to Hamara to save her marriage. In reality, she was sabotaging it from the start. A sense of fear from the cruelty she harbored made him feel something he seldom felt in his life: pure and unequivocal hatred. Jarahad heaved as he tried to calm down before he harmed Talgel. She was being honest, and he hoped it was her little way of apologizing. In the end, Henrietta's sorrowful face was proof she followed his command to avoid sabotaging Talgel's plans, which ultimately backfired. Jarahad's anger soon melded into remorse from the revelation, and he sighed. "Would you know who she has been seeing? Is she with her lover right now?"

"Oh yes, Hamara loves him deeply, and she will soon want Soremin to dissolve her wedding vows to marry him… under the harlequin custom."

A quip in Jarahad's lip suggested he knew who the lover was. "She wants to marry Hurrujat, am I correct?"

"Hurrujat will be a loving husband, even though I feel bad for Tioja. Jamad is your friend, and you only want the best for him. But you must agree Hamara felt miserable with him. She married too young and didn't know what she wanted."

It was a painful revelation, but Jarahad had to agree with her. He could have tried to stop Talgel's plan if Hamara had fallen for a peasant, but Hurrujat was their widowed ruler, whose children perished in the second purge. Even if Jarahad wanted to salvage their marriage, for Jamad's sake, it would be at the high price of creating unwanted animosity with the harlequins.

Talgel's face was showing its genuine facial expressions without the intrusive mask. She was enjoying this, and it scared him to the bone. Was she always this cruel, or was she lashing out because of her handicap? Her expression and the equal remorse on the usually upbeat Henrietta meant even more secrets were waiting to be unraveled.

"What is going to happen to the clan?" Jarahad asked.

"At least for the next few decades, Almjarhad will continue to prosper. Sharad will remain in the palace doing his personal projects, and you will continue to rule alongside Jamarnid. I will even reveal a little tidbit to keep you motivated: you will summon a phantom beast. I do not know when it will happen or what the beast looks like."

The revelations filled Jarahad with hope. His sense of joy soon became switched for concern because he was certain Talgel was keeping something important. He soon realized why. "And the harlequins?"

"Save for a select few with solid ties to the elves, they will all leave. There is absolutely nothing you can do at this point to stop it."

Tears welled in Jarahad's eyes when he understood the severity of the revelation. If Talgel had the confidence of revealing it to him, it was bound to happen. He had previously heard unpleasant news from her, yet this one hit him particularly hard. After trying to garner some composure, he again spoke. "I need you to tell me two things, Talgel."

"I am all ears."

"One, is any of this my fault? Two, will I see them again?"

It was a tricky question, and Talgel smirked. "The harlequins consider you their friend and don't harbor animosity against you. They unanimously appreciate Sharad as well. Even though they detest Jamarnid, they made their decision for other reasons. The harlequins wish to create a suitable underground city to rule. They harbored these feelings for a very long time. Now that Hamara has admitted she wants to become Hurrujat's wife, a sense of patriotism has reignited because Hurrujat might give them a new heir to carry on his legacy after his death. If you do your best to soften the gap between both clans, they will remain our allies. I believe you will see the Great One at least once."

"The Great One?"

After waiting for Talgel's nonverbal approval, Henrietta's face soon became invaded by a smile. "Talgel saw a vision in Hamara's future. She is going to have a son with Hurrujat after they leave Almjarhad. He is a halfling of great power, and his future extends beyond any vision Hamara had seen. Not even the immortals of this city have ever shown a leyline as extended as this unborn child."

"Does that justify Hamara's cheating? And leaving us?!"

Henrietta frowned. "I wouldn't be the best judge of the morality of altering the future. Talgel saw flashes of you meeting the Great One. It will be important, albeit Talgel doesn't know the motive yet."

Talgel interjected rather abruptly. "I will reveal it to you someday when I find out. The Great One must be born at all costs, which requires you to grant the harlequins the chance to create their new city. If you show Hurrujat your complete support, you will have an easier time requesting the Great One's help when the time comes."

Hearing so many revelations prompted Jarahad to pace around the room in circles while cleverly dodging Talgel's boxes of jewelry and clothing. After pondering enough time to drive most people mad, he finally stopped. "I will speak of this privately with Hurrujat before I set the alarm. If my father discovers Hurrujat plans to leave us, he will think it was treason, and he could act irrationally."

Talgel nodded at once. "Confirm it if it makes you feel more at peace with your conscience. Even invite Soremin to garner a neutral perspective of the matter. If Soremin hears the bad news in person, he will give Jamarnid proper counsel and avoid unwanted bloodshed. Even though I feel uncomfortable staying here, Jamad might lynch me when he finds out."

Jarahad was glad Talgel made this decision and would do his best to avoid aggravating Jamad. If he had to lock him up in a prison cell, he would do it for the clan's sake. Jarahad bowed at Henrietta, kissed Talgel's hand goodbye, and soon found Soremin pacing through the palace hallways with his usual carefree attitude. "I need you to do me a huge favor."

"What do you mean? Is a student of mine causing you any trouble?" Soremin asked.

"Far from it. I need you to accompany me to visit someone. I will tell you everything along the way."

As both elves passed through the city wearing suitable outdoor robes under the drenching rain that never seemed to stop, they eventually arrived at a series of tents inhabited by the harlequins.

Now that Soremin and Jarahad knew the reason why the harlequins purposely clustered together, it made sense. While both elves saluted the harlequins standing outside in the rain, most of them acted with indifference, which only made Jarahad more suspicious.

They soon arrived at Hurrujat's tent, and Jarahad rang the outdoor bell. It was an ugly thing that made an unpleasant noise, but Hurrujat couldn't hear anything else, so it had to do. Before long, a familiar gorgeous halfling dressed in a bathrobe greeted the door.

Hamara gasped at once. "Lord Jarahad! Why are you here?"

After taking a deep breath, he spoke in a stern tone. "We have to speak to Hurrujat immediately."

"Oh, I am not presentable! My assistant Hamara is nursing my aching back." Hurrujat's screechy voice replied from afar.

Soremin could never put up with lies and stormed into the tent. The abode had ostentatious rugs on the floor and a potent and cloying odor permeated the air. Hurrujat enjoyed the best cuts of meat, and it was clear from the two plates of half-eaten steaks on the table that Hamara had been eating the second one. As expected, Hurrujat's tiny frame with a frumpy and frail constitution was resting on a soft fur bed.

Jarahad averted his gaze from the disconcerting sight. "I apologize for visiting you like this. Would it be possible for you to wear something first?"

"Ho! Ho! A pleasure indeed for the great Lord Jarahad!" Hurrujat tried to grasp the camisole next to the bed, but his arthritic hands couldn't reach it with ease. Hamara rushed to his side and dressed him with a smile on her face. "Thank you, my dear. My shining light."

"Your're welcome, my Lord."

Jarahad wanted to vomit out of respect for his betrayed friend, but he tried to keep a sense of reticence to confirm his doubts. Both he and Soremin bowed at the harlequin and sat down. "I will get to the point. I know Hamara wishes to dissolve her wedding vows with Jamad and marry you under the harlequin custom."

There were zero doubts in Jarahad's mind that the tint of resignation etched on Hurrujat's face meant Talgel's story was true.

Soremin sighed. "What you have done is a grave sin, Hamara. The elvish custom allows a marriage to be dissolved, but you were not supposed to commit adultery before you did it."

It was Hamara's turn to turn defensive. "Hogwash! That isn't my religion, and I didn't know what I was doing! I should have never married when I was a teenager. I feel disgusted just thinking of it!"

Soremin frowned even more. "According to the elvish custom, you became of age when you turned twenty. You were more than old enough to understand the implications of your decisions. Please remember I performed the ceremony and would have done nothing that goes against the tenets of my country. If you wished to marry someone else, you should have spoken to me first, and I would have given you counsel."

"If you wish to blackmail me into salvaging my ruined marriage with Jamad, forget it!"

Jarahad turned around. "Soremin, we both know you will have to dissolve the marriage. Try to find a way for Hamara to find repentance without forcing her to become your student. There is no reason to continue aggravating this issue even further at this point."

"Very well, my Lord. Since you were never a fervent believer of your elvish vows, nullifying your marriage could be an option. May Hamara find peace with the false prophets of the harlequin gods." While Hamara smiled with glee and caressed Hurrujat's eager face, Soremin remained grave. "In exchange, there is one thing you will have to do. Jamad must give up his wedding vows as well."

Jarahad didn't like the sound of this. "Jamad would never do that! He will keep his vows until the bitter end."

"That may be so, but since it looks like Hurrujat wants to find a new home, we don't have another option."

Hamara's and Hurrujat's faces became pale at the same time.

Hurrujat began mumbling in the human dialect rather awkwardly. "I told no one about those plans! They were just foolish ideas I had after bedding Hamara!"

Jarahad shook his head. "The seer revealed the truth to me ahead of time. If she believed it was safe to tell me this, it means you have already made your decision. I should just give you my blessing with Soremin present so that Jamarnid doesn't suffer a fit when he finds out. I respect you, Hurrujat. Given you wish to live in a harlequin city instead of Almjarhad, I will do my best to make this transition as smooth as possible."

Soremin nodded in agreement. "You have a heart of gold, Hurrujat, and I had many misconceptions of your people for far too long. I disagree with Hamara's behavior, but I know your feelings for her are true. We should strive to maintain our friendship for as long as possible. I will miss you very much." He then bowed at the harlequin with genuine politeness.

Hurrujat felt humbled by the comment and patted Soremin's shoulder. "If you give us your blessing to leave, we shall do it in good faith. Thank you so much."

After the room's ambiance soothed from the respite, Jarahad quenched his curiosity. "Will you leave us soon?"

"I will speak with my people and invite all of those who wish to come. If all goes well, perhaps we shall leave before the sun becomes intolerable. I prefer to get on the move when the weather is at its best." Hurrujat replied.

"That will happen in five months. Why wait so long?"

"Wishing to evict us so soon, Jarahad?" The snarkiness in Hurrujat's voice was embellishing.

"Not at all. I found it odd because there are only several dozen pureblood harlequins in the city and many of them are married to elves."

"Some will stay if their ties are strong enough. But I need time to speak to the halflings as well."

"What?!"

It was Hamara's turn to speak. "I am not the only halfling who clamors for their harlequin heritage. Many of us want to learn more about our mortal origins and embrace them. Convincing them to abandon their families will be difficult, so we may need more time. We will be gone before the sun reaches its pinnacle and will never return unless it is for something urgent. Please come visit us once we settle down."

When it became apparent Talgel had told the truth all along, Jarahad sighed in relief. "Seems like I will complete my training, after all. I was worried Charon would leave immediately."

Hurrujat chuckled at once. "As a token of my goodwill, I promise to remain until you finish your initiation. It is exhilarating! I would love to be present when you do it!"

"I thought nobody could watch the last test."

"Fellow initiated such as me and trusted members of my clan can watch because we will not spoil the secret. I hope you comply with the oath of secrecy as well."

"I will."

Both elves stood up, bowed at Hurrujat politely, and soon departed together. Much to their joy, the rhythmical beating above the tent had vanished, and the sky was clearing. It was going to be a delightful afternoon, after all.

Jarahad's mind was racing at full speed during the voyage back to the castle. Talgel was right in her assertion that Hamara and the harlequin clan were leaving. If that is so, he had an increased urgency to master his sorcery before Charon left.

Jarahad stood before the recently finished doorway to the throne room, accompanied by Soremin. It was a godsend that Talgel encouraged the priest to hear Hurrujat's side of the story yesterday, so that he could attempt to reason with the ever-volatile clan leader when he listened to the bad news.

Strangely, the increasing omnipresence of Sharad's exceptional craftsmanship would briefly delay tense moments like these. Over these past few months, Sharad had established a carpentry shop in his bedroom, and he volunteered to carve the doorways of at least some of the palace's principal rooms. For the time being, most rooms would have to conform with curtains, but Sharad didn't mind as long as he freely decorated his creations.

A carving of the downfall of Teryoura City suitably decorated the imposing twin throne room doors. Sharad could even replicate the architecture of his lost home with a striking semblance. The square-shaped Teryoura Palace was in flames as grey elves were slaughtered by Äimite guards. Standing on one tower was the imposing figure of Lord Hormandra during his brief rule. Hormandra's identity was easy to pinpoint from the wing-shaped appendages on his arms while he lifted a pipe that emanated deadly attacks. The masterpiece was a stark reminder of their tragic loss so that the younger generations would never forget where they came from. Sharad couldn't have chosen a better theme for these doors.

"Are you ready for the inevitable, my Lord?"

Jarahad inhaled and nodded. "Let's see my father Soremin and pray we can avoid bloodshed. The sooner we get this over with, the better for both sibling clans."

"Very well then." Soremin pushed both heavy doors open. The circular-shaped room had rows of stone bleachers for the public alongside the walls and a frontal dais. Small windows illuminated the gold-domed ceiling near the top, aided by torches on the walls. There was plenty of time in the future to build much more refined lamps.

Jamarnid sat on the most oversized throne chair while wearing his customary black silk robes. The velvet pouch containing Sharad's ring was dangling from his neck. Sharad was by his side and dressed in a ceremonial grey robe highlighting his cheerful face. From the stories Jarahad heard growing up, it was the custom of Salman's palace to dress all visitors in the heraldic color of their clan.

Citizens filled the bleachers to the brim, save for a handful of soldiers standing guard around the city. Skimming through the room, Jarahad found Hurrujat seated among his people and Jamad on the other side, along with several other pureblood elves. Hamara was nowhere to be seen. A bad omen.

Jamarnid's dark green eyes lightened as Jarahad and the priest approached the dais. "Welcome, my son, to this strange meeting assembled by Priest Soremin under complete urgency. I am sorry we don't have a third chair for you. Lord Sharad took your place."

"No offense taken, my Lord. I am glad he is present to hear beforehand what we must say." Jarahad replied with a bow.

A cunning grin appeared on Sharad's face as he was playing with a wooden yoyo he made to curb his irascible boredom. "It sure is a pleasant spot. I can see everyone present, and the sound quality of the room is just amazing. Listen! HELLO!"

A colossal vibration emanated from the echo of Sharad's hollering and bounced through the roof and back again. The sound slightly hurt Jarahad's ears. Sharad's pervasive childish behavior was a small price for having him back in his home.

Jamarnid's right hand tried to caress Sharad's chest. "Yes, my son, this palace is a marvelous piece of architecture we all worked very hard to build to please both you and Lord Hurrujat."

A brief chuckle could be audible from afar. Jarahad frowned because he knew Hurrujat found the comment to be funny. He let the offense pass for the greater good. "I agreed with Soremin to organize this special meeting with every able-bodied adult member of the clan to make an important announcement so there are no misunderstandings or hearsay."

"Well, come on, my son, spill it out!" The tone of Jamarnid's voice rumbled with increased concern than before.

Jarahad inhaled once again. "Lord Hurrujat has agreed we will split apart our clans from this day forward."

"What?!"

Jarahad knew his father would feel riled from the announcement. He never expected to feel mana invading Jamarnid's body and his phantom beast heading his way with no time to prepare.

"Watch out!"

Before Jarahad could even react from the shock, Soremin stood by his side and summoned his fire beast that attempted to stop the onslaught of magic from harming them both on the brink of time.

Soremin's face soon became covered by sweat as his hands continued repelling the attack of Jamarnid's phantom beast. "Calm down, Lord Jamarnid! You'll kill your child and the city's inhabitants if you don't stop!"

"Shut up, Soremin! So you've been feeding ideas into my son and betraying the harlequins, aren't you?! I'll kill you both for kicking them out of our city!" As if on cue, Jamarnid's earth beast became increasingly vicious as it prowled and scratched Soremin's helpless firebird in its attempt to kill them both.

The throne room became filled with anguished shouts and the stomping of hurried feet towards the exits at full speed. Jarahad extended his hands and absorbed his father's phantom beast while he devised a desperate plea. "Father, don't kill everyone! You must trust us! We never insulted Hurrujat's people! You know me! Please listen, for god's sake!"

The apparent act of hostility only angered Jamarnid even further. "How dare you raise your hand against the father that birthed you! You worthless, disgusting creature birthed by that vile whore. I knew I made a serious mistake when I didn't murder Chandrice when I had the chance! If it hadn't been for you, I would have continued to be a guard, and our clans would have continued to live in peace in their ancestral lands."

Before anyone could react, it was Sharad's turn to stand up. With a firm grip, he grappled Jamarnid's arms. "Stop hurting them!"

"Jamarnid's Lusenia is going to destroy the ceiling!"

Jarahad attempted to raise his hands and absorb the beast before it obliterated the delicate support structures of the building. Before he knew it, someone was quicker than him. The instant before the Lusenia hit the ceiling, a greater force made it vanish. Jarahad sighed in relief when Hurrujat took advantage of his superior command of harlequin sorcery to devour the beast on the brink of time.

The elderly harlequin was standing with a face covered by unexpected disdain. "Please stop fighting! And as for you, Jamarnid, I can see that you have shown your true colors by insulting the memory of my granddaughter. A cherished child sired by my deceased son and the heiress of an important human merchant so that he could reach a favorable trade agreement. Chandrice didn't know about the laws of the Eirmite guard when she slept with you. I suffered immensely when I first discovered she was being held hostage in the kingdom thanks to the letter written by Lord Serumo, who begged for my help. If you want to blame anyone for risking it all to save your pitiful life, blame it on the good intentions of your deceased cousin, Lord Serumo. You're nothing but a traitorous oath-breaker!"

The room soon fell silent as Hurrujat heavily breathed upon finishing his rant. He harbored these intense feelings for a long time, only now that Jamarnid's derisive behavior brought them afloat.

Soremin relaxed his shoulders and stared at Jarahad's face with concern. "Did he injure you?"

Jarahad shook his head as he stared at his hands marred by first-degree burns. "No wonder my father was so headstrong during my training growing up. I've never ended up injured absorbing a phantom beast attacking me before."

Sharad stood in front of Jamarnid and crossed his arms. "You fool! I know I have no right to demand respect from everyone, but I believe you owe poor Chandrice an apology! I was just a little child, and perhaps I never fully understood everything going on during the chaos. However, I know Chandrice was worried about your wellbeing, and she would cry in her bedroom every night for hours as her baby continued growing. She knew they would execute you the instant Jarahad was born. Committing suicide to spare your life was impossible because Master Salman sent Äimite guards to keep a close watch on her. Even my brother Hormandra found Chandrice to be a redeeming person. And yet you choose to insult her memory despite knowing the punishment for sleeping with her from the start!"

Jamarnid eventually recovered from the shock of seeing Sharad's act of assertiveness. Instead of apologizing to anyone, he pitifully rubbed his face with his wrist as best as he could and turned away. "Reclaim the leadership of the clan, Lord Sharad. I am unfit to rule. Save the alliance my foolish son has ruined for some unknown motive!"

Sharad shook his head and bowed at Hurrujat with overt politeness. "As an honorary member of your family, I urge you to accept my apology on behalf of Uncle Jamarnid. Living in exile with his injuries has left my relative without a sound mind, and he can sometimes say horrible things. If there is anything I can do to convince you to stay, I will be more than happy to help you."

Jarahad sighed in relief. Maybe Sharad could try to convince the harlequins to remain after all!

Talgel soon stood up and cleared her throat before Hurrujat even spoke. "Nonsense, Lord Sharad! All of you are getting ahead of yourselves! Despite Jamarnid's pathetic tantrum that nearly killed all of us here, we did nothing that prompted the harlequin clan to make this hard decision. Tell them, Hurrujat!"

Talgel's ability to know his plans took Hurrujat somewhat aback. There was a part of him that wondered if her sorcery granted her other unforeseen abilities. "Thank you, dearest Talgel. Too bad you already declined my invitation to accompany us to our new home." Jarahad frowned upon hearing this and wondered if Talgel had any additional agendas of her own. Hurrujat continued speaking without a care in the world. "We appreciate the hospitality of the Grey Clan. Despite Jamarnid's hurtful words, we are not angry at you. There is a reason why harlequins are also known as the wretched race. We change into our new skin during irregular intervals, eliminating prior blemishes and growing a new pair of wings. Our skin suffers from the dreaded rotting disease that can cover our bodies with painful growths and end our lives after an agonizing ordeal." To further prove his point, Hurrujat pointed at the lesion growing on his nose. "There is no longer any cure for this. Eventually, this vile growth will invade my eyes, and I will die. I have reached the eve of my life and feel prepared for the inevitable. But these people can still be saved. Even though the halflings have prospered in these desolate lands, we purebloods suffer exponentially during the summer. Maybe if we had moved to a forest, we could have adapted decently enough. These lands have a hostile climate for us. After discussing it with my kin, we have made this tough decision to leave your city soon."

Murmurings from the elves and harlequins invaded the throne room as everyone tried to understand Hurrujat's position.

Jarahad stared at Soremin and spoke in a softer voice. "I guess we managed the impossible and did the right thing by announcing the split in front of everyone to avoid misunderstandings."

Soremin nodded. "I concur. If you had told your father in private, he could have mortally injured you. My medical knowledge is deficient, and you would have likely perished, which could have worsened things. At least the harlequins will leave under favorable terms, and you will still be allowed to finish your training."

Despite being a sadistic bastard, Jarahad knew Soremin always offered sound advice. As everyone continued speaking and Sharad was once again occupied playing with his yoyo, Jarahad stared at Soremin's face with increased seriousness. "Hurrujat will invite as many citizens as possible over the next few months. Do you think your students will leave as well?"

Soremin shrugged his shoulders. "Technically, any student that completes their apprenticeship may leave this city without being punished. I did my best to guide them back to the path of virtuousness and hope they spend their days rethinking their lives and doing something good with it."

"Will you brand the ones that leave before they finish their training?"

"They would have to suffer that fate. However, given that Sword Master Charon will probably accompany them, Almjarhad will no longer have any mages capable of performing those spells."

"Fair enough. I am quite surprised the harlequins invited Talgel. She never told me."

"She is a cunning woman. I sense some darkness in her, albeit she covers it very well."

"Huh? What do you mean?"

Soremin was no longer paying any attention as he noticed the group of pureblood elves was ready to speak.

A lanky male elf with wavy blue hair in a ponytail stood up. "Members of the harlequin tribe. On behalf of the last survivors of the Grey Clan, we thank you for everything you did for us. We bid you good luck. None of us plan to leave Almjarhad, but once you settle down, please tell us the location so we can stop by. You will need a few mana donors to build your city."

The harlequins began clapping in approval from the generous offer. Everyone started leaving the throne room when Sharad waved goodbye and left without saying a word. After a lot of persistent pleadings from the servants, Jamarnid finally accepted their offer to be carried to his wheelchair and ushered away rather unceremoniously. Jarahad doubted Hurrujat would ever want to forgive him after his tirade.

After Soremin left to speak to his students, Jarahad paced across the palace hallways to organize his thoughts. Talgel was obviously up to something, which worried him. If she rejected Hurrujat's generous offer, it was because she remained loyal to the elves despite being an orphaned half-breed with no genuine ties to either clan. His pacing edged to a halt. Someone was missing from the meeting, and it ate him inside. He stormed to the outdoor patio, where a group of children was playing.

And then he saw her, the halfling willing to cause a rift in the clan to satiate her selfish pursuits. Hamara sat on the stairs watching the children without a care in the world. Much to Jarahad's annoyance, she was chewing on a slab of jerky. "Mind if I join you?"

"Oh my, Lord Jarahad!" The snickering in her voice was proof she no longer had to maintain the charade. He decided for the greater good to let her insult slide for this one time.

"I was expecting you to be present at the meeting."

"Someone had to babysit the children."

"How convenient! While your lover was busy defending his tainted honor and explaining his perfectly valid motives to leave Almjarhad, you were here this whole time acting the role of subservient wife."

Hamara growled as she continued munching on her slab of salted meat. "I have agreed with Hurrujat to continue living with Jamad for now."

"Tell him the truth. He deserves to know you wish to leave him!"

"This isn't just about me. Tioja needs his mother more than anything in the world. Even though the thought of sleeping with Jamad disgusts me, the elves don't know the truth yet. Hurrujat and his closest aides have agreed that it would better serve our ulterior motives to avoid causing a scene while they try to convince the halflings to join us. Even though I still respect you as the clan leader, I urge you to keep this information to yourself. When the time comes, I will leave Jamad."

"Very well. I will only agree to this because Talgel cornered me to the wall. Try to be mindful of Jamad's feelings. He doesn't deserve to be treated so poorly. I also urge you to follow Soremin's request. If you plan to remain in Jamad's home for a few months, try to maintain the peace. Hopefully, he will give you his blessing to marry Hurrujat. If he doesn't let you leave, I will use my authority as the interim clan leader to force Charon to place a brand on your body."

Hamara shrieked at once. "You wouldn't dare!"

"As a halfling who has remained allied with the harlequins, you know better than most how powerful those spells are. What kind of curse would you prefer? One where your skin can never touch sunlight again? Or how about one where you will suffer from terrible agony if you use harlequin sorcery? Maybe Charon should place a curse where you will find sleeping with Hurrujat unbearably painful, even though the brand causes you to become irresistible to him. Maybe I will ask Jamad to choose your curse."

"You vile, ruthless, annoying, pitiful…."

"At least I have values and care about my friends, Hurrujat included. If you decide to continue prolonging the inevitable by living with Jamad, the condition for my silence is that you must convince him to dissolve the marriage. Find the way, and you will be free to leave and return to this city whenever you fancy. I hope you don't involve Tioja, or else the deal is off. Good day, Hamara."

As Jarahad walked away, a feeling of dread invaded him. It was a minor victory for Jamad's sake, but he knew Hamara would leave him, no matter what. He just hoped Jamad and Jamarnid would both come to grips with this cruel truth sooner rather than later. Talgel's ability to know his plans took Hurrujat somewhat aback. Likely, a part of him wondered if her sorcery granted her other unforeseen abilities.

CHAPTER 19 ♦ JARAHAD

The moment he had been anxiously awaiting finally arrived, and Jarahad was so excited he couldn't fall asleep all night long. In just a few more hours, Charon would place the final tattoos on his face. On that very same day, he would perform the second and far more difficult last test of his initiation.

These elated feelings did not derail his everyday duties. While he tried to give the departing harlequins ample freedom in their recruiting efforts, it was sometimes difficult to settle the inevitable discord when they attempted to go overboard separating families. None of the pureblood elves wanted to leave Almjarhad for apparent reasons, and he ordered the harlequins to avoid harassing underage citizens.

Jarahad stared at the barren stone ceiling of his bedroom and sighed as he stretched his arms. His fingers twitched upon the realization he unconsciously kicked the blanket off the bed during the night. This was an old habit that prompted more than one heated argument with his father in the past. He then made a despairing realization. The fact Jarahad didn't feel chilly from the approaching dawn was a sign spring was fast approaching and, along with it, the imminent threat of the clan being split in two. Initial excitement of completing his long-awaited training was soon replaced with the dread of losing many people he had grown to appreciate over the years.

"Will the clan have enough people to till the lands once they are gone?" That was a ridiculous comment. Talgel assured him that Almjarhad would prosper, and his position as the interim ruler would continue. After meandering in his thoughts while sunrise arrived, Jarahad finally became fed up with his pervasive thoughts and sat up.

Since he was born, Jamarnid educated him in the only way he could by mimicking his harsh Äimite training. As Jarahad stared at the array of robes, he felt a slight pang of guilt. He was also a member of the clan's noble family, yet Jamarnid's upbringing always enticed him to opt for the most practical option. He selected a slightly more elegant peasant robe for the special occasion.

Jarahad then stared at his bedroom. The large windows offered a pleasant view of the ocean. Besides a few cushions and rugs, his circular-shaped room was devoid of decoration. This was because of Jarahad's disdain for frivolous displays of wealth and guilt for the squalid living conditions of his people.

After placing his robes in a basket, Jarahad did yet another repetitive activity because of his father's insistence: he lifted the blanket from the floor. With an elegant motion, the fabric floated in the air until it nestled on the cushion of the elevated flatbed lying atop a hollowed stone slab. His hands meticulously pushed the blanket to remove any crevices and irregularities until he felt sufficiently satisfied.

"Lord Jarahad, are you awake?"

"Come in."

Sharad stormed inside while wearing a cotton sleeping robe and was brushing his insanely long hair. Jarahad believed the blue robes only highlighted the countless freckles adorning the blond elf's fair face.

"This is unexpected! You never gave me the vibe you were a morning person," Jarahad said.

"You sure got that one right! I just wanted to say hi because you will be out most of the day."

"I still have one last chance to convince Charon to let you come with us."

"The cranky old chap with a loose tooth that wiggles in his mouth? Nah, I already asked him for permission, and he outright said no." With no hesitation, Sharad sat on the bed and ruined Jarahad's recent attempts to keep his private quarters tidy.

The forced smile on Jarahad's face twitched from Sharad's accidental mischief. "That's a shame. Did he care to tell you why?"

"Well, he says I can't be initiated because I don't have harlequin blood. We both know I couldn't care less about learning how to use your weapon; I just wanted to support you. We are family, after all."

It felt odd to have the rare chance to enjoy Sharad's company. Even though both elves were almost the same age, Sharad spent so much of his time depressed or wandering around while Jarahad was busy ruling the clan that they were practically a pair of strangers. In an attempt to mend the rift that destiny formed between both cousins, Jarahad sat alongside Sharad and patted his shoulder. "Well, at least you got to see Charon place the remaining vantage points each month."

"Yeah, that looked painful! And I am squeamish, like, really much." To further emphasize his point, Sharad caressed one of the stud earrings in his ear. "I went to this place in a pirate haven to, you know, look rougher on the edges and blend in. One guy got his lower back inked with a Kraken, and it was a great tat, by the way."

"Your point is?"

"Oh yeah, I think I'm rambling a bit like usual. What I mean is that to sort of fit in and stuff, the guys encouraged me to do something with my body. And look at this." Sharad pulled his sleeve and revealed an irregularly shaped blue blotch on his skin.

"You tried to get a tattoo on your elbow?"

"I know, pretty stupid. The artist showed up with this big needle, and it hurt. Man, it was awful, and I screamed like a sissy and shoved him away. Everyone was making fun of me. I probably would have ended up hurt until I decided on getting something else and got my ears pierced instead."

"Well, you look nice with those earrings."

"I do too! Too bad your daddy scolded me when I first came back a few months ago. His exact words were: I didn't sacrifice my legs and hands for the true heir to my clan to dress like a caveman. I love my uncle, but he's just all sorts of square."

"My father suffered a lot. You shouldn't mock him."

"Okay, I will behave and try to act nice to him, even though he gets on my nerves. Well, I am feeling famished. You are probably busy, so I will let you do your thing. If things go well, we have to celebrate! I know this great tavern in a nearby town."

"Sharad, you are not leaving Almjarhad. I urge you to stay put, at least for now. If Lord Froylan spots you outside, you won't have another chance to return to Almjarhad in one piece like the last time. I'll order someone to bring alcohol, and we can celebrate in the privacy of my room."

"Okay, okay. Hey, do you want me to invite Talgel? Or how about that devilish friend of hers? She looks sort of cute."

"Henrietta?"

"Oh, what a pretty name!"

"Don't even bother trying to hook up with either woman."

"Why not?"

"You know perfectly well I want to marry Talgel and Henrietta…." Jarahad was about to spill the secret about Henrietta's identity until he clasped his jaw shut and shook his head. "She is already taken as well."

"Aww, shucks! Well, invite them over anyway so I can enjoy their company. See ya!"

Sharad promptly ran off. Jarahad mended his wrinkled bedspread and walked outside. Today was going to be a great day, and he was ready to face anything. Jarahad had been concocting plenty of romantic ideals of the importance of his initiation, only to feel disappointed he spent so many endless hours attending to everyday clan matters in the throne room alongside his father instead.

After the last visitor departed and the door was finally closed for the day, Jamarnid rested his aching back on his chair and turned around. "So, are you going to do it? Sell your soul by binding yourself to that terrible weapon for the rest of your life?"

The discussion was inevitable. Jamarnid knew some secrets behind the cursed swords only high-ranking nobledemons could use to protect their clans. Jarahad would have felt disgusted if his father didn't feel concerned. Fortunately for Jarahad, Hurrujat assured him that training hybrids was acceptable in harlequin society. To further stress his point, Jarahad's distant blood claim to rule Hurrujat's clan as his great-grandson would satisfy even the more traditionalist harlequin factions. "It would insult Hurrujat's honor if I back down now. Besides, you should be aware of their innate power."

Jamarnid stretched his arms and flexed his shoulders as a few servants swept the floors. His caretakers were standing at a close distance with a wheelchair waiting for both parties to finish discussing to usher Jamarnid away to his dormitory. "You humiliated Lord Froylan so easily with an incomplete training, proving you will become a formidable warrior. I guess I should not be the best person to judge. The first person I murdered was early into my Äimite guard training."

The shocking revelation prompted Jarahad to slip from his chair and gasp in astonishment. "You're finally going to reveal one secret of your training? I had been prodding you for ages, and you never wanted to share anything!"

"That was before Lord Froylan nearly murdered Lord Sharad. A pleasant chap whose only crime has been to drink with thugs for reasons I still have difficulty comprehending. I would never feel comfortable sharing everything, but this little tidbit of knowledge is menial enough. Not every elf that joins the guard is a hardened warrior. Nobleelves such as me learned to fence from a very young age because that is the custom of the kingdom."

"Does everyone become good at it?"

Jamarnid shook his head rather nonchalantly. "Most nobleelves never become remarkable at fencing. It is more of a show for the civilians and to deter human migrants from causing havoc. Summon a phantom beast before a human thug, and most will scamper off without batting an eye. You already know my capabilities using sorcery." The effusive nod of approval coming from Jarahad was proof he agreed with his father. "Peasants employed as rangers typically end up attracting the interest of an Äimite guard after a battle or two. There is a reason why rangers always have an Äimite captain instead of an ordinary foot soldier to function as their immediate superiors."

"Because lower ranked Eirmite guards cannot invite anyone to the guard."

Jamarnid nodded in agreement. "I was talented but just another medium-sized fish in a gigantic ocean of the country's best warriors. Only a handful of exceedingly capable guards become captains, and the kingdom has fewer than fifty senior guards. If you are wondering, Äimite guards never promote members to the coveted Senior status. The Elf King selects them because they are his most trustworthy servants."

"Such as Lord Froylan."

"If Ferhyr dies, I am certain Lord Froylan will end up as the commander, and he will bring forth a reign of terror among my former allies. I feel sorry for them. Ferhyr is strict, but he is also a man with good morals. Froylan meanwhile is a homicidal maniac with a shady past."

"You told me a long time ago the bastard was a convicted criminal. Hard to believe your old friends would trust him to be near Salman."

"I don't understand it, but his loyalty is unbreakable."

"Well, where are you trying to get with all of this?"

"Long story short, unlike rangers that attract the interest of recruiters by showing off their combat prowess in a real battle or hardened criminals like Froylan that weasel themselves out of trouble, I was a capable fighter in the safety of friendly competitions but completely untested in a real fight. Äimite guards have private lives, and I won a fencing competition with ridiculous ease. Intrigued, they all set a bet on who could defeat me and asked if we could have a friendly duel. I agreed upon a set time in the privacy of a desolate field. One by one, I defeated them all."

"Wow! Quite an achievement! Too bad you didn't do it in your family's castle."

"In Teryoura Palace? Nah, too many watchful eyes. The only suitable patios for fencing are the rooftops of some of the adjacent hallways connecting the myriad of towers, and they lack protective railings. Ask Sharad, and he will swear those patios are a death trap. His deceased older siblings probably fell more than once dueling each other while he eagerly watched as a little child."

"There weren't any gardens in the palace? A throne room, perhaps?"

"And risk having swords damaging the mosaic decoration of Serumo's throne room? The garden might have been an option if it hadn't packed together so many trees. I think it was better the way things happened. I defeated a group of rowdy guys in a private setting, and they all ran off to their captain and begged him to invite me."

"Without even seeing your skills firsthand?"

"I had to perform a repeat of my prior endeavor and humiliated him, too. He still thought it was a fluke and sent every guard he could find within a nearby radius. I defeated them all and earned my letter."

"Your family must have freaked out when you showed up with your letter."

"Among the noble circles, situations like mine are unusual but not unheard of. Most applicants from noble families end up bumping into a prominent guard while fending an attack. Meanwhile, my combat prowess during a friendly duel seems rather minuscule in comparison." At that very moment, it was as if Jamarnid's green eyes glistened with the small trickles of light permeating the windows as the day reached the late afternoon, imbuing them with a yellow hue almost reminiscent of a coppery glow. Seeing Jamarnid fondly recalling an auspicious moment of his life made Jarahad pleased. He would keep a mental note to continue prodding his father for other pleasant stories from happier times.

"What was the training like?" Jarahad asked.

"Brutal, endless, they push you beyond your limit, only to keep it up the next day. The first phase of the training is mostly physical. They tested my body to ensure I didn't have chronic injuries that would make me worthless as a guard and verify if I was truly as good in combat as the letter claimed. They also pressured applicants to perform pointless tasks such as scrubbing fountains with toothbrushes for hours in silence. Drill sergeants purposely caused strife between candidates to see if anyone would falter and disobey orders."

"Seriously? The guard would invite talented candidates only to screw with their minds, so they had an excuse to reject them?"

"The country invests a fortune training each guard to serve and protect the Elf King. No point in wasting ten years on someone who would break under pressure and punch Salman's face in the moment's spur."

This comment prompted Jarahad to giggle. From Jamarnid's previous stories, Jarahad concluded Salman was an intolerable jerk and felt glad Froylan seemed disappointed he was an unsuitable candidate for the guard because of his ancestry. Jarahad would have probably ended up hating Salman with a seething rage. "So, what happened during your training?"

Jamarnid sighed with a twitch of his lips and the hint of a sneer. "The initial training is straightforward and not a state secret. Most of the rejected candidates simply tell their peers they spent their time doing exercise and combat in perfectly manicured situations. Perhaps a lot more rigorous and emotionally draining than the training rangers get, but nothing out of the ordinary. The true Äimite training is a whole other situation once you start wearing your apprentice uniform. One of the first things they do is separate guards with actual combat experience from candidates invited due to intriguing skills such as me."

"Why?"

"Tell me, Jarahad, what did it feel like to kill someone for the first time?"

This thought made Jarahad's eyes widen from the gravity of Jamarnid's odd tone of voice. "He was a human soldier charging in my path during one of the first battles of the second purge. Just came rushing in my direction with a sword held high like a fool. He was probably some farmer who agreed to kill every harlequin he could find with a sword he bought in exchange for gold from his king. I try not to think about it."

"Exactly! It is one thing to swing a sword during a competition; it is another to take those skills to a life and death situation where you don't have any time to think about the morality of killing. You are just trying to stay alive."

"They separated you into a group where you had to murder people."

"A hard pill to swallow. I believe it is better to take your humanity away from the start so that you aren't at a disadvantage with the other apprentices. They did not give us any prior warnings during our first few special outings into the forests near our training camp. They would just send us into the open, and we had to perform routine tasks such as finding and returning a flag. Imagine the horror and anguish of starting a perfectly harmless team activity, only to be ambushed by hordes of human mages."

It was disheartening to listen to the words Jamarnid had to say with a graver tone than before. On all accounts, Jamarnid never felt remorse for joining the guard and seemed to enjoy his previous life. And it made a lot of sense. Why select an elf with superb combat skills like Jamarnid and have him pass his ten-year training without taking a life? Would he hesitate when the time arrived to protect his king from danger at the very last minute? "Who were those humans, anyway?"

"The Elf Kingdom offers work permits to humans during certain times of the year. Most of them do seasonal agricultural work. Others perform many commercial endeavors. The permits must be renewed, or else the person risks prison followed by deportation. They can only visit specific cities with it. Ordinary humans may never visit the capital where Master Salman lives."

Jarahad didn't need to prod Jamarnid for more information. He already knew the answer. "Those men were condemned criminals."

"Rangers do most of the grunt work, which saves the guards a lot of free time. Any elf with a menial ability to control their phantom beast can defeat the average carriage mugger. Occasionally, they will find one adversary most rangers can't defeat. Many of these exceptional humans can cause a lot of problems. That is where the supervisor captains come along. Whenever a ranger informs them about a dangerous criminal, the captain shows up, and tries to defeat their opponent without killing them. A ranger sends them off to Eurfouyr Prison with a bow in their heads as an offering."

"That prison… you were there, weren't you?"

Jamarnid nodded. "It is located very near the capital and within the protective magic of the energy field. We only send the most dangerous mages. Depending on the crime, they will either serve long sentences like any regular convict… or get the death penalty."

"They gave those humans you killed a deal, right?"

"Foolish you are not, my son. If they had convicted you of a capital crime and offered the chance to get deported in exchange for killing a few elves in a secluded forest, wouldn't you accept?"

"Do any of them get deported?"

"I have heard some stories. There is one recurrent legend where a powerful human mage murdered all the apprentices, and the full-fledged guards in charge of the post chained him up and organized a meeting. After thorough research, they confirmed the human had very distant elf blood ancestry and invited him to the guard because he had earned his way in."

"That story is bull, and you know it, father."

Jamarnid shrugged his shoulders. "It's a famous urban legend. Some variations vary the tale. One even stated the guards felt convinced about his ancestry because part of his hair was violet."

It was plausible. While most elves had hair colors that seemed very normal for human standards, at least one of the pureblood refugees in Almjarhad had royal blue hair, and another had lilac.

Feeling satisfied with the conversation, Jamarnid nodded at his servants, who promptly settled him in his wheelchair. Before servants ushered him away, Jamarnid turned around. "Remember this conversation during your ceremony tonight, son. I hope this advice will serve you well because I may not be there for you in person. I bid you good luck, and the doors of this palace are always available whether you pass or fail the test."

After speaking with Jamarnid, Jarahad felt less skittish than before. A part of him had a hunch Jamarnid wanted to address this topic for an ulterior purpose. He had a small dinner as Talgel suggested, only enough food to avoid feeling weak. As nightfall arrived, he stood in front of the palace where a carriage was waiting. Hurrujat accompanied Charon while they wore elegant black harlequin jackets that reached the ground with green stitched creases and a silk sash belt.

Jarahad continued wearing the same attire he wore all day. He bowed at both harlequins with the most utterly high respect. "Good evening, my Lords."

"Ho, ho ho ho! I expected you to wear something more formal for the occasion!" Hurrujat's gleeful voice was unwavering.

Charon grunted. "Let him be. No rules stipulate the apprentice must be initiated while wearing a particular robe. I believe the robes he is wearing are suitable enough. Let's get going. I want to finish this so we can pack up and leave."

Jarahad sat in the back alongside both men, and the vehicle set off. Twilight had imbued the little city with a dazzling array of colors, while some inhabitants had reestablished their tents in the city's lowlands. As the carriage traveled away from the city and into the mountains, Jarahad frowned at once. "We are going to the same cave, aren't we?"

Charon nodded. "That is correct. The elves can not see the initiation. Only those loyal to our cause will be present."

Hurrujat sighed. "I am the last member of my people to wield one of our sacred swords. Too bad everyone in my family is gone, buried unceremoniously in the tomb of my former city."

The words hurt Jarahad because it was apparent Hurrujat never considered him to be his family. Perhaps it would be better to accept this truth now that Hurrujat and his people were about to leave. As long as he followed Talgel's suggestions, he hoped they would remain friends. The carriage traveled in silence until it reached the fearsome mountains with jagged but stunning cliffs covered by a thin blanket of wildflowers. The carriage arrived at a nondescript ridge with a large cavernous opening. Several harlequins stood guard.

Hurrujat spoke as he prodded the carriage door open. "Everyone present to watch your initiation knows everything, and they will keep the secret. I hope you abide by these sacred traditions as well."

"You know I would never betray your trust."

Charon cleared his throat as he stood up with the aid of his cane. "I hope so, or you will face the consequences."

Hurrujat interrupted Charon's train of thought with a subdued growl. "My great-grandson will prove to us he was worthy of your steel! We all know he has what it takes!"

Good to see Hurrujat believed in him, and it injected a sense of self-confidence into the halfling. The group passed by the guards and entered the same large artificially enhanced dome Jarahad visited a year ago on the same date. It had curved indentations carved with harlequin earth sorcery. Several torches were adorning the walls, which granted sufficient light to see his surroundings. It was still rather bleak, even with his superior eyesight. Jarahad spotted two stone chairs and an adjacent stone table for Charon's tools. Apparently, Charon would begin the ceremony with the inking. Also standing on the table as a prize to be awarded was his sword. According to the harlequin customs, upon passing the first test, the initiated had to spend as much time as possible near the weapon to form an energy bond. Jarahad already mastered the incantation of several spells that could activate with the sword, albeit he only practiced those spells with ordinary wooden swords. These exercises were done while Jarahad placed his sword inside a magical cloth bag. Charon was very insistent with these rules, and Jarahad had followed them to the letter. Accompanying the two harlequins were a few dozen halflings, and pureblood harlequins that all seemed excited to see him. After a polite hand wave, Jarahad's eyes soon caught sight of two familiar faces. He gasped at once. "Talgel! Henrietta! Why are you here?"

Henrietta was wearing a stunning bright red human dress that reached the ground. Her shoulder-length black hair had several pins, which made her seem more feminine than usual. "Of course, we would come to cheer for you!"

Talgel seemed somewhat ambivalent but friendly enough. She wore an alluring black dress, which seemed unusual because she usually opted for lighter tones. As usual, she wore excessive jewelry, and her medium-length grey hair had two pigtails ending in braids. "Good evening, Jarahad."

Hurrujat chuckled at the bewilderment present on Jarahad's face.

Charon, meanwhile, trudged towards the group and grasped Talgel's hands. "You are a mightily fine halfling, my dear. It is such a shame your sorcery took away your eyes. I feel remorse for not initiating you before you awakened your mana. You could have passed the test so easily."

Charon's odd behavior towards Talgel only confused Jarahad even more. On all accounts, he recalled Talgel's childhood and never thought she was remarkable with the sword. He cleared his throat to gain everyone's attention. "Excuse me, Sword Master Charon. Why would you believe such a thing? Even though I admire Talgel's many qualities, I never saw her defeat anyone in fencing when we were growing up."

Instead of feeling angry, Talgel's mouth formed a cruel sneer that startled the elf. "There are other things harlequins consider before initiating someone. You could have the right blood claim with extraordinary fencing skills and still be completely worthless."

Charon nodded in agreement without showing insult to Jarahad's previous question. "Under normal circumstances, I would have never initiated you, Jarahad. And it is not because of your mixed blood or because you are the son of that useless bastard Jamarnid. I cannot tell you the reason until after you perform the test, but I believe you have the hidden qualities I search for in every candidate."

It was a sufficient, albeit somewhat vague, response that satisfied Jarahad. He then stared at Talgel, who seemed to enjoy herself for some odd reason. "Were you invited by Charon?"

Talgel grinned. "Hurrujat was skeptical at first, but I convinced him all right. Good luck in your initiation."

Her words of encouragement seemed sincere and injected Jarahad with even more confidence. He kissed Talgel's hands, politely nodded at Henrietta, and bowed to the other guests. "Thank you all for being present during my examination. I know the fact I will remain in Almjarhad might seem like a waste of Charon's invaluable steel. I swear I will pass this examination and use the knowledge your people have shared with me to be repaid tenfold. If your people are ever in need of my help, I will always be more than glad to help you."

Pretty much everyone bowed at him in return.

Charon finally sat on one chair and retrieved the materials from his box. "Sit down, Jarahad, and let's perform the simple part."

Recalling the physical pain he always experienced from the prior inking sessions, Jarahad swallowed some saliva. Hard to imagine at this point being subjugated to the most extended tattooing session to connect every vantage point in his body would be easy. Knowing he had until sunrise to complete the test or risk being barred from wielding a harlequin sword forever, he promptly sat down and stared at Charon's piercing iridescent pink eyes.

The old harlequin lifted his hands, and strange glowing markings appeared on his own body. He touched Jarahad's hands, filling his body with pleasant, pulsating energy. Soon enough, the markings Charon previously placed on Jarahad's body during the prior inking sessions were glowing, and he examined them. "Remove the shirt and pants to see where I must work."

Trying to avoid feeling any shame from stripping himself almost completely nude in front of a large audience, Jarahad complied.

Henrietta gleefully stood by his side. "I will take care of these things for you. You sure have a nice body! Yum!"

"Quiet, young harlequin! Go away before you interrupt me during this critical initiation step!" Charon growled.

"Sorry!" Henrietta soon scampered away.

Jarahad then spoke while sitting on the chair and resting his hands on his lap. "Is there anything else you need from me?"

"Put the gag in your mouth. I will ink various parts of your body to connect the thirteen vantage points. Stay still, close your eyes. If you need the harlequins to hold your body from the pain, just blink three times in a row without saying a word. Any movement you make could be disastrous."

Jarahad placed the wooden gag in his mouth and bit hard. Knowing this was a critical step in his training, he closed his eyes and focused his mind on Talgel. He didn't understand Charon's reasoning behind inviting her if she wasn't strictly loyal to their cause. Perhaps she was present as moral support. The instant the needle pierced the skin on his chest, Jarahad's eyes flinched. The pain was just as bad as the prior sessions, only magnified a little because of the pulsing energy coming from his tattoos. One instant, Charon would ink his chest. The next, the old harlequin's hands grasped his calf, followed by his right shoulder. A gratingly tedious hour passed, and Charon was not even remotely close to finishing his task. It seemed like this session didn't have prominent tattoos. More like Charon was drawing tiny ones all over his body. It didn't take long for him to issue his first of many commands. "Stand up."

Jarahad complied without flinching while sweat fell from his temples from the pain and increased heat in his body. He could hear Charon's tired gait as he stood behind and began tattooing on his back. The pain only increased as he performed this task.

Perhaps to lift his spirits, Charon spoke. "You are probably wondering why you are in so much pain. Our special spells connect through the spinal cord. Now that I have placed all the peripheral vantage points together, they are convening in your back. The pain will increase exponentially with each energy point that I connect. Prepare yourself and do not move at all during this portion of the procedure."

Just as Charon claimed, ever-increasing pulsating burns bombarded Jarahad's body, followed by a dull thud in his spinal cord he had never felt during his prior sessions. For a brief instant, as Charon worked tirelessly on his buttocks, he wanted to steer away from the pain. Knowing he couldn't let anyone down, Jarahad focused his mind on his meditation sessions in Soremin's little temple instead.

Among all of Talgel's suggestions, when she first found out he would be initiated, she stressed he needed to learn ways to focus his mind. Assuming his father Jamarnid might help, Jarahad approached him with great enthusiasm. After one session, Jarahad soon realized Jamarnid's approach proved to be useless because he only focused on resisting torture. Jarahad then asked Soremin to teach him proper meditation. Despite his shortcomings as a person, Soremin was a patient teacher, and Jarahad focused on imagining a leaf trailing across a river while he breathed at controlled intervals. The heat increased, but it no longer bothered him. As he focused on the leaf twirling around in a bend, his mind inevitably wandered to Talgel's beautiful face, prompting him to fight the urge to smile and risk ruining Charon's work.

"I have connected most of the points. Please give me a moment." Jarahad was unsure of Charon's vague words until he felt a soothing sensation in his body. Charon was placing a numbing ointment on his newly tattooed bloody skin, reducing the pain to a tolerable level. It did nothing to mitigate the burning energy on his back. "In case you are wondering, Jarahad, there is no turning back. I am now obliged to tattoo your face, or you could risk death from heatstroke. The only way to reduce energy is to connect the vantage points with the crown. You may open your eyes, dress in your robes, or sit on the chair and let me finish."

As tempting as it was to cover his body, Jarahad opted to sit down instead. Charon was never a trickster, and he was sure there would be no problem if he didn't fetch for his robes immediately. He opted against it because there was little point in covering his robes in blood. Let the fresh wounds dry out and worry about them later. Charon remained focused as he grasped Jarahad's forehead to inject it with his strange magical ink in silence. This part of his body hurt even more than anywhere else and soon reached his pain tolerance threshold. Jarahad remained dutifully still as Charon continued with his gruesome task. It wasn't long before Charon's hands grasped his left ear, followed by the right one, descended to the jawline, and began a series of even more painful injections on his neck. Jarahad had no clue how much longer this portion of the session would take. Before he felt tempted to open his mouth to protest, Charon rapidly turned around and was working on the back of his neck. Something even worse soon replaced the prior pain. Jarahad thought he had experienced pain while training under Jamarnid's stern watch. None of that could compare to the physical agony caused by Charon, causing tears to fall from his eyes.

When it seemed like Jarahad was about to give up and run outside, Charon chanted in Harlequin. "I call upon those who died in the gallows before their time to awaken from thy slumber. Assist this new member of our kind in reaching the pinnacle of his endless potential. Raise and come forth, I now implore!" With a clever hand motion, despite his advanced age, Charon intertwined his fingers in a prayer position. His index fingers touched the upper portion of Jarahad's spinal cord connecting to his skull. Increased energy bombarded Jarahad, who soon felt like he was elevating into a higher plane for a brief instant. This was followed by weightlessness he had never experienced before. Wishing he could remain in this strange world filled with joy and freedom, Jarahad felt his body becoming heavier until he ultimately collapsed on the ground while tears oozed from his eyelids. Steam soon evaporated from his body until the pain vanished. It then became replaced by a sense of dread that they had deprived him of that incredible sensation of true freedom because of the imprisonment of his flesh.

In the recesses of Jarahad's mind, he wondered if the clapping and cheering of the guests were because they were laughing at his failure. He felt a soft hand caress his shoulder. After wiping the tears from his eyes and tossing the gag on the ground, Jarahad turned around and saw Talgel's face without the intrusive mask.

She was smiling. "You fulfilled the first part of the initiation. Do not cry about your loss. You still have a lot of duties you must fulfill in the living world."

"That floating sensation, is that where we will go once we die?"

Charon chuckled as he placed his tools back inside the box. "You are half right. The spell releases so much energy that a part of your spirit briefly flies out of your body, and you share the freedom only a wandering ghost can enjoy. The sensation is very addictive, albeit chances are you will never experience it again. You might still feel it for brief moments if you are on the brink of death." Charon turned around, and Jarahad soon realized sweat covered him from overt exhaustion. "I need to rest for a few minutes. Can someone place some numbing ointments on Jarahad's skin? Maybe you should heed my suggestion and put on some clothes, too."

Jarahad sighed in relief. He didn't know why everyone present considered the second part of the test to be worse; the inking of his body proved to be tiring enough. Jarahad sat cross-legged on the artificially smooth stone ground while a few harlequins were busy wiping his sweaty brow with a moist towel. Other assistants applied the same ointment on his neck and face, which soon diminished the horrible pain. Jarahad then stared at the bloodied skin where Charon worked a while ago. The bleeding had stopped. After allowing the harlequins to scrub most of the blood off, Jarahad retrieved his robes from Henrietta's eager hands. With her help, he once again dressed and stood up. "You are all so kind, thank you."

The harlequins nodded in acknowledgment and scampered off. Jarahad then stretched his muscles while feeling a new sensation of energy in his body. The previously dormant mana was now invading his body with full force. A portion of his mind felt the urge to speak, but he shut those feelings away because he had to focus on the last test.

After resting for a few minutes on his chair, Charon eventually stood up and retrieved a small ceramic bottle from his box of tools. "Feel the energy flowing in your body, Jarahad. I have never felt so much energy in an initiated before. You will probably become the best student I have ever had if you pass the genuine test that will forever bind you to your sword."

The vagueness in Charon's words made him frown with discretion. The elderly harlequin approached him with a ceramic cup while Hurrujat offered him his sword.

Jarahad grabbed the weapon without knowing if this was adequate or not. Pulsating energy echoed from it, clamoring for release. He knew better than to succumb to temptation and stared at the harlequin leader. "Am I supposed to touch this weapon? I thought I had to stay far away from it during the last test."

Hurrujat shook his head. "The vantage points have been united so now you can touch it. Don't summon any spells yet. Your binding remains incomplete."

After securing the weapon on his belt, Jarahad grabbed Charon's ceramic cup. "What am I supposed to do with this?"

"Drink the beverage and leave the cave immediately."

"Huh?"

Hurrujat chuckled at once. "No, we are not kicking you out, Jarahad. We only want you to stand outside for a few minutes while we prepare for the last test. When we are ready, we will call you. Please go."

Jarahad obeyed and was soon standing outside. He had never realized it before, but the inking session and whatever happened to his body afterward took several hours. A part of him was concerned as he studied the alignment of the stars meant dawn was soon going to arrive. His chances to pass the test would vanish if he didn't hurry.

"Fail the test."

Jarahad's heart began pounding as a strange, intrusive voice resonated in his head. "What?"

"Fail the test. Run. You are worthless."

He turned around in every direction, but he was alone. "Hello? Are you a harlequin?"

"Run, you fool! You are unworthy of me."

And then Jarahad's body jolted still as he stared at the weapon resting on his belt. "The sword is speaking to me?"

"You are slightly intelligent, but I do not need that."

Either Jarahad was going mad from the initiation or… He soon realized something. Charon offered him a beverage during his first test, which tasted very different from this one. On that occasion, he desired to kill everyone in the room but remained dutifully still in a small energy circle. His last test might have just begun, and he stupidly never realized it.

"Leave me and run, you coward."

Jarahad smirked as he remained still. The sword had never spoken to him before, albeit Charon was insistent during his training to never recite the harlequin spells near the weapon at all costs. Jarahad was working out a reason when Hurrujat soon appeared from the cave entrance while holding onto something in his hands.

"Good to see you are still here. Wear this in your eyes and return with me."

Jarahad realized Hurrujat was carrying a long scarf that he fastened on his eyes. He was now rendered fully blind.

"Can you see anything?"

"I see absolutely nothing, my Lord," Jarahad replied.

"Good, very good! Hold on to me, and let us return for the test."

Jarahad was unsure of the vagueness of Hurrujat's words. While he fought with all his might to ignore the nagging feeling in the deepest recesses of his mind to say a series of words on the tip of his tongue, he soon stood on the familiar sleek stone floor in the dark. He did not know what he was supposed to do because the harlequins were utterly silent. He assumed he would have to attack an adversary with the weapon. And yet several minutes passed, and nothing happened.

The strange voice booming from the weapon was laughing. *"Why are you doing nothing? Don't you want me? Do you want my power? Run. You can never tame me!"*

Jarahad listened to the weapon speaking to his mind while trying to understand the hidden meaning. The test might have been a riddle, and his sword offered the clue. A clinking far away then attracted his interest. Metal? A collar? Chains?

"You hear it? Do you want me? To become bound to you forever? This is your one chance. Take it!"

Jarahad ignored the taunts and remained alert to his surroundings without saying a word. The sword only kept on pestering him even more. Above everything else, Jarahad was feeling a familiar burning sensation in his chest.

"You want it? Blood? I clamor for it, and so do you."

"I will not savor blood to satiate your needs, strange sword."

In that instant, someone unleashed the blindfold, and an incoherent sight bombarded Jarahad. Seated right in the middle of the cave was nothing else than a human toddler who was chained to the ground while he pulled the chain somewhat playfully. The oddness of it all dumbfounded Jarahad. "What is a child doing here? Where is everyone?"

He looked in every direction, but the harlequins purposely only placed a few candles around the child, who did not know why he was there. Jarahad could hear the harlequins breathing in the dark cave, albeit he did not know what they had in mind. The burning in his body was only getting worse, along with a sense of dread.

"You want him, don't you? The life of an innocent. Yes, I want blood. I need it!"

"Shut up!"

Jarahad frightfully covered his ears and turned away. He wanted to run outside and scream at the sky for what the sword wanted him to do. He would never hurt a child. Why would he? He might have killed humans before, but it was always in self-defense. And now he was inside a cave with a talking sword that was likely a figment of some hallucinogen he drank that was ordering him to feed it blood. He then realized something: this was the test! The sword wanted to bind to him by a blood pact!

With a sudden realization, Jarahad unsheathed the weapon and aimed it at the palm of his hand. "If you want blood, feed on me!" The sword sliced his left hand, and he closed his eyes from the surge of pain. Blood soon spilled into the weapon, and it glowed in an intense green hue alongside flickers of white energy that invaded the cavern until the weapon settled upon a light green color. The strange reaction of the weapon startled Jarahad. He had seen harlequins ignite the true colors of their weapons a few times, and now that his sword was finally doing the same thing, tears welled in his eyes.

The moment of joy soon vanished as he felt something from the weapon. This novel sensation was evil, pulling him aside and only taunting him further. *"I accept you, Lord Jarahad. Now finish the binding and kill the innocent!"*

"No! I will not kill that child!"

"Then you will fail, and I shall take you as my prize!"

Before long, a desire to protect the child burned through his mind while he also mentally clamored to kill it. Two opposing factions fought for control and the evil that inhabited his sword was winning. He initially assumed the weapon was trying to take control of his body to kill the child. Instead, his hand aimed the weapon at his unprotected abdomen to commit suicide, and he shrieked upon realizing something: "My father… he had to kill to become a guard."

Whether Jamarnid knew about the cruel truth or telling his story was just an odd coincidence, Jarahad blessed the heavens they had spoken earlier that day. To become a guard, Jamarnid not only killed criminals. He was also probably forced to kill innocents as well. Jarahad could now appreciate why the harlequins told him repeatedly that the initiation was far more challenging than just a physically painful procedure. The initiated had to embrace the dormant evil hidden within his self-conscience. He knew he would forever hate himself for doing this, but there was no turning back. While tears welled from his eyes, Jarahad fought against the pull of the sword's mental control. His hands clasped the scabbard and pointed the weapon at the child. The poor little creature probably did not know why he was sitting there. It no longer mattered to Jarahad at this point. While reciting a small prayer in Elvish to clamor for the child's eternal rest, Jarahad charged forward and struck the child's heart in one clean blow. As life vanished from the child's little beady brown eyes, Jarahad placed his weapon to the side and grasped the child's trembling hand until he passed away. The sword resonated once again, and the puddle of blood combined with the blood still spewing from Jarahad's hand was soon lured by the dragging energy of the weapon, which absorbed the vital red liquid until it felt satiated.

Upon passing the test, Jarahad felt neither pleased nor disgusted at himself for what he did. In reality, not even the lingering pain of an imminent attack from his blood-borne disease was at the top of his mind. The energy surrounding his body was mana, and he wanted to release it while he could still understand how or why to do it. He focused on these words to distance himself from the unpardonable crime of killing the child. They seemed strange and familiar like he had wanted to say them his whole life and didn't know why it was necessary. These words were in the pidgin tongue he spoke most of the time with his people. If he truly wanted, Jarahad could have uttered the words in either Elvish or Harlequin since he felt comfortable speaking any of his three birth languages. Despite being unable to understand the purpose, he voiced them out loud: "I summon thee my phantom beast, the Demonic Armor Rashin!"

The energy unleashed from Jarahad's body jolted him awake. As the writhing pain from the blood attack increased, he opened his eyes and gasped at the sight. The group of harlequins still surrounded him, whose pink eyes were now open as they stared at him with equal awe and reverence. And then he noticed something on top of his body. It was made of white and green material, very similar to the color of his demonic sword when it was glowing just a few minutes ago. Awestruck, Jarahad turned around and realized the strange object surrounding his body was his phantom beast which adopted the unique shape of armor covering his body like it belonged there.

"You have done the impossible. Congratulations. I knew you would achieve it."

Much to Jarahad's glee, Talgel was standing right in front of him with a massive smile on her face. Concern soon replaced the moment of joy when he saw a small ceramic cup. He instantly knew what it was. "I will never drink the blood of an innocent human."

His reaction only prompted Talgel to shove it into his hands with increased insistence. "You will faint and could risk your life if you keep on using mana nonstop while suffering an attack. The child never deserved to die, which is the entire purpose of this test. Therefore, the harlequins could never reveal it to an applicant. He was a prostitute's child who would be killed anyway, so the harlequins bought him in a slave market as a sacrifice instead. Hate their kind forever or throw the sword away. At least do me a favor and honor the child's passing by taking a token of his life for yourself. Don't let his death be in vain. Remember this moment to protect the weak for the rest of your life."

With those words said, Jarahad cautiously grasped the cup, said a prayer of gratitude to the child for his sacrifice, and drank the blood. It tasted beautiful and sweet, just like the child's clean conscience, sadly ripped away from this world before he even enjoyed it. After he swallowed the blood, the energy surrounding his body was easier to control, and he locked it away, at least for now. Much to his relief, the strange armor vanished into the shadows, and he collapsed to his knees.

Charon grabbed the weapon and observed it. "You accomplished passing the test and even summoned the phantom beast lying dormant deep inside. Congratulations, Lord Jarahad. You have succeeded with your initiation in the secret harlequin arts."

CHAPTER 21 ◆ TIOJA

The separation of both clans was convened during a meeting a few months ago. In Tioja's simple mind, he always felt like it was a distant supposition. It wasn't until after Jarahad returned to Almjarhad one early spring morning, looking unusually weary and covered with minor bloodied wounds on his face, that the harlequins were busier than ever.

Like any child, his father Jamad would ask him to visit the market to purchase things or fetch pails of water. Tioja's face became riddled with concern when the harlequins would walk away, paying no proper attention to him. While a few harlequins remained married to their elf spouses, Tioja saw many couples visiting Soremin's temple for reasons he could not entirely understand.

One minute a couple would walk side by side holding their hands, only to descend the hill back into the city separately and later melt their wedding rings. He even saw one woman holding onto the hand of a fellow harlequin while her now former halfling spouse walked away in the opposite direction without even turning around. Tioja couldn't understand what enticed the harlequins to abandon their spouse in his feeble young mind. Why were the harlequins setting their tents around Hurrujat's modest residence?

Little did Tioja know as he hurried off to the basins for a pail of water that a familiar young halfling around his age planned on doing the same task. They recognized each other immediately and smiled. "Nurran!"

"Hey, Tio! Good to see you!" Did your father send you?"

Tioja nodded and looked at the basin. During the winter, the clan's newly minted hybrid elf mages had been busy training under the tutelage of a pureblood harlequin water mage named Sou. The new mages spent all winter carrying ocean water and sifting it through a series of specially designed open-air stone water reservoirs to remove the salinity. The water they sifted still kept a slightly sour aftertaste, but they deemed it safe enough to drink in small quantities. Most city inhabitants used it for washing dishes or bathing and only drank the highly purified water extracted by the clan's pureblood elves.

After Nurran fetched his pail, he kicked the dusty ground. Because of the rains, there were still a lot of pesky wildflowers. A stubborn patch of plants had found a good place to grow beneath the basins because children usually dumped droplets of water every time they scooped water. Tioja shoved some violet wildflowers to the side and sat down, careful not to kill them.

The city was bustling with life, albeit it increasingly seemed to be divided into two separate groups. Nurran sighed as he watched the truth unfold. "The harlequins are going to leave in a few days."

"What?! I thought those were stories Kashin said to spook us."

"I think my brother wants to leave with them." Nurran's foot kicked a meandering stone, which rolled away.

A horrid void invaded Tioja as he tried to make sense of everything. "My uncle… is leaving us? But…"

"You just don't get it! Hamara has been filling Kashin's mind with strange ideas all winter, saying she knows he wants to be initiated in the sword like Lord Jarahad. It's like she wanted to find his weak spot. I fear my father might disown him for leaving us. Chances are we might never see him again."

"My uncle…" Tioja shook his head without believing Nurran's haunting tale. "My mom wants to take him away? Bullocks! She loves me, and we are all a big family! Maybe Kashin can learn the sword and then come back!"

"Stupid Tio! You understand nothing about harlequins. Our leader Jarahad will stay here with his sword because he is Hurrujat's illegitimate great-grandson. They reached this agreement many years ago. The rest of us are just ordinary peasants, and the harlequins will force my brother to serve Hurrujat for the rest of his life. Hamara got into a nasty fight with my mama the other day because she wants to convince me to come too."

"Please don't go!"

Nurran smiled at once. "Jarahad ordered everyone to back off and not force the underage halflings to leave Almjarhad if we don't want to. I don't care things are still difficult in this place. This is where I was born, and I am staying put. Hamara can promise me the moon and the stars. I will not go with her. My mom told everyone she would only go if Jamen agreed to go with her, and we all know he would never leave Almjarhad."

"I am happy that your parents are staying. Why would Hamara want to leave Almjarhad? She loves my daddy!"

"Seriously, Tio? Your mom hates Jamad! She is probably smooching with her new boyfriend right now!"

In that instant, Tioja's world fell apart. As much as he appreciated his uncle Nurran, some things were best left unsaid. Ignoring the bucket of water, Tioja ran back home, hoping Hamara would hug Jamad and be happy like before. Much to his horror, he encountered a massive group of people while Hamara was taking things out of their tent.

Jamad soon rushed outside and grasped Hamara's wrist. "Where are you going?!"

Hamara yanked her arm free and rubbed it. "I'm sick and tired of pretending, Jamad! My people are packing, and I am going with them!"

"No! We are husband and wife! I am not leaving Almjarhad! Tell him, Soremin!"

While everyone present was harlequins and halflings, the elegant priest focused his sea-green eyes on Hamara's face with seething rage. "You lied to everyone, Hamara. You made a promise several months ago to both me and Jarahad that you would not leave Jamad for your new lover until he gave you his blessing to visit my temple and let me perform the dissolution ceremony."

Whereas it shocked Tioja to discover Nurran's story was true, Jamad was utterly terrified as he stumbled backward and nearly collapsed on the supporting beams of his tent.

Jamad gasped with disgust. "Im...possible! Is this why you insisted on sleeping in a separate bed for the past few months? Because you are someone's mistress? How could you hurt me?! Why?! I only wanted to save our marriage, which is why I gave you so much freedom these past few months!"

Soremin didn't seem impressed by Hamara's deceit. "Hamara has cruelly taken you as a fool, Jamad. I regret I didn't visit you a few months ago when I discovered Hamara fell in love with Hurrujat."

If discovering Hamara's adultery wasn't bad enough, the fact she had done it with the harlequin leader filled Jamad with so much rage that he soon stood up and tried to shove the harlequins away to harm Hurrujat. "Let me pass, you morons! Hurrujat is going to pay for this!" Jamad became increasingly irate and did something entirely careless: he summoned his phantom beast and attempted to shove them away.

Nobody seemed to care. The harlequins and halflings loyal to Hurrujat expected Jamad to react this way. After lifting their hands in the air, they absorbed Jamad's phantom beast until he collapsed on the ground with exhaustion.

Hamara grinned at his foolishness and nodded at the group of onlookers. "Thank you for helping me by stealing his mana. Now he will be too tired to visit Hurrujat and harm him."

"You vile, lying, deceitful, horrible… awful woman! I would have moved heaven and earth to reignite the love I still harbor for you, and you only wish to humiliate me! Do you hate me so much that you would convince Hurrujat's servants to sabotage me?! Why???"

Soremin stared at Hamara's face with scorn. "You had several months to tell Jamad the truth about your endeavors, Hamara. He deserves an explanation."

It was Hamara's turn to growl with disgust. She felt tempted to lift her clenched fist to punch Soremin. For a moment, the fine vibration in her hand showed he compelled her to do it. In the end, she relaxed her shoulders and nodded at the priest. "I apologize for lying to you, Jamad, and feel glad Soremin and Jarahad kept their promise. Do not get angry at them. They didn't betray you. Perhaps I don't like you all that much, but you deserve to get some closure. I should have never gotten married when I was so young. Soremin will claim the religious ceremony he performed was legitimate according to the Elvish customs. Looking back, I had a gut feeling things would not be right. We are too different, and there is no way for you to understand I have thoughts and desires of my own. Unlike most halflings, I am not ashamed of my harlequin ancestry and wish to learn more about it."

"You are an elf! We already had this argument many times!"

Soremin stood in front of Jamad and shook his head. "What Hamara did to you is beyond reprehensible, Jamad, but your stubbornness is not helping you gain any sympathy. I apologize for performing the religious ceremony when Hamara's vows had been a sham from the very start. You have the full right to request a marriage annulment."

"What? No! I will not agree with this!"

A grave voice was suddenly audible. "Yes, you will!"

Tioja turned around and gasped at the strange sight. Standing among the hordes of people was Jarahad, whose face, torso, and arms were still covered in bandages from the recent inking while he wore loose-fitting peasant robes. He approached the group of bickering elves with a wobbling gait from the lingering pain.

Jarahad stared at Hamara, shook his head in disbelief, and agreed with Soremin. "It seems like Hamara finally confessed everything."

Soremin nodded while still looking upset. "She broke her promise of requesting Jamad for the annulment, which was the agreement we reached a few months ago. She will have to stay fully bound by her wedding vows and live with Jamad for good."

A cruel grin invaded Jamad's face when he heard that. "Do you mean I get to keep my wife?!"

"No! Don't you even dare, Jamad!" Hamara then stood up to protest. "My wedding vows were never sincere because I do not believe in the Elvish religion." To further emphasize her point of view, she grabbed her wedding ring and tossed it on the ground. "I was never your wife, Jamad. Under the eyes of the elf gods, I am not suitable to betroth you because my vows were lies. In the eyes of the harlequin gods, I am still single and never committed adultery. Release me from your vows so that I am not forced to be branded by orders of Lord Jarahad."

"Branded? What in the hell?" Jamad couldn't understand anything and even less Tioja as he continued watching the elves bicker.

Jarahad sighed at once. "The day Hurrujat announced the separation of the clans, I had a private word with Hamara. She promised she would confess the truth to stop hurting your feelings. In case of failure, she agreed to let you select whichever curse you wanted. I will not hesitate to use my authority as the interim clan leader to oblige Charon to have her branded for life. Since it looks like Hamara waited until the very last minute to do this, I would deem you can select whichever punishment you want."

Soremin agreed with the proposal as well. "Hamara would not be the first halfling that ended up exiled with a curse for breaking the law. I believe the punishment is fair because she insulted our gods by letting the lie of her sham marriage continue. As the affected party, you may select something from a series of curses. I believe Charon can make Hamara's skin impervious to sunlight. Would you like it if she had to spend the rest of her days imprisoned in a lead coffin during the daylight hours as fair retribution for hurting you in exchange for her freedom?"

Jamad was aghast at such a ridiculous proposal. "I do not allow Charon to harm her! I just want Hamara to remain as my wife!"

"Why would you hurt me like this, Jamad?! Soremin made an honest mistake by performing a ceremony that is completely void. Release me and enjoy your immortal life with a new lover that will appreciate your company!"

"No, Hamara. I will not let you do this to me. Why would you lie to me all winter when you loved another man? Why return home and continue to hurt me without shame?"

"I did it for Tioja because I love him!"

As if on cue, Hamara stared at poor Tioja. Feeling horrified he was the center of attention in a fight that was not his own, Tioja shook his head and clenched his tiny fists. "No! I don't want mommy and daddy to leave!" The poor little thing ran off and went to the only place that made sense to him. He rushed up the hillside and eventually reached Soremin's temple and cried himself to sleep on the altar where his parents married almost twenty years ago.

Evening arrived, and someone touched Tioja, prompting him to wake up. Much to his surprise, it was Talgel while her assistant, Henrietta, and Soremin accompanied her.

Tioja wasn't sure why Talgel had visited him, of all people, but it seemed rather important. He rubbed the tears from his eyes and bowed at the seer with forced politeness. "Hello, your ladyship. Is there anything I can do for you?"

Talgel sighed and sat on a little pillow. Without engaging in eye contact, she stared into the void. "Your future is uncertain, young one. In a few days, the harlequins will leave Almjarhad, and there is nothing you can do to stop it from happening."

"No! I like them! Are they leaving because we were bad to them?"

Talgel shook her head. "The harlequins appreciate the hospitality of the elves, who suffered just as much as them when they lost their homes. Their skins sadly do not tolerate the sun in these lands very well, and they have to leave to ease their suffering. Listen, Tioja. Whatever happened to your parents is not your fault. You did nothing wrong, and they are not angry at you. Your mother loves you and will always be there for you."

"But why does she want to go away? Why would she hurt my father?"

Soremin interjected at once. "Hamara is… a difficult person. She only thinks about herself and tries to act like a victim because most of us don't understand her true feelings. She did something terrible to your father, and it is up to him to decide whether he should forgive her."

Talgel then continued speaking. "Listen, Tioja. Your parents are going to separate. It is their destiny. These things happen in life, and you will someday grow up to understand. I will remain here, and so will all the pureblood elves. There is something strange about your future. It is fluid and wavering. I want you to stay here for a few days so that you make your decision without having either parent pressuring you. I know you will choose what you want the most, and it will be the right choice."

As commanded by Talgel, Tioja remained in Soremin's temple while accompanying the priests to the morning prayers and eating modest dinners. While he helped them sweep the floors as best as possible, the servants prepared his meals and didn't want him helping them clean the dishes. He remained fully isolated regarding the events of the city he could spot from afar.

Whenever he felt the urge to visit his parents, an apprentice priest would always stand in his way. "Please, Tioja, follow Soremin's command. You must remain here. It is for your good."

"I want to be with my family!"

"Lady Talgel has determined you must stay here. You can help us tend to the garden or rest in your room. Until we settle everything, you can't leave the temple. Any command of Talgel is a command from Lord Jarahad himself. You don't want him to get angry at you for breaking the law, right?"

"No, I would never do that, sir! I am sorry." With that settled, Tioja spent the following few days wholly isolated from the city's events. As he helped the priests with their daily tasks, he noticed several were pureblood harlequins. A female one with startling pink eyes soon prompted his curiosity, and he approached her. "Umm… excuse me?"

The harlequin stopped accommodating food supplies in the pantry and stared at the tiny elf. "Yes, Tio?"

"Well, I was just thinking. Hurrujat wants to leave, but my grandmother Svetlana will stay here. What about you?"

The harlequin shook her head and resumed her tasks. "I am honor-bound to stay here by decree of the city. I committed some crimes and must pay my debt to the city or become branded for the rest of my life."

"Don't you want to go? My mommy and Hurrujat don't want to stay!"

The harlequin seemed unimpressed. "They are free to choose their lives while I am not. Perhaps once I finish my training and become ordained as a priest, I will visit the harlequins. Chances are they will no longer accept me because I am being taught to follow the Elvish religion, and I will have no choice but to remain here."

"The sun… does it hurt?"

"Soremin worries about our wellbeing, and we stay inside the temples to pray during the summer. He is an excellent teacher, and I learn new things daily. Staying here is a better punishment than being branded."

Tioja swallowed some saliva, thinking about his mother. "Is being branded terrible? Jarahad told my mother she must get branded. I don't want her to suffer."

"I don't think that will happen to her. Harlequins leave it as a last resort because there is no way to break the curse. It is likely a ploy so that she makes the right decision. Some of my peers have considered getting branded to leave with Hurrujat, but I doubt they will follow suit. Better to live here as servants of the gods than to suffer from a curse that will severely hinder your life for the promise of a new life that might not be as good as the one we have in Almjarhad. I hope I have answered your question."

Tioja spent the next few days staring at the ocean and thinking about Talgel's message with utter concern.

Talgel and Henrietta eventually arrived and stared at him. "The day has arrived. Please go to Almjarhad Palace."

"Thank you, your ladyship!" Without even waiting for Soremin's permission to leave his temple, Tioja rushed down the cliff and ignored the seething pain in his gut from running too fast without rest. He blinked in disbelief upon seeing the harlequins had stored their tents in carriages.

A guard was standing on the road and smiled at him. "Come with me to Almjarhad Palace. The time to make your decision has arrived."

Under the uncomfortable agreement Jarahad reached with Talgel, he would only speak to each adult family in the privacy of this throne room and the clan's highest-tiered advisors.

After witnessing a few brawls in the street between the vicious rainstorms, Talgel offered this solution, which seemed to bridge the severing gap between all parties.

The proposal still left a bitter aftertaste as Jarahad entered his throne room dressed in more elegant robes than usual, accompanied by Sharad, who once again carried a wooden object in his hand.

Dressed in the same blue silk robes as the day the dome was settled in its permanent place, Sharad ambled with a surging fluidity, considering his mind was preoccupied carving off scraps of wood with a tiny pocket knife.

"Sharad, my friend, I am concerned about this meeting."

Sharad kept on pacing without even bothering to lift his head. "I finished building a third chair so the three of us can be present. I'll decorate it when I have more time."

"This isn't about the chair you kindly built for my father," Jarahad surmised.

Sharad stopped moving and stared at Jarahad's face with unusual seriousness. "Then he will have to sit in a wheelchair for today. Lord Hurrujat deserves to sit on something suitable, and you haven't been giving me more wood to work on."

"I don't mean that, and I apologize. We can't barter more material for your carpentry projects for now."

"Look, you don't have to worry about that. The harlequins will soon leave, and I believe they deserve to find a home where they can be happy. Hurrujat is a good person, and he can count on us for anything. Stop overthinking everything!"

Jarahad stretched his arm to grab his cousin's shoulder. Sharad's pace was too frantic, and he was soon on his chair on the dais.

With a sigh, Jarahad sat on his chair between his cousin and father Jamarnid, who was seated in his wheelchair while he spoke to Soremin standing behind him. Jarahad found the priest's company odd and then realized something embarrassing. "I beg to apologize for not granting you a chair, your eminence."

Soremin shook his head with a neutral expression. "Lord Jamarnid requested my help." Everyone turned their attention to Sharad, who was too busy carving his wooden toy to pay attention. "I abused the city's limited resources with my petition to build Almjarhad Temple while most of the city's inhabitants are still suffering in sodden tents. I believe I can tolerate standing for this session and offer any useful insight for giving me preference over the civilians."

Jamarnid nodded in agreement as he watched Hurrujat approaching the dais from afar. "We can't stall this separation any longer."

Hurrujat's face had its usual cheerful demeanor as he settled on Jamarnid's throne and snuggled in place. "A most impressive throne chair indeed. Your city's artisans are the most talented."

Sharad replied from afar. "Good to know you liked my hard work, Old Pops!"

"How do you feel about splitting our clan?" Jamarnid asked.

Hurrujat didn't even need to reply. He proved his point by pointing at the scab growing on his nose. "I appreciate your company and friendship. Too bad I can't continue living under this dreadful sunlight any longer."

Soremin's face remained somewhat disinterested as he chipped in the conversation. "None of the pureblood elves will leave Almjarhad."

Hurrujat crossed his arms. "Indeed, indeed! I cannot blame them. After the threat to Lord Sharad's life from the Elf King's army, their lives are irremediably tied to this city. Contrary to the rumors you might have heard, my men have not pressured the elves to join us. Even though I would welcome their company, we cannot guarantee their safety if the Eirmite guard attacks us."

Jamarnid spoke in a sterner tone of voice. "I heard the harlequins threatened a few married couples. Any news?"

Jarahad realized his father was specifically speaking to him and blushed at once. "I had to separate a few troublemakers before we got into worse problems. Some harlequins expectedly riled Jamen and Svetlana when they wanted her to leave her husband."

"Nonsense, my boy! Svetlana should never feel guilt for following her heart. Bless her soul for choosing love over the bonds of her blood, and I wish her well." Hurrujat couldn't help but chuckle as he attempted to downplay the seriousness of the confrontation. Diverting problems by brushing them under the rug was the hallmark and weakness of Hurrujat, which irritated Jarahad to no end. He would never dare voice such blasphemous opinions about him in the open when tensions were already so high.

It wasn't long before the first group of people approached the dais. Standing before the group was a small family unit of pureblood harlequins, undoubtedly a group of humble peasants based on the attire and lack of weapons.

Hurrujat couldn't help but smile because he already knew their answer. "Good morning, my dearest Parlok. Welcome to the repatriation committee. Tell us, will everyone here agree to the same decision?"

Parlok stuttered rather sheepishly. "Yes, my Lord. We are all planning on staying united."

Hurrujat grinned at once. "So then, are you planning on staying in Almjarhad, or will you join me regardless of the perils of finding a new home?"

The man straightened up, looking firmer than before. "We wish to go where our king goes. Even if we risk facing death, we will follow you."

Jarahad expected this reply. "We wish you good luck. Will your family accompany you as well?"

"Thank you for your worries, Lord Jarahad. We plan to accompany our king," The woman replied.

Jamarnid nodded without showing emotion on his face. "Very well then. The page will now place a red stone bracelet marking all of you as future emigres, and we wish you good luck in your new life."

An assistant wrote everyone's name on two separate logbooks. Jarahad would store one in Almjarhad, whereas Hurrujat would bring the second one to his new home. Whatever he planned to do with the population data was no longer Jamarnid's concern. The assistant then fetched a red stone bracelet from a box that was fashioned by Talgel and Henrietta over the past week. The family swiftly left the room with little ado.

A solo individual ambled inside with a wobbly gait. Daedoman arrived at the dais alone, wearing his artisan uniform with pockets filled with brushes and other odd utensils. Even though it was obvious he planned to stay, Jamarnid was still required to issue the verbal statement for the sake of order. "Good morning, Daedoman. I can see you never rest from your workshop."

"We have to bring money into this city by engaging in commerce with humans. The sooner the city becomes self-sufficient, the better."

Jamarnid continued. "I will assume you will remain here."

"I plan to stay in Almjarhad except for brief business trips and will probably die in these lands."

Without wasting time, the assistant wrote his name on the logbooks and placed a blue bracelet on his arm. Daedoman frowned as he inspected the trinket, sizing it up and practicing a few wrist movements. When he realized he could still work on his projects without significant issues, he bowed to everyone present and marched outside to keep working without rest.

The first few hours passed where most of the clan made rapid choices that were not even remotely unexpected. Jarahad selected the turns very well to move things ahead, but things would get trickier from now on.

One such couple was a pureblood elf, his wife, and two children. Boshi was yet another one of the clan's elves who ended up marrying a pureblood harlequin. Everyone surmised it resulted from boredom more than anything else. Jarahad disliked the man's rumored infidelity and wondered why they didn't ask Soremin to dissolve their marriage months ago and get it over with.

Realizing the room didn't have any attractive females overseeing the process, Boshi yawned and stared at Jamarnid. "We are staying."

Unexpectedly, the shrill voice of his wife Shimai filled the room, who clenched her tiny fists and growled at her husband. "You liar! You told me we were moving with my parents!"

Boshi chuckled at once. "Hurrujat offered you to leave me. You stupidly didn't when you had the chance because you know you will never find a man as handsome as me. We are staying put."

"You will respect your wife!" Soremin stood forward with clenched fists.

"She is my wife and rejected leaving me. Therefore, I can choose what to do with her and my children."

Jarahad felt tempted to stand up and punch the man. Before he did, Jamarnid's hand rested itself on his lap. "What is wrong, father?"

Jamarnid smirked as he stared at Soremin arguing with Boshi. "You were wise in selecting the easy family units first. This gives us more time to reason with the troublesome cases. Now you know why I specifically wanted Soremin to be present." Before Jarahad could continue arguing, Jamarnid stared at the elf with scorn. "Citizen of the Grey Clan, Boshi!"

Boshi's brown eyes lightened when he realized Jamarnid was speaking to him. He briefly bowed. "Yes, my Lord?"

"You are a disgrace to my people. Every harvest always has a few rotten apples, and you just happened to survive the two purges unscathed."

"Ha! I am a pureblood elf. Therefore, I get to dictate some rules!"

Soremin sneered. "Such as defending your adultery?"

Boshi clenched his fists and growled in return. "You have no proof!"

It was Sharad's turn to speak. "Misty, Shiori, and Ameru are all pregnant. Nice job giving the clan more halflings as handsome and dimwitted as yourself."

Boshi blushed at once. "How could Sharad know?"

Jamarnid grinned as he observed Sharad playing with his toy without a care in the world. "Sharad knows absolutely everything that happens in the city. Those children are sure going to be attractive. They might even inherit your lilac hair like your two legitimate offspring."

When Boshi became increasingly defensive, it was Shimai's turn to growl and pull her children far from his reach. "How dare you! Tell me, Boshi! Did you sleep with those women?!"

"What would you have done? They are gorgeous halflings without your sharp teeth! I have to spread my seed somehow! It's for the good of the clan! Right, Jarahad?"

Jarahad smirked with overt disgust. "I have never lost my sanctity and swore to remain that way until I am blessed by the sacred bond of marriage."

Jamarnid nodded in agreement and stared at Soremin. "Boshi, we must reorganize this room because your family unit is incomplete. Guards, bring those three women at once!"

"Yes, my Lord!"

As the minutes passed, Boshi walked around in circles, arguing with his enraged wife and mistresses to justify his prior behavior, which amused Jarahad.

Jamarnid stared at his son and blinked. "You're a virgin? Seriously?"

The question took Jarahad by surprise, making him blush. "I… uh… I believe it is important for a man to commit himself to his wife. I want to grow with her and believe it is improper to sleep with a stranger."

Jamarnid chuckled. "You would have made a great Äimite guard."

"Impossible! I would never serve Master Salman!"

Jamarnid didn't reply as his face seemed amused by his son's awkward explanation. Perhaps his naivety was why Talgel was unwilling to correspond to his love. Even though Jarahad was confident everyone would ridicule him for his odd confession, he didn't care.

After it looked like the pitiful spectacle would go on forever, Hurrujat seemed too irate to let Boshi continue defending himself. "Shut up, will you?"

Boshi stared at Hurrujat and shrugged his shoulders somewhat derisively. "Everyone is angry at me, and I don't seem to understand. You slept with a married woman. Can't you understand I have needs?"

Jarahad stood up and clenched his fists. "Don't put yourself in Hamara's position. You are a pitiful excuse for an elf! Hamara had already agreed with Head Priest Soremin because her marriage was never formalized. I believe Soremin will dissolve your marriage against your will because it is clear to everyone you have four wives."

"What?!" Boshi stared at the eager women who giggled as they spoke in Harlequin.

Jarahad and Hurrujat were soon laughing because the women were comparing Boshi's sexual prowess in bed and felt pleased they would probably get a beneficial deal. Jarahad soon recalled harlequins prized marrying for prestige, which gave him an enticing idea. "Bring Priest Harselon immediately."

The guards soon ran off, and Jamarnid stared at his son quizzically. "What are you planning to do?"

"Trust me."

Harselon soon appeared from the side hallway, looking rather annoyed because the guards fetched him while he was halfway into his meal. He was licking his bloodied fingers as he stared at the whole commotion. "What is going on? I thought everyone would leave me alone once I accompanied Hurrujat to our new home."

Jarahad grinned. "We are at a cross bend. Boshi wishes to remain in Almjarhad. However, he has sired children with four different women, and it seems like none of the mistresses are happy they aren't his wife. His cheated wife also wishes to join the harlequins."

"So why did you drag me here without notice? Soremin offered to dissolve his marriage, and he refused."

"I order Soremin to dissolve that marriage because Boshi has broken his vows and insulted his poor wife with his adultery. As long as these women agree to remain in Almjarhad, I want you to bind him in marriage under the harlequin custom," Jarahad commanded.

Soremin stared at Jarahad with incredulity. "All of them?"

Jarahad nodded with a grin. "Harlequins may betroth over one wife but under one condition: the husband must treat them with equal kindness. He can't choose any favorites, and they have the final say on whether they wish to live under the same roof or a separate one. The husband has to provide for them and is forbidden to commit adultery, or the wives get to eat him. Is that correct, Hurrujat?"

While Boshi screeched upon hearing the uncomfortable proposal, Hurrujat chuckled. "Almost nobody in Orsenmuray bothered to betroth two wives because it is prohibitively expensive. I am quite surprised you knew about that rule, considering you follow the religion of the elves."

"My father taught me to learn about a lot of subjects to become a good leader."

Jamarnid nodded with a smile. "I know you will make me proud, son."

Feeling glad his father agreed, Jarahad took a deep breath. "Harselon, how quickly can you perform a marriage ceremony?"

"I uh… immediately."

"I am quite pleased with that. Boshi, as interim ruler of the Grey Clan and with the company of my father and Lord Sharad as acting witnesses, you will be forced to dissolve the elvish vows of sacred matrimony. The wife you offended will have the final say whether you repay her economically so that she may leave Almjarhad in peace. Or she can decide no later than sunrise tomorrow to marry you under the harlequin custom."

"I am an elf! I am not a follower of their religion!"

Soremin grinned rather cruelly. "You are a disgrace to our kind and will never be welcome in my temple again. You have turned your back to the true gods and are deemed a heretic. May you find peace in knowing you will never be allowed in the doors of our heavenly afterlife and shall seek counsel with the false harlequin gods."

Harselon wasn't sure what Jarahad had in mind and shrugged his shoulders. "Well, I can initiate a pureblood elf into the harlequin beliefs, although I am not planning on staying here."

Soremin interjected at once. "Several students finished their training and studied under Harselon's tutelage. Perhaps I can allow them to perform the more innocuous harlequin ceremonies."

Jarahad nodded with a grin. "Then that is settled. We will no longer consider Boshi to be religiously an elf. Therefore, Harselon will betroth him to any available woman willing to remain with him in Almjarhad. If he has to marry two women or twenty, he cannot object. I want Charon to place a brand on his body to ensure he remains faithful to his wives." Boshi's cocky face became devoid of color, and he collapsed to the floor while Misty fanned his face. Jarahad had little patience for philanderers and even more if they were supposed to be virtuous elves. "I will let Charon select the punishment. The women who opt to marry Boshi cannot dissolve their marriage and will maintain the peace. If they want to sleep with him twenty or forty times a day, Boshi can't oppose. He must fulfill his husbandly duties." Sharad laughed hysterically and would likely eavesdrop on him during his intimate moments. Feeling morbidly curious to know how many women would be foolish enough to betroth the city's most obnoxious scoundrel, Jarahad smiled even more. "I will be present during your wedding tomorrow morning in this throne room. I am not increasing your dowry without mattering whether we force you to marry one or fifty women. You might have to find useful employment. I'd get some rest if I were you. Charon will brand you tonight, so I expect you to stay sober. A few of my most trusted guards will accompany you, so you can't escape Almjarhad."

As they dragged Boshi outside, hurling constant insults at Jarahad, all four women remained in Almjarhad. It was puzzling. "Are those women seriously going through with my insane plan?" Jarahad pondered out loud.

Sharad chuckled from afar. "An additional five of his lovers might also choose to remain here. I wonder if there are assistants to the groom in harlequin weddings."

While the guards were ushering the women outside and fetching the next family, Hurrujat chuckled. "Blood relatives always serve as witnesses to our weddings, and the parents assist the lovers. Since Boshi's family is deceased, I guess Harselon will grant you the honor if you ask him politely enough. Want to see someone getting branded?"

"Are you serious? Those curses are terrible for the spirit," Soremin mused as he crossed his arms.

Jamarnid smiled at the offended priest. "You just condemned him to an eternity in hell. Brands that vanish after the condemned meets the conditions are far more benign than permanent curses. He will get more than he asked for depending on how many women are foolish enough to betroth him. I believe the punishment is harmless enough and applaud my son's efforts."

Hurrujat agreed. "I would have never thought about exploiting those obscure religious rules myself."

Feeling pleased with the rather satisfactory result, the next family arrived. On this occasion, the halfling wife and pureblood elf remained with no spectacular bickering. As the day was reaching its pinnacle, the last family came. Jamen, his wife Svetlana, and all his children, including Hamara, appeared. Jamad and Tioja were nowhere to be seen.

Jarahad lifted his eyebrows at the odd sight. "Hamara, why are you here?"

Hamara spoke with contempt. "Assisting my family, of course. I may accompany my parents, right?"

"Yes, but…"

Hurrujat spoke rather abruptly, giving no hints about his feelings for Hamara. "Has the family made their choice?"

Before Jamen could speak, his second oldest son Kashin stood forward. "I will go with my master, King Hurrujat."

Svetlana grasped her son's beige shirt while tears fell from her eyes. "Don't leave us! I beg of you!"

Hamara grinned rather ruefully. "I will leave with Kashin and ensure he reaches the pinnacle of his potential."

It was Jarahad's turn to gasp in disbelief. "What is going on?"

Hurrujat seemed complacent as he stretched his arms. "Once we reach our new homeland and Kashin lends us a hand in building the city, I have promised he will be initiated, along with several other highly promising elves."

Kashin beamed as he wiped the tears from his mother's eyes. "Don't feel sorrow, dear mother. I love both of you very much and respect the elf lords of this city. My sister Hamara told me I have the qualities the harlequins desire to become initiated. As long as I swear an oath of loyalty to your clan and serve under his lordship Hurrujat, I will become a nobledemon. I know you wish to remain here with papa Jamen and you made the right decision. I promise to make you very proud and will return with an enormous chest full of gold so that you can live in comfort forever."

Jamen stepped forward. "My child, are you sure of this? Will you be allowed to visit us?"

Kashin nodded. "As long as I finish the training and promise to leave the sword within the city limits as a safeguard, Hurrujat will let me visit you. Nobody coerced me." He then stared at a rightfully angered Nurran and petted his hair. "I know you are angry at me, and I forgive you. Someday, you will understand." Kashin walked toward the assistant and proudly lifted his fist with the red bracelet.

With a sigh, Jamen spoke in a sorrowful voice. "We are staying here."

As Jamen and his family had a blue bracelet placed on their wrists, Hamara conveniently walked towards the door and dragged an infuriated Jamad and their son Tioja inside.

Jarahad was unsure about Hamara's intentions and spoke out loud. "Guards, is there anyone else?"

"Hamara and Jamad are the last citizens, my Lord!"

The response was displeasing, but it was inevitable. Jarahad briefly wondered if Hamara's insistence on being the last person was Hurrujat's idea. "Jamad, have you made your decision?"

"I spoke to my son Tio, and we are staying. My wife stays with me where she belongs."

"No, I am not!" Ignoring Jamad's furious glare, Hamara knelt in front of Tioja and brushed his hair. "My dearest child. Your mother and father are going to separate. I am leaving with the harlequins. You may choose."

"Please stay in Almjarhad!"

While Jamad grinned contemptuously, Hamara shook her head and walked toward the assistants. "Contrary to what Jamad thinks, I will go with the harlequins. Give me my bracelet right now."

While the assistants began scribbling her name on the logbook, mana invaded the room. Jarahad stood forward with sweat covering his brows. "Get out of there! Now!"

The next seconds flashed with the blink of an eye. Jamad's phantom beast crashed against the stone table, covering the air with a layer of papers tossing in every direction and red and blue beads tumbling against the floor. Before Jarahad used sorcery and stopped the tirade, Sharad's Artica began a vicious battle against Jamad's amorphous water beast, biting and gnawing its hide.

Sharad stood straight with an extended arm and sweat covering his brows. "Arrest Jamad!"

Jamad was now busy punching the horde of bodyguards approaching him while trying to keep his phantom beast active. Little did he realize; someone began absorbing his mana.

It was an expectedly enraged Hamara who absorbed Jamad's beast. "You are a disgrace of an elf and a sloppy warrior. You forgot halflings can steal mana."

The throne room became a cacophony of chaos as bodyguards yanked away Jamad, who was hollering insults. Dozens of worried citizens stormed inside to see the commotion. Sharad collapsed into his chair and fell to the ground.

Jarahad was the first to rush by his side. "Sharad!"

Much to his delight, the elf chuckled. "I guess we need to pause the ceremony until Jamad calms down. And maybe fix those logbooks as well."

Traveling into the realm of future events was daunting. Talgel's body constantly ached in wilting exhaustion whenever she returned from her endless visions.

"Your ladyship?"

The vision dissipated into the customary darkness as Talgel returned to her usual self. At first, she surmised she was in her old tent until her hands felt the soft fur of a bear pelt Jarahad once killed for her, prompting her to sigh. She was in his palace.

Having Henrietta by her side at all times was growing on her, partly because of the vision she had just saw a few moments prior. The halfling sat on the border of her bed and absentmindedly stared at her odd friend. "Would you like to know about your death?"

The shifting of the harlequin's legs hinted at her likely answer. "I, uh… appreciate your offering and feel honored your phantom beast saw my fortune. However, I don't wish to change my fate. May things happen the way the gods intended."

"That is a lie."

"Not at all! I always prize sincerity and wouldn't want you to tell me my fortune!"

"The gods our kin worship don't exist… or if they do, they don't care about us. We are just peons in the greater scheme of things." The sigh emanating from the harlequin was proof Talgel hit the nerve she wanted. Like all harlequins, Henrietta was deeply religious. It was as if they tried to hide the depravity of the things they did with excuses the gods would someday forgive them.

As she grabbed a brush and combed her hair, Henrietta sat on a chair with a false tone of joy in her voice to divert the touchy subject of Talgel's blatant atheism. "Why didn't you join Hurrujat?"

"Because I need you to be with me."

"I uh… am flattered you enjoy my company despite our differences. I feel you would have been thrilled to leave this city."

"I never intended to make Jarahad suffer out of spite. Contrary to the many lies he told you, I broke our marriage agreement for a different reason."

"Will you ever tell me why?"

Talgel remained silent for a while as she tried to revisit the visions of Jarahad's fortune. "I still love him. But I do not intend to stay here because I wish to see him suffer or plan to marry him. I also appreciate Hurrujat and will always enjoy the company of his kin." It felt strange in Talgel's tongue to savor the truth spilling from her mouth for a change. It was almost…. liberating.

Her confession only piqued Henrietta's curiosity even more. "Talgel, what false future awaited you if you accompanied Hurrujat?"

Talgel grinned at once. "I could have enjoyed true happiness if I served under Hurrujat. It's that… the price of leaving Almjarhad to its fate was too great."

"Fate? Is something bad going to happen here?"

"That is correct. I first must locate the Cursed One. Only I can pinpoint his identity and warn Jarahad ahead of time."

"This mage, you know who he is!"

Talgel knew Henrietta was intelligent and insightful, just never to this degree. "I bet Soremin finished performing Jamad's marriage dissolution. I have been moving the strings of these puppets, and they have been most obedient. Everything is marching to plan."

"You are a monster."

"I have never felt more pleased to be awarded a more suitable compliment. Thank you, my dear friend." Talgel wiped a tear from her hollowed eye. Perhaps there was still a figment of her long-lost humanity that was not stripped away from her after all.

That evening, Talgel finished dressing in the attire and hairstyle of the future vision she wanted to recreate the most. Accompanied by Henrietta, they reached Jamad's prison cell. Jarahad was standing in the hallway, fuming nonstop.

The second Jarahad saw Talgel, his characteristic unwavering footsteps stomped in her direction. "Lord Talgel! I am so glad for your presence!"

"I am well aware of that. Tioja is with his mother while she tries to coax him to accompany her. You must release Jamad immediately to say goodbye."

"Impossible! He attacked our clan leader!"

"I don't care. Force Jamad to do community service for as long as you wish, but he must speak to Hamara and his son. You must also be present because Hurrujat and his kin are leaving immediately."

"What?!"

Henrietta was sent to do Talgel's dirty work earlier that day and easily convinced Hurrujat to prepare their entourage while Jarahad, Jamarnid, and Soremin were too busy meddling with Jamad. Sharad was going to be the trickiest individual to manipulate. Talgel made Sharad an offer he couldn't refuse, under the condition he remained outside Jamad's tent while wearing his brand-new armor.

After hearing Jarahad argue with the guards, they hauled Jamad outside. Talgel didn't waste any time grabbing a key from the bodyguard and unlocking Jamad's manacles.

The sound of clinking metal against the ground combined with Jamad's gasps was like music to her ears. "Why are you liberating me?"

"I already agreed with Sharad that as long as you say goodbye to Tioja and Hamara while being as polite as reasonably possible, we will pardon you with just a warning. You will agree to the inevitable departure of your wife, and that is the end."

Jamad wished he could punch her. Talgel recalled one potential leyline in her visions where Jamad followed his dormant violent instincts to be most enjoyable because he ended up being executed. Much to her dismay, Jamad didn't even lift his fist. He knew she was playing with his feelings like a mouse trapped in a maze, and he no longer wanted to be her peon. The drolling footsteps hinted Jamad simply walked away.

Henrietta sighed. "Let's continue your plan and visit the tent."

Jamad's tent was still on the outdoor patio of Almjarhad Palace. Efforts to build permanent dwellings for the city's inhabitants became delayed because of the drama of splitting the clan apart. Talgel couldn't care less about these minor inconveniences. She wanted an excellent future to occur and felt satisfied that her plan was working.

They soon reached the patio and became bombarded by Tioja's shrill squealing in Hamara's arms. He was a strange and somewhat obnoxious child, in Talgel's opinion. But she knew he would be helpful with her ulterior plans. Before Jamad's little tirade, Tioja was supposed to be unable to choose because of his age.

As expected, Jamad was oozing with rage. He was about to harm Hamara in front of everyone when Jarahad grabbed his wrist and growled. "Don't do it."

"What in the hell are you doing, Lord Jarahad? Half of our clan wishes to abandon us!"

A sigh escaped Jarahad's lips. "I can understand your indignation because you are one of the ousted immortals. Care to remember these harlequins ended up left homeless as well."

Hamara rudely cleared her throat. "I am no longer your wife, Jamad. I have chosen my side."

"You're an elf, Hamara!"

"I'm a HALF elf, Jamad. Don't forget that. While you were a noble husband that never struck your hand, I have made my decision."

Talgel felt even more pleased Hamara was now busy caressing Hurrujat, whose labored breaths and stumbling gait were easy to tell apart. The future she wanted was about to be sealed.

"How can you do this to me, Hamara?!" Jamad pleaded.

"Let me remind you that despite his appearance, my new husband is much younger than you, Jamad."

Jamad's breathing became more profound, and he could barely resist the urge to drag Hamara back into his arms. However, he didn't dare contradict Jarahad's authority. After thinking for a few moments, Jamad sighed with disdain and tossed his ring at Hamara's feet. "I liberate you from the bonds of our marriage vows, Hamara. May your mortal life be full of joy with your new husband."

As expected, Hamara squealed almost as much as Talgel did deep inside while she feigned an inert facial expression.

Hamara approached her bewildered son and hugged him. "Tioja, your mother loves you very much. Please come with me to our new home to be happy."

This was the final defining moment of Talgel's plans. If Tioja left Almjarhad, it would be an uphill battle to ensure the future she wanted for her ulterior plans. While Tioja engaged in a pitiful spectacle most expected of a troublesome brat, he hugged Jamad and sealed his fate.

Talgel could no longer care about Jamad's speech and instead focused her attention on Hurrujat's labored breathing, who correctly surmised she was the culprit behind Tioja's decision to remain in Almjarhad. With a huff of indignation blended with sorrow, Hamara stood up. Talgel could hear her footsteps approaching her lover, with a callous disregard for Tioja. The way Hamara only saw her child as a pawn for her own selfish desires was quite wicked, even by Talgel's standards.

Hurrujat chuckled at once without displaying in public his irritation regarding Tioja's decision. "Ho, ho, ho! This is very good! I will indeed miss the company of all of you. We shall continue to be friends, even if both sister clans must separate forever."

Hamara's voice increased in softness. "Lord Jarahad, I appreciate your help. We will remain as allies. You can count on us."

Jarahad didn't seem too pleased with Hamara's sudden loss of interest in the little child she would leave behind. Neither did he realize all his actions this evening had been planned by Talgel the whole time. Like a good puppet, Jarahad had the firmest strings that never tangled nor lost their way. His predictability was his greatest weakness, yet Talgel always found his naivety to be his most irresistible trait.

Jarahad's speech about friendship and past loyalties was of minor importance, but Talgel had to feign interest out of politeness. She whispered in Henrietta's ear. "Is Sharad wearing his sword?"

"That is correct. You told Hurrujat he needed a suitable sword made of normal steel. I can't believe Charon finished it on time. It is indeed exquisite looking. Albeit I don't know why you asked Hurrujat to do that instead of something that directly benefitted you. Wouldn't you have wanted fine robes or gold? You always enjoy dressing up on special occasions."

"Nonsense. Sharad is a fool, but he has his merits. The sword has no magical powers, yet it will be a driving force for him. He will need to become stronger when the time comes."

"Oh, how fascinating! Will he learn to fence?"

"I don't care if he does. The sword is just a symbol of his unpaid debts to the harlequin clan. He will eventually make a payment worth tenfold of the weapon's value."

Henrietta asked a few more menial questions that no longer interested her. The conversation now reached the pinnacle regarding Jarahad's invaluable sword. Talgel knew beforehand that Hurrujat had to make an uncomfortable promise to lend the sword to his great-grandson. Yet, hearing Jarahad cower at the man that never truly loved him was a fruit she must savor. She would miss Hurrujat because his future was going to be entertaining, and he made her laugh. Listening to Jarahad suffer because he had no other choice only made Hurrujat's departure more salient.

Henrietta was right: she was a monster. And she wanted to embrace it.

CHAPTER 24 ♦ JAMARNID

Life became rather dull after the harlequins left. Jamarnid had difficulty accepting he missed Hurrujat's obnoxious laughter and carefree attitude toward life. He was always too jovial for Jamarnid's taste. And it only worsened after the second purge. Jamarnid believed his suspicions were correct. Perhaps the last string of sanity left the decrepit creature when his children died, and Jarahad became his unwanted heir.

"Where is my son?"

The servant assigned to cut his nails today lifted his face. Tanato was a halfling with remarkably pronounced harlequin physical traits. He was also one of the first few students of Soremin that became his apprentice without having a prior criminal history. The price of his enthusiasm was equaled by how much he wanted to taint the true elvish religion with his vile harlequin beliefs.

Soremin enjoyed the challenge Tanato offered because he had to find increasing proof that the elvish gods were real. Doing so only enticed Tanato to perform even more gruesome summoning rituals within the safety of a magical barrier field to contact some random false harlequin god.

Jamarnid promised Soremin he would allow Tanato to continue his twisted experiments as long as nothing he did could harm his city as a special favor to his friend. He believed the spells were utter nonsense, and Tanato would come to his senses soon. Still, the fact the apprentice priest was disrespecting Jamarnid's absolute rule with such defiling behavior prompted him to hate him. The instant Tanato engaged in eye contact without being granted permission, Jamarnid swatted the halfling's temple with his forearm out of spite.

Tanato collapsed on the ground from the unexpected act of violence. Just like the other times, he kowtowed in his presence, showing no resentment. "I am deeply remorseful for having caused you hardship, my Lord Jamarnid. I hope you accept my sincerest apology for whatever wrong I have done."

"Your existence is wrong, you skinless mutt. Deprived of the sanctity of immortality and forced to shed your skin and drink the blood of innocent animals to live. You act like a messenger of the gods, yet you are the full embodiment of sin. Get out of my presence and bring Jarahad here."

"I shall obey his lordship immediately. May I continue caring for your hands before I leave?"

"Get out!"

Tanato scrambled away with the right amount of politeness and speed to his impossibly high standards. Making other people feel uncomfortable was one of Jamarnid's favorite mind games. Jarahad never approved it, but he couldn't do anything to stop him. The only elf in the clan that would be capable of putting Jamarnid in his place was too busy playing with the sword Hurrujat gifted him the day he left a few months ago. Jamarnid loved his nephew Sharad very much and felt sure the aloof elf would someday accept the ring. Meanwhile, if learning to fence helped him, all Jamarnid could feel was pride.

It didn't take too long for Jarahad to appear. He was breathing heavily while dressed in his armor. "Is something wrong, father?"

"From the sweat on your face, I will presume you are Lord Sharad's mentor."

Jarahad felt relieved his father wasn't in danger and sat on a chair to clean his face. "I told him I am not a master swordsman, yet he insists I have to be his teacher."

"I think he made the right choice. It is the custom of nobleelves to be taught by their kin."

"A fencing teacher taught you. Am I wrong?"

"I was a prodigy in my own right and was mostly self-taught. My tutor was married to a lesser family member, so I never truly deviated from tradition. How is Sharad doing?"

"Honestly, Sharad is wasting his time."

"Huh?"

"He insists he wants to use his weapon instead of first learning how to fight with a practice sword."

"He is going to hurt someone! No wonder he asked you to teach him."

"More likely, he is going to sprain his shoulder. Carpentry has kept his body strong, but I can't teach him anything with my unbreakable sword."

"Do you want me to speak to him?"

"Try it if you must. Sharad will still do whatever he wants. I plan to continue the charade until he inevitably tires of wasting his time and finds something else to occupy his thoughts. If you must excuse me, I must monitor him."

Jamarnid waved his hand. "Tire him while ensuring he doesn't harm anyone and continue with the tasks to finish our city."

"I shall, father."

Overcoming Sharad's authority was one of the few things that made Jamarnid feel uncomfortable. He didn't care if they accused him of being racist, intolerant, or useless because of being disabled. While he still struggled on occasion, he had gotten used to his body and was more than capable to use his sorcery to teach any detractors a lesson.

In reality, it was the backstabbing behavior of his subjects that truly got on his nerves. As expected, Boshi was unhappy with his punishment, and the reasons were quite obvious. After being forced to marry an unprecedented number of sixteen women who were constantly fighting with each other for some bedtime or more expensive dresses, his guards caught Boshi fleeing the city on foot. Nobody cared because he would not get very far.

And watching Boshi crawling into the throne room a few days later while he sniveled in utter agony was all too enjoyable. On this occasion, Jarahad and Sharad were too busy training in some nearby mountains to witness it. Jamarnid would have wanted Soremin to be present, but the priest declined because Boshi became excommunicated and was no longer his problem. Therefore, Jamarnid was forced to have Tanato, of all people, by his side. A curse seethed through his teeth because of Soremin's little prank.

As expected, the sixteen wives stood around their husband and laughed nonstop. It surprised Jamarnid that one of them was a pureblood human from a nearby village who couldn't even speak the local tongue. She was the one who issued the alert to her conspirators, and they all activated the curse together.

And behold, Charon couldn't have chosen anything better for the occasion! Boshi was lying on the stone floor of his throne room, grasping his privates with both fists with a puckered red face. "Help me, Lord Jamarnid! I beg of you!"

Amongst the relentless giggles of the women, Jamarnid took his time. "I am deeply sorry. Can you remind me what your name is?"

"It's Boshi! Boshi! BOSHI!"

"Hrm… Never heard of him. Are you sure you are not an Äimite guard on a mission to claim my head?"

Misty giggled even harder. "He looks like my husband, but this guy is taking forever to explode. The elf I have loved so many times was quick."

Boshi's moans were worse than before as he supplicated for mercy. "None of them want to forgive me. I don't understand. I left the city to make ends meet."

This amused Jamarnid even more. "Oh really? Apprentice Priest Tanato, would you mind if you refreshed my ailing memory?"

"Not at all, my Lord! Charon placed the ring brand on Boshi's… uhh… male anatomy. His brand was linked to all his wives. Boshi is virtually their slave, and they can cause him terrible agony whenever they wish. I am not entirely familiar with this brand because I have never seen its full effect in action until now. As a fellow man, I can understand the pain he must feel for being unable to release the seed that continues to accumulate inside. Have you been able to relieve yourself during the days you were away, dear elf?"

"Of course, I can't, you sniveling brute! I want to ejaculate so badly, and this disgusting thing Charon placed on my skin has kept it locked inside. Please, save me!"

As much as Jamarnid wanted the clan's worst citizen to continue suffering for his entertainment, he felt Boshi endured enough. "Dear ladies, I urge you to release him. Boshi could perish and leave you without his joyful company. You wouldn't like that, would you?"

One wife cheered out loud. "You heard our clan leader. It's time to release our husband from his misery!" Every woman stood in a circle and grabbed each other's hands as a gold symbol etched on their hands reacted with the branding on Boshi's body.

Jamarnid closed his eyes and heard Boshi's squeals of release, followed by dripping noises on the dais. He didn't want to know what it was, but Boshi would clean up the mess. "I hope you have learned your lesson, dear citizen. You cannot go against my son's back and ask me for a larger dowry. If you cannot earn enough money to support so many wives, I can find you better sources of employment. I will also urge your wives to be more agreeable to their demands. However, do not forget that you belong to them for the next few centuries and are responsible for raising your children. The next time you leave Almjarhad, you must ask for everyone's permission. They cannot harm you as long as your chastity remains intact. Tanato, do you know what would have happened if he had defiled a new lover and his wives activated the curse?"

"An agonizing and painful death."

Boshi lifted his head and screeched.

"Well, seems like someone is listening. Go clean up the mess you made in my throne room and cuddle with your wives, Boshi. I encourage them to visit me as frequently as possible so that I can listen to their complaints. Don't forget, I have a lot of free time and enjoy a story with a happy ending."

Upon hearing the news of Boshi's public humiliation, Jarahad didn't think twice before he stormed into Jamarnid's bedroom. "You went too far!"

As usual, Jarahad was too soft when it came to corporal punishment. A real irony, given he was the culprit of Boshi's current situation.

Jamarnid grinned. "I never told Charon to place that specific curse on the brute. Nor did I encourage Boshi to leave the city and visit a whorehouse, either. He was lucky his wives activated the curse before he killed himself. That was all on him."

"We have to protect the pureblood elves!"

"And what better way than to keep him trapped inside the same tent with his sixteen promiscuous wives and children all clamoring for his attention? I am certain he will be very obedient from now on."

"Why are you so bitter?"

Jamarnid sighed as he focused on his hands. "If I had remained celibate like I was supposed to and ignored the temptation, my people wouldn't have died."

"And I would have never been born. I see you only view me as the embodiment of your mistake."

"No! Son, I… I am sorry for hurting your feelings. Maybe I am not the best person to say this. What I mean is I could have never been worthy of a better person to be my child. If one good thing came from all of this, it was you."

Jamarnid hugged his son, whose face was plastered with a furrowed brow when the door opened. Both elves gasped at the unexpected arrival of Talgel and Henrietta.

Much to Jamarnid's annoyance, Talgel was still living under his roof for Henrietta's well-being because of the oppressive summer. "Leave, Talgel. You are not wanted here."

"Oh, quite the contrary. I had many chances to speak to both of you, but I wanted to enjoy a rare display of love towards the son you were not supposed to have. Most touching indeed."

"Why… you little tramp!"

Jarahad stood between both parties to remain neutral. "Is something wrong? Why pay us a visit with such urgency?"

Talgel's hands unfastened the ribbon that held her mask and stuffed it into her pocket.

A sneer escaped Jamarnid's lips from her impolite behavior, yet a part of him was curious to know the motive for her visit. "Why did you remove your mask? Do you wish to be punished?"

Talgel shook her head. "The story I plan to reveal today is critical. I believe it would be easiest for all parties if I revealed my true facial emotions to prove I am serious. I had a vision some time ago, and I had to wait until the harlequins left and things to calm down before I could share this information."

Jarahad's hands were shaking because he was sure something was wrong. "Is someone going to die?"

The sheer vagueness of the question was tricky to answer, and Talgel's lips twitched for a few moments. "Perhaps. I have been completely supportive of the clan's attempts to locate more mages, and I am certain it will serve an ulterior purpose in Almjarhad's survival."

"You are just evading the answer. Speak up!" Jamarnid demanded.

Talgel clucked her tongue rather rudely. "I had a vision that is very important to our clan. I do not know the identity of this mage, but a citizen of our city will endanger us all."

"Huh?" Jamarnid and Jarahad stared at each other and swallowed saliva.

"This is not good, father. Could it be possible one of our people is going to kill Sharad and conquer the city?" Jarahad asked.

The creasing in Talgel's eyebrows softened. "Not exactly. The Cursed One has a magical ability that is too dangerous and uncontrollable. Keep your eyes open. Once we discover the elf's identity, we must evict him from the city. You will know when the time comes. Good evening."

As the woman walked away alongside her assistant, Jamarnid slumped in his chair and remained pensive.

Jarahad stared at his face with a frown. "Could this be another one of Talgel's ploys to split the clan even further?"

"I seriously doubt it. Have the apprentice mages caused any trouble?"

"Not at all. I sometimes visit, and at least one halfling has been working hard to summon their latent mana. Could it be possible one of these children will summon a dangerous phantom beast?"

"I would not discard that possibility, son. Keep your eyes open. If the twerp's warning is true, we must evict that elf immediately to protect Sharad's life."

"Please don't say that! Maybe I can save him!"

"And risk the city?!" Jamarnid shook his head and averted his gaze. "I have suffered through two purges and seen many friends perish. If I must kill this cursed elf to safeguard Lord Sharad's life, then so be it."

After Hamara's departure, Tioja's relationship with his father only worsened. Jamad never cooked or cleaned. So, Tioja frequently visited Svetlana's home for help. When he heard his father weeping, Tioja huddled on his bed and covered his ears. Tioja was sure he caused his parents to separate, and he would forever hate himself for it.

As dawn arrived, Tioja's stomach grumbled, prompting him to get out of bed. "Father? Do you want me to bring you some food?"

"Leave me, Tio. Go play with your friends. I don't care."

Seeing his father withering away into a miserable husk was pitiful, so Tioja went outside. "I will bring you something to eat. Take care."

Almjarhad experienced a remarkable change over the years. Food shortages ceased to be a problem, and the elves bartered their surplus harvests for building materials. Engineers had the time to develop a reliable map of the regional topography and commence the construction of a sewage system. Wastewater was diverted into faraway basins to be converted into compost for the farms, and they erected houses in safe areas.

Even though the harlequins left, the clan still had ample amounts of earth mages that cleared the beach and diverted the sharpest rocks into strategic posts. When word spread that Almjarhad Bay was now accessible along with a newly constructed stone dock, merchants arrived in large numbers for trade and commerce. Whenever it became too overbearing to stay with his depressive father, Tioja would rush to the bay and watch human sailors gawking at the city. Almjarhad boasted new stone roads alongside small gardens adorned with palm trees. Narrow walkways had intermittent fountains that became the favored resting place for the city's youth in their free time.

The tents had been replaced long ago by manicured stone houses in large swaths of land that could be easily changed with earth magic as families increased in size. Jamad's modest home, in comparison, seemed cramped. Not that Tioja cared too much. The house was cozy, and it offered a delightful view of the beach. When he became fed up being near his father, the yard offered Tioja the chance to tend to his little vegetable garden.

As the city continued to prosper these past fifteen years, Tioja could finally receive much-needed formal education. Svetlana taught him basic Harlequin in the privacy of her home as long as he didn't use it elsewhere. He then alternated his time between doing community service, going to the city's first school, and learning magic.

Tioja was an extraordinary prodigy and the first halfling attuned to two elements simultaneously. Even his father Jamad gawked when he used air and water magic. As the elf remained in the garden that morning, his fingers flickered, and leaves were attracted to the whims of his powerful air magic. They would tinker sideways, lift off and rise into the sky.

"Wow, Tio! I am so jealous of your magic!"

Tioja blushed when Nurran showed up unannounced. He was now almost a full-fledged adult with medium height and a muscular build. Nurran's face was devoid of handsomeness, instead characterized by eager red eyes with a perpetual hunger for adventure. On this occasion, the sweetness of steamed fruit and some kind of bread infused the surrounding air. Tioja couldn't resist the temptation, and his hands lifted the fabric of Nurran's basket. His mouth salivated at the sight of several pastries. The second he attempted to grab one, Nurran swatted him hard. "Ow! Why did you do that?"

"They are not for you." Nurran grabbed the pastry Tioja wanted and chomped it down in one gulp. "Maybe if I eat more, I'll awaken my second element and join you!"

"Silly Nurran! You are supposed to be my role model and act like a child!"

When both halflings stared at each other's sweaty faces, they laughed at once. "Don't you ever bathe, Tio?"

"Don't you have any manners, Uncle Nurran?"

After wiping the scattered tears from his eyes, Nurran seemed to be in a jollier mood. He shoved the basket in Tioja's hands. "I lied. My mom cooked them for you. Give them to your old pa. How is he doing?"

From the outside, Jamad's home presented a false appearance of normalcy because of Tioja's fervent cleaning. However, the fact his father hadn't even bothered to close the front door meant he remained in bed. "He's still heartbroken. He doesn't even go to the tavern with his friends anymore. On one occasion, he caught me speaking to a neighbor in Harlequin, and he went back inside without saying a word. It's like he wishes to overcome the attitudes and behaviors Hamara disliked in a foolish hope she will return."

"That is a real bummer. Has Hamara sent you a message or anything?"

"Not at all. I think a few citizens visited their city last spring for a brief visit, so I am certain they found a new home. But I know nothing else."

Nurran's eyes darted around as his frisky hands rummaged into the basket and nabbed another pastry when Tioja wasn't looking. "Is Jamad still on probation after all these years?"

"I think Lord Sharad has not released him from his sentence on purpose so that he has an excuse to leave the house without starving to death. He went to the palace last week to polish his lordship's boots for a few hours. The mundane tasks seem rather strange to me. When I found out my father tried to injure our leader, I assumed he would get a long prison sentence."

"Heard the seer got him out of jail for some reason. You just never know what Talgel is up to."

Upon hearing Talgel's name, Tioja twitched his ears. "Has she ever visited you?"

"My mother was summoned to her tent a few weeks ago. I have tried prying for answers, but she has remained rather elusive. What about you?"

A flash of remembrance from Talgel's speech prompted Tioja to avert his gaze. "She told me I will become a great mage someday, but my future is still uncertain. It was as if I was supposed to do something important. I wished she could have been more specific."

Nurran shook his head in disbelief. "Silly Tio! What if your magic is evil, and she wants to force you to learn it on purpose?"

"Are you referring to the legend of the Cursed One?"

"Obviously, you dope! Lord Jarahad has kept his eyes open on the lookouts for new mages. I am getting worried."

"What do you mean?"

"Ugh, you're so clueless! He wants to evict that elf!"

"That is silly. Lord Jarahad is the best mage I have ever met. He can defeat anyone!" The instant the sun was reaching its peak, Tioja squealed in anxiety. "Oh, my! Jamen told me to go to the beach today at midday!" Upon leaving the basket inside and rushing to the street, Nurran chased after him.

"Why are you in such a hurry?"

"Because today is the day! Jamen told me I was going to summon my phantom beast!"

"Wait!"

Being the world's most gifted seer elicited two very different responses. Elves and every law-abiding harlequin viewed Talgel with reverie and considered it a great honor to be seated on the visitor carpet of her new beachfront residence. Some of Almjarhad's inhabitants were never summoned, whereas other people might visit her several times in a given year.

"I am deeply sorry for wasting your time," Talgel seethed with gritted teeth to maintain appearances.

"Wait! I swear I will pay you anything! I heard you are the most talented fortune teller in the world! You correctly predicted the attack of a horde of pirates!"

Even though unsuspecting humans viewed Talgel somewhat favorably, someone misinformed them about the scopes of her abilities.

And one such human was groveling her feet this morning, prompting Henrietta to giggle nonstop. Both women had grown accustomed to these frequent visits from desperate humans. It had been agreed upon that Talgel had to allow visitors to beg for her help. They had to sign a magical scroll with their blood to accept her answer or, in this case, the lack of one. The visitor must leave the city without harming her at all costs or risk being executed by Jarahad. It annoyed Talgel to no end because she had less free time to pursue her hobbies. However, offering usually disappointing predictions was an excellent source of steady income for the city. Even though most visitors abided with the rules without issue, some would return, hoping that Talgel might give them a far better prediction.

Her current visitor was a combination of persistent and pitiable. Talgel stood up from her chair, rubbed her legs, and walked around the visitor room in circles. The room was both luxurious and suffocating. Silk and velvet cushions of all colors littered the ground, her indoor slippers paced against a finely weaved red carpet, and the sweet aroma of dozens of orchids invaded the stone walls growing in every crevice. Red and gold semi-translucent curtains covered the room's windows, granting it an eerily dark atmosphere that further fed into the allure of her mystical powers. The rhythmic sound of waves crashing on the faraway shoreline alternated with the agonizing whimpering of the man.

None of this mattered to Talgel. The man could continue begging until he died of thirst for all she cared because he never read the job contract. Using a technique she honed over time, Talgel knelt in front of the man while a scornful twitch of her lips adorned her otherwise expressionless face. "I cannot share the future of a visitor I have not seen."

"I don't care if my fortune is bad. Please help!"

"Look, I know why you are so desperate. Your feudal leader was very much the same as you. He once paid me a large sum of money to grovel for my help. I had to shoo him away because I had no useful visions to offer. Several months later, I saw his fortune and sent him a letter to return on short notice. You must understand I have never seen your fortune. Even if I did, it would have probably been an utter banality, such as visiting the market or scratching yourself. I can't force myself to see the vision of a specific person, nor can you demand me to help you. If I see a vision that concerns your livelihood, I will be more than glad to request your return. Please leave my home."

"Please! Tell me something! Anything!"

Henrietta stood up to drag the man outside and turned around. The harlequin knew Talgel was up to something. "I know that expression, your ladyship. You do have some information that can be relayed to this man."

As the man's breathing hastened in glee, Talgel smirked with restraint. "If you had bothered to read the job contract, dear Pishkadela, among many other things, I can never tell a lie to a paying customer. I would never harm my reputation because it would taint the honor of this city. I have never seen a vision where you appear, not even as the background character of someone else's future." Even though the man conceded defeat, Talgel was kind enough to continue speaking. "There is one small amount of information that could be useful to you."

"What would it be?!"

"Leave Almjarhad immediately. For your safety."

"Huh?" The way Pishkadela was shifting his weight and swooshing his clothes around marked his skepticism. Perhaps he suspected Talgel had some goons waiting for him outside.

Much to Talgel's chagrin, Henrietta patted the man's shoulder to appease his fears. Damn traitor. "Please do not be afraid. I can assure Talgel never harms her clients unless they attack her first. She is possibly telling you some kind of fortune, and you should pay close attention. Right, my ladyship?"

Talgel sighed in defeat. Even though her roommate never divulged her visions, Henrietta had recognized her subtleties and wrongly presumed this warning was another one of her mind games. "I have seen the fortune of several city inhabitants, and I urge Mr. Pishkadela to leave at once. Abide with my suggestion, and I promise to send you a message if I see a vision. Thank you for visiting me."

Despite the reassuring speech, getting rid of the stupid man still took several nudges. The instant the door closed, Talgel covered the curtains and turned around.

"The fortune you told him isn't serious, is it?" Henrietta's abilities to predict her moves never ceased to be astounding.

This was a tricky question. If she had had more time, Talgel would have offered a more appropriate explanation. A shrill chime of an enchanted bell echoed from the windowsill, signaling it was midday. Instead of explaining anything, Talgel grabbed her walking stick and stormed outside with Henrietta trailing behind.

Henrietta knew Talgel's behavior signaled it was serious. "Oh, my! Something terrible is going to happen to this city! Is it a pirate attack?" Much to her relief, there weren't any strange ships in the bay today.

Talgel was in too much of a rush to appease Henrietta's concerns. She could answer Henrietta's questions, but it was more fun irritating her out of pettiness. The two women reached the sandy beach that was dotted with palm trees. In the middle, a small but growing crowd of onlookers was cheering at a teenage halfling with messy grey hair and modest peasant robes. A young adult halfling and a pureblood elf stood nearby.

Talgel stopped to admire the spectacle from a safe distance. "I am glad we have arrived on time."

"What do you mean? I just see an elf talking to those halflings. What is so great about this?"

"Keep your eyes open and watch."

It didn't take long before mana surrounded the little elf, and an imperceptible thickness invaded their surroundings. Everything melted into a dizzying blur until Talgel stumbled before her demon. None of this made any sense.

"What? How is this possible? I didn't use my phantom beast!"

Unlike their prior encounters, the demon seemed less ethereal, more distant. Its reptilian blue scales soon convalesced, and they stood together on the beach alongside Henrietta.

Talgel saw her friend offering encouraging words that didn't seem to matter. Her voice was there, but the sounds were garbled. And then… Talgel understood. "Is this the strange prediction I have been trying to revisit?"

The demon floated in the sky and flapped its wings. "You are sort of correct. Do you enjoy seeing the world with my eyes? This is the second effect of a critical prediction. You always failed to relive it, no matter how much you tried. Since I am happy because the first requirement of my plans has been accomplished, I will share this knowledge: The next time you have a critical vision of your own future, you will see the world in this split state. Time-altercating damage can be done if you are not careful."

"And Henrietta isn't seeing all of this?"

"We are in a parallel timeline that intercrosses different futures. Your body is moving by itself like a doll while I remain invisible."

Something intrigued Talgel. While she was sure this was the pivotal event she yearned to see, the little elf collapsed on the ground and stopped using mana almost as quickly as he started using it. "I thought I would finally discover the identity of the Cursed One… but I was wrong."

"Come back here at midday in exactly 5 days, and the future you correctly predicted will happen. You missed the date."

"What?"

"Summon me in 6 days, and we shall see each other again."

And then the reptilian beast vanished, and everything returned to normal.

***

A commotion ensued, and it wasn't long before Talgel had to dodge an elf running towards the beach at full speed. From the wretched smell, it had to be Jamad. She could sniff the slob's malodorous body a mile away.

Booming voices and stomping reverberated in every direction. Henrietta opted to hear the gossip, whereas Talgel soon lost interest and returned home. Taking advantage of this rare moment of peace, Talgel snatched some of her most poignant orchid petals, cruised to a low-rise table, and began crushing them with a pestle. Soon enough, the door slammed open, and Henrietta rushed inside, prompting Talgel to seethe with gritted teeth.

"What is wrong, your ladyship? You left the beach and didn't wait for me," Henrietta heaved in exasperation.

"My mistake. I thought the prediction I wanted to witness would happen today. At least I didn't embarrass myself in front of a paying customer."

"No harm done! I have big news!"

"Really? What could it be?"

"A young halfling has just summoned a phantom beast for the first time! Almjarhad now has another mana donor! Isn't it wonderful?" By this time, Henrietta sat on the other side of the table to rummage through Talgel's perfume bottles and sniffed them with glee. When they first started living together, both women bickered a lot because Henrietta had no sense of respecting other people's personal space. Talgel had given up long ago on remediating this terrible habit and tried to ignore her to maintain the peace.

Despite the good news, Talgel remained unconvinced as she fastened a cork to a glass bottle. "While I recall sensing trace amounts of mana, the beast must have vanished only a few seconds after the halfling summoned it. Even Jarahad kept his Rashid active for a minute or two when he first summoned it."

From the crumple on Henrietta's clenched hands, Talgel might have gone too far by insulting Jarahad's achievement. If Henrietta had shown any offense, she didn't address it out loud. "Remember that little boy named Tioja?"

"Oh, so he finally summoned his phantom beast? Splendid. I knew he would prove his worth soon enough."

"Well, I am certain he is more gifted than you think. If it hadn't been for a pair of demonic wings that grew on his back for no apparent reason, I am certain he would have continued using mana."

This strange observation prompted Talgel to bite her lip. "That makes little sense. Since when does a halfling grow wings when they summon a phantom beast?"

"I know! I believe I have seen the skin of at least one halfling turn a few shades darker, and that woman named Yunisha always grows a splotch of black hair behind her ears when she summons her beast. A pair of wings must be a first. Poor little kid was squealing in pain because the wings pressed against his shirt, and that is why he stopped using mana so quickly."

Talgel crossed her arms and frowned. "Well, we will continue to learn more surprises. Do you know where Jamad took him?"

"Lord Jarahad paid Jamad a visit to see if Tioja needed help. I brought Jarahad a snake to feed the little guy, just in case."

"Then Jarahad is doing his job, and I can resume my hobby in peace."

"How delightful! Are you planning on making one for me?"

"What for? Make your own perfume!"

Instead of feeling insulted, Henrietta lurched in Talgel's way, covered her in a bear's hug, and kissed her hair. During times like these, Talgel wished the dratted woman would take her cue already and move out.

***

Tioja's health had recovered, and he returned to the same spot 5 days later alongside his grandfather, Nurran, and Jarahad. Unlike the first time, almost every city inhabitant was reunited under a few palm trees. Talgel stood a safe distance and tapped her red slippers repeatedly.

Bemused, Henrietta patted her shoulder. "You should have heeded my suggestion to visit the beach earlier. Now that Tioja is wearing suitable robes that accommodate his new wings, he can summon his phantom beast without distractions. I can't wait to see it!"

"I am not annoyed about standing too far away; I am worried about the bystanders. Nobody knows what Tioja's phantom beast does, and everyone is stupidly standing right in front of him, making drooling noises like rabid dogs. It's annoying."

"Ha! You're just jealous you haven't seen a vision that features Tioja's… wait, he's summoning his beast!"

Just like the other day, Talgel was no longer paying any attention. The reptilian demon stood nearby. Instead of addressing her with its usual quips, a deep crevice formed where Talgel was sucked inside. A primal feeling of terror enveloped the deepest recesses of her mind that far surpassed the usually terrible fortunes she had seen in the past. If the prior master vision was seductive by its overreaching power on its own, this even greater vision surpassed it tenfold, and Talgel soon knew why. Alone in the dark, she regained her eyesight and saw many gold leylines shoot in varying directions. Realizing these were her future possibilities, she chose a random line and floated into a seemingly endless hall of mirrors that showed windows in the days ahead. The visions on this path were most mundane: walking in the desert alongside Henrietta and inhabitants of Almjarhad mulling about. The mirrors that reflected this future continued for a long time until Talgel stopped with a sigh. "This future will never happen. The leyline is too long."

Flustered, Talgel soon returned to her launching point and chose another path. Much to her chagrin, this line abruptly ended when she was in Jarahad's bed. For a moment, her heart thumped with anticipation. Unlike her typical visions, this one didn't grant her the chance to feel the pleasure of reaching ecstasy as Jarahad pounded her naked body. Initially envious of her doppelgänger, Talgel soon realized there was a reason the leyline ended at this scene. For some odd reason, as Jarahad was reaching the most incredible heights of pleasure, his hands clenched on the other Talgel's neck and squeezed hard. Talgel stifled a whimper upon seeing the projection of herself scratch and prod for Jarahad's release until she perished from suffocation the instant Jarahad reached orgasm. It didn't take Talgel long to realize while it was a grandiose way to die, this would not be her future either. And so, she returned to the vantage point once again.

On this third try, the reptilian demon was awaiting. "You can continue traveling the leylines all you want until you grow tired of seeing this house of lies."

"You promised me a vision that would surpass the first one that involved me. So far, I feel cheated."

"Given your mana is running short, let me take you to one future that might pique your interest."

A cold, firm hand gripped her unwitting wrist and yanked her in another direction. In this future, Talgel abandoned Almjarhad. The demon was clearly mocking her pride.

"This is the stupidest thing you have ever done for me. Why would you want me to see this false future where I wander in the desert all alone without being able to see anything?" Talgel protested.

"I would guide your way and for an excellent purpose."

The desert soon became replaced by greener vegetation until they reached a nondescript field with scant trees. Talgel initially thought she was all alone until the soft whimpering behind a flock of trees enticed her to approach it. Hiding behind the trunks was a male halfling of frail build, towering height, and glowing white tattoos covered his bare chest. There wasn't a harlequin sword in the initiated halfling's possession. A part of Talgel wanted the demon to explain the purpose of this vision, but he remained tight-lipped. Despite appearing uninjured, the man's huddled body suggested he seemed terrified of the sunlight. A soft voice made her freeze. "Mother, I can see your demon. He's terrifying, isn't he?" Mother, are you there?"

As the man lifted his face, Talgel screeched upon seeing a stranger that looked a lot like herself. His crimson eyes were beckoning. If seeing this man wasn't terrifying enough, his trembling hand caressed her face, and she saw yet another vision, much worse than any other she had ever seen.

The demon was cackling nonstop as Talgel gawked at the sight of her body with restored eyesight and dressed in elegant ceremonial robes. She greeted the same man from a while ago in a dark throne room. This Talgel looked much older than her current self. Standing on the sidelines was a myriad of the halflings that joined Hurrujat's clan and the pureblood elves of Almjarhad.

The strange halfling man knelt in her presence with great humility… alongside a devout Jarahad who wore elegant armor. The man spoke once again in perfect Elvish. "Your eminence, I have returned from my voyage and have brought a little gift."

The instant he placed a small white box imbued with the twin griffin insignia in front of her feet, Talgel rushed past Jarahad, removed the top, and gloated as she yanked Salman's severed head high into the air as everyone in the throne room cheered.

"The Elf King is dead! The Elf King is dead! Long live Lord Talgel, ruler of Murdorhiolan!"

"Thank you, Lord Elias, my beautiful son. You have finally exacted revenge for the murder of our people."

"Long live Lord Elias, slayer of kings!"

Talgel soon understood the purpose of this vision and cowered behind the demon. She would never grant it any modicum of respect under normal circumstances. Still, the sight of this impossible future was so sinister that even she had a hard time believing anyone could dream it.

Not that the demon showed any offense as this vision dissipated into smoke. "In case you are wondering, Jarahad isn't Elias's father. If you visit the harlequin city, you will inevitably marry the right man."

Taken aback by this odd confession, Talgel lifted her head. "I could love no one else. Perhaps I only make Jarahad suffer, but my heart belongs to him."

"Foolish mortal. Since when do harlequins marry for love?"

And then it all made sense, and laughter escaped her lips. "You're telling me I will marry Hurrujat's child and give birth to a halfling capable of murdering the Elf King?! Are you out of your mind?!"

The demon's sharp black teeth glistened in this dark enclave from amusement. "I told you this was the best vision you will ever see in your lifetime. As long as you leave Almjarhad before the first trouble mage arrives, you still have a chance of birthing Elias and claiming your long-held revenge. The choice is yours."

As the demon slithered away and darkness enveloped Talgel again, she became overwhelmed by an irrational sense of fear for unknown reasons. Screams and the sound of people running in every direction didn't concern Talgel. It was the strange magic that lurched from her shadow, a power so uncontrollable that it could rip her apart without a second thought.

"Watch out, your ladyship!" Henrietta grabbed her in the nick of time, batted her wings, and flew back to safety.

"What's going on, Henrietta?!"

"No time to waste! I can feel strange sorcery coming from Tioja! Lord Jarahad has stayed behind to subdue him before he kills anyone."

And then reality hit Talgel very hard once again: Tioja was the Cursed One, and he had sealed the future the demon wanted from the beginning in stone.

CHAPTER 27 ♦ JAMARNID

Jamarnid spent all afternoon keeping a close watch on the young halfling as he rested in his bedroom. Conscious of the need to stop Tioja without causing severe injury, Jarahad sliced a coconut with magic. The coconut hit Tioja's skull, which only required a few stitches after knocking him unconscious. Jarahad had to assuage the city's inhabitants for the better portion of the day. It riled Jamarnid to no end the lengths his son would take to protect this accursed monstrosity.

Jamad stumbled inside Tioja's bedroom with a bottle of strong liquor in one hand while wearing a dirty beige shirt covered in vomit. Jamarnid couldn't have expected less from the poor elf. "Fate has been unkind to you, dear Jamad. I apologize for not stopping Jarahad from training your son before it was too late."

"Jamen did this! He listened to Talgel's prediction and enticed my son to summon his beast! You should punish her!"

"What's the point? Talgel will feign ignorance of the consequences of her actions, and my son will defend her to the bitter end. Even Lord Sharad will side with them because he has a crush on her."

"Set me free from my sentence! Let my voice be heard and enact my revenge on Talgel for taking Hamara away from me!"

"I wish I could. Only Lord Sharad can liberate you. I am powerless to oppose." Jamarnid's hands twitched in an automatic spasm, forcing him to shut his eyes. Even though this chronic affliction seldom occurred, Jamarnid always experienced painful electric jolts on his oversensitive fingers.

As usual, Jamad didn't come to his aid, preferring to gulp even more alcohol as his favorite solution to ease every woe. Jamad offered one last look at Tioja, who remained in the deep bliss of unconsciousness. With a shake of disapproval, he stormed outside.

Once the pain subsided and Jamarnid could regain control of his inner thoughts, he concluded Jamad had just severed his final emotional link to the wife that would never return. If Jamad disowned his son, evicting him from the city would be much easier.

Jarahad soon returned and sat by Tioja's side, accompanied by a deathly silence that lasted hours. The instant Tioja's reddish-green eyes fluttered open, Jamarnid's hair stood on end, and he controlled the urge to summon his phantom beast to kill the miserable creature.

Tioja became jostled by the churning agony of a blood attack which required Jarahad to fetch a venomous snake Henrietta had placed in a basket earlier in the day. Jamarnid's anger increased a notch upon seeing Jarahad perform a harlequin prayer as his sword beheaded the creature, and he filled a cup with blood. "Please drink some blood, dear Tio, before you faint."

With trembling fear, the pitiful child slurped the cup's contents and heaved until the attack receded.

Feeling fed up, Jamarnid couldn't take it anymore. "Blubbery misfit creature that should never have been born."

Jarahad growled as he turned around. "Please stop it, father. What happened today was merely an accident. It could have happened to anyone."

"Vile creatures that ruined our clan. They have infected our citizens with their filth. My existence has befallen from grace for nothing! Nothing!"

Jarahad sighed at his father's endless nonsense and smiled at an increasingly confused Tioja.

"Why is Lord Jamarnid in my house?"

Jamarnid growled from Tioja's perceived rudeness. "As an honorable Äimite guard, I have to ensure that you don't murder the last true members of my clan."

"Stop it, father!" A growl escaped Jarahad's lips as he tried to divert the topic before angering his father further. Feeling satisfied, Jarahad focused on Tioja. "Before I explain anything, could you please tell me what happened when you summoned your Lehart earlier today?"

Tioja set the bowl beside his flatbed and thought. "It was bizarre. The second I finished the summoning spell, it's like I could feel everything around me."

"Could you explain further?"

"I could see the waves, the trees, and all of you, but I didn't see things in the normal sense." Tioja's face became increasingly strained as he focused. "It's like I could see everyone from the viewpoint of their shadow, my Lord. Something in the back of my head taunted me to rip them apart."

"I knew it!" Jamarnid pounded his badly mutilated right fist against the armrest of his wheelchair and emitted faint grunts of pain.

Jarahad's face became increasingly grave, and he stared at his father. "The seer was right. Tioja is the one."

"The mortal that will kill his clan with his vile demonic sorcery!"

Tioja's eyes shot open in remembrance. "Those explosions that caused everyone to run in fear... Did I cause them?"

Unlike Jamarnid's relentless anger, Jarahad tried to exude unwarranted compassion. "Please don't feel guilty, Tioja. Fortunately, nobody was seriously hurt. Now that we know the abilities of your phantom beast, I promise I'll train you to master the ability as well as I can."

"Expel him from the clan, Jarahad! He's too dangerous to live among us!"

***

When Tioja first confirmed their suspicions he was the Cursed One, a nasty argument ensued that only ended when Jarahad marched outside in a horrible mood.

After watching Tioja's relentless whimpering until he fell asleep, Jamarnid felt mildly at ease the pest wasn't an imminent threat for now and returned home.

The following day, Jamarnid's wheelchair was being pushed through the circular ramps of his palace. Guards told him Jarahad brought the monstrosity into his castle covered in a heap of blood. He had a hard time controlling the urge to murder his son.

Jamarnid's wheelchair was pushed towards a dormitory, and he spotted Jarahad marching back and forth through the hallways as the echo of Tioja's shrill screams was audible inside. "Explain why you brought that disgusting thing into my home!"

Jarahad lifted his head and remained a safe distance from his father. "Something is wrong with Tioja."

"Yes, he is the Cursed One!"

"Father, he's just a child and only needs help."

"Bollocks! Why is he screaming anyway? Are your men torturing him?"

"No... Tioja was starting to shed in the middle of the badlands in broad daylight. His relative Nurran told me it happened abruptly, without warning."

"What? And you stupidly brought him inside of my castle to kill Sharad?"

"Father, are you even listening to the poison that spews from your mouth? Tioja is shedding his skin before it was supposed to happen. I think it has something to do with his strange wings, and I ordered my men to have them severed. With all the blood he has lost today, he will not have enough mana to summon his beast. You are overreacting like usual."

An adamant Jamarnid stared at the servant assigned to care for him today. "Take me inside. I want to confirm my son's nonsense." Much to Jamarnid's dismay, he confirmed the veracity of Jarahad's story. They strapped a screaming Tioja to a stone bed as two halflings sliced off rotten flesh from his skin. Jamarnid shut his eyes and averted his gaze. "Take me back to my office."

A few weeks passed, and Tioja's skin had regrown enough to be allowed to walk outside his guestroom with bandages that covered his still growing new pair of eyes. Jamarnid kept a constant close watch on the poor halfling's movements and soon realized whenever Tioja felt sunlight on his healed skin, he huddled against the wall out of a sense of self-preservation for unexplained reasons. Whenever someone coaxed the troubled halfling to go outside, they were met with shoving, pulling, and relentless wails until they released Tioja so he could rush back to safety.

Feeling fed up with his unwanted guest, Jamarnid ordered his son to visit his office at once. "Well? Have you given up and evicted the Cursed One?"

"Absolutely not! I have already spoken to Lord Sharad, who has sided with me. I will train Tioja so that he learns how to control his gift before you do something stupid, like assassinating him."

"How dare you disobey my orders by feeding lies into our leader! Curse you!"

"Father, I beg of you to give me a chance. Expelling a child who has harmed no one is ludicrous, and I will prove you wrong!" As Jarahad stormed outside, Jamarnid heaved with seething hatred.

"If you don't believe in yourself, you will never master your demonic beast."

Tioja shook his head upon recalling Jarahad's warning. It had been three months, and despite Jarahad's everlasting patience and guidance, he was still incapable of taking his mind away from those horrifying thoughts.

Frustrated after yet another failed evening fencing lesson where Tioja spent most of his time sniveling in front of Jarahad, Tioja ran towards the outskirts to wallow in self-pity. The tired gait of stuttered footsteps prompted the elf to lift his head and gasp at the sight. "Who goes there?!"

"I am not your enemy, little Tio." The voice was profound yet feminine with a raspy quality that hinted at exhaustion. As the footsteps became more audible, a medium-height halfling met Tioja with a bright red cotton dress that reached her ankles, a series of leather belts, and her grey hair in two pigtails equally covered by colorful beads. Talgel was wearing her mask as she stared at him with impassive indifference. On this occasion, Talgel was not being accompanied by Henrietta.

Out of a sense of respect for the seer, Tioja felt compelled to slide to the side, and Talgel sat on the boulder as he focused on the errant clouds in the dark sky.

"Cursed One."

"How dare you call me that?! Everyone hates me! You did it!"

A cruel grin invaded Talgel's lips from the blight. "I was certainly not lying. You are born with a curse."

"Nonsense! You see the future!" And then a sense of realization hit the halfling that made him whimper. "You knew this would happen to me, yet you still encouraged me to learn sorcery. I hate you!"

It was then Talgel's turn to shake her head, and her shoulders lurched in defeat. "I… Look, I knew a halfling of the clan was going to summon a demonic beast that was imbued with a dangerous curse. My sorcery told me this would happen, whether I wanted to stop it or not. I sped up the inevitable because the Cursed One must abandon the clan at all costs."

"You're lying!"

Birds nestled on top of the olive tree fluttered away as Tioja slapped Talgel in fitful rage. She unfastened the ribbons to remove her mask. There were no hints that Talgel felt offended by Tioja's act of violence as she rubbed her swollen left cheek. "This will be the last time we will ever speak to each other, Cursed One. Perhaps you are angry at me, and I know you will not forgive me. I can offer you a hint of insight about your future, and I hope you will let me explain."

Ashamed, Tioja turned his head away as tears invaded his eyelids that freely flowed to the ground. "So selfish. You knew a clan member was cursed, and you encouraged me to learn sorcery for your purposes. Lord Jamarnid wants me dead, my father has disowned me for no reason, the clan almost unanimously wants to drive me away, and my mother…."

"Hamara will be your salvation."

A gasp escaped Tioja's lips. "My mother? Is she well?"

Smiling never came easily to Talgel. She lost part of her humanity the fateful day she summoned her sorcery at the expense of her eyes. Tioja glimpsed her slightly uneven teeth with an imperceptible hint of sharp molars, thin yet luscious dark pink lips, and a strange wholesomeness on her face as the smile reached her lower eyelids. "There is something you must do at all costs, Cursed One. This is a decision only you can make. I will tell you your fortune as long as you promise something."

Tioja averted his gaze from the warning. He couldn't determine if it was because of the shame or the sense of dread that Talgel's prediction had an ulterior motive. "I will never return to Almjarhad, will I?"

"Perhaps you will return. I couldn't care less if you do, and I can guarantee nobody will miss you."

Tioja shut his eyes and clawed at his thighs. "I understand. You don't have to tell me anything else. I will leave tomorrow."

"Thank you for following my suggestion. Visit the third resting pagoda on the trade route heading north with any belongings you can fetch from the castle and stay there. Don't even bother speaking to Jarahad. He will only be a hindrance and ruin everything like usual. The trip will be long, so bring some nonperishable food and sufficient water. You won't need any weapons or money."

"Huh?" The increasing vagueness from Talgel was enticing Tioja's curiosity more than anything else. Before he could protest, Talgel stood up and gave her back to him as she fastened the ceramic mask. "This is our goodbye. Good luck and be kind to him. You will know what I mean when the time comes." As perpetually cold as Talgel was vague, she soon drifted away from Tioja's life with as much mystery as the first day she spoke to him.

Tioja didn't know what to think as the clouds drifted away, granting him the chance to see a few stars in the sky. Was this the last time he would see Almjarhad? Was he indeed the Cursed One, or was Talgel planning on using him? Perhaps Tioja would never know those answers, so it no longer mattered. If his destiny was to wander the world and be feared by everyone, he would prove he was indeed a monster.

The unconscious swallowing of saliva halted Tioja at the last minute. Could he accept his fate and become evil? After thinking about Talgel's words for a while, Tioja reached a harrowing conclusion. The seer was never wrong, and if his destiny was to leave the city, he would always hold Almjarhad dear to his heart. It was the least he could do.

With a hurried pace, Tioja took advantage of the darkness of the moonless evening and soon reached Almjarhad Castle without bumping into anyone. The security guards stared at him with lifted spears in the constant fear that Tioja would summon sorcery. Tioja couldn't care less at this point. The sooner he fetched his belongings, the easier it would be to leave without enduring the painful process of saying goodbye. Reaching his bedroom was simple enough. As usual, guards had ransacked the room under Jamarnid's command in the lookouts for weapons, which made Tioja waste precious minutes locating any clothes he could find.

There was nothing edible in his room. After packing an oiled raincoat, Tioja reached the desk and grabbed a pen. His trembling hand filled the quiver with ink as he garnered his thoughts. After pondering for a moment, Tioja set the pen aside and shook his head. If Talgel wanted him to leave, she would undoubtedly use her influence to ensure a search party never left the city to find him, so he didn't need to write a note. After staring at his room one final time, Tioja descended to the first floor and reached the pantry. Tioja lifted a candle he ignited with a match, and the small storage room became invaded by a warm light. He then filled his travel sack with a few hard loaves of bread, dehydrated vegetables, spices, and salt. His eyes set on a bottle of blood wine. Given the trip would be long, it made sense to grab one. Jarahad would understand and forgive him.

With a whiff of air, Tioja set the candle on the floor. He then continued pacing through the aisles until he bumped into the one person he tried to avoid at all costs. "Jarahad!"

Jarahad was wearing sleeping robes as he stared at him with a tint of disdain on his face. "You're leaving, aren't you?"

"I…" Jarahad's gaze concerned Tioja initially, but it wasn't because of mockery or malice. His eyes reflected a sense of resignation instead. "You couldn't save me, my Lord. I thank you for being the only person in Almjarhad that believes in me, but I am weak and unfit to remain here."

"I failed you."

For a brief instant, Tioja lifted his head and saw the sense of weariness in Jarahad's gaze. "Thank you for everything, my Lord, and forgive me. I will miss you." With a heavy heart, Tioja bowed at his leader with relentless politeness and ran off as fast as his tiny legs could travel before he regretted this decision forever. As expected, nobody chased after him. After filling his water skin from the wells, Tioja soon reached the third pagoda upon the first rays of sunlight on the horizon. With increased sunlight, Tioja breathed more heavily and stared in every direction. He felt a strange urge to rip the wooden structure and rushed off to the sand and trembled relentlessly. "Why??!!"

"Why what?"

The voice was sugary and soothing. Knowing an innocent was nearby, Tioja huddled in a fetal position. "Go away! I am dangerous! Please run for your life!"

Instead of hearing footsteps rushing off, a pair of soft arms embraced him. Tioja was bombarded by a poignant scent of cinnamon and blood intertwined with something closer to his heart. He lifted his head and saw Hamara smiling at him. "Mother!"

Among all the strange things Talgel had said or done, Tioja would have never believed her if she told him he would greet his mother. Feeling bombarded by a flurry of conflicting emotions, all he wanted to do was hug the elf he missed so dearly and promised he would never let go.

CHAPTER 29 ◆ JARAHAD

This had never happened before. He was furious. It was a feeling Jarahad seldom felt during his upbringing alongside Jamarnid or the hopeless battles to defend Orsenmuray and the three-year trek in the desert. And yet the instant he felt compelled to run after Tioja to force him to stay, Talgel stood in the way while pushing Jamarnid's wheelchair. Even more damning was that Jarahad's father still wore the same robes from earlier that day.

"You did this. You drove him away!"

Jamarnid grinned with a strange sense of satisfaction, and his mutilated hands rubbed both palms eagerly. "Yes, our mongrel seer has finally proven her worth by helping us pinpoint Tioja's true identity and ensuring he will never bother us again."

Treason was not a word Jarahad would willingly use against any law-abiding citizen. Such an inflated sense of satisfaction on Jamarnid's face only angered him more. "I was training him!"

Talgel laughed at once as she played with her hair. "Tioja only became increasingly self-conscious, making his beast even more unstable. It would have only been a matter of time before he killed someone. Is that what you wanted? To kill the last remaining members of Almjarhad to satisfy your ridiculous dream of keeping the clan united?"

"Hogwash!"

Jamarnid growled at once. "Talgel warned us ahead of time. As usual, you didn't heed her warnings and only made things worse for everyone. You are lucky I will forgive this one mistake and let you continue ruling my clan. Don't forget that, son."

Jarahad couldn't believe it. Talgel and Jamarnid hated each other, yet both purposely waited to see Tioja's departure. Offended by such an act of betrayal, Jarahad punched the wall with his clenched fist. "Dammit! You didn't give me a chance! Tioja deserved better!"

Talgel shook her head. "Tioja was wise to leave before he killed an innocent. I feel sorry for him. But I must make some sacrifices to keep the clan safe. You said goodbye to him, and he appreciates it. Don't make things any harder for everyone by going after him."

Jarahad suspected Talgel was up to something and lifted his head. "Where will he go? How will he survive out there? He has nobody!"

Jamarnid cleared his throat. "As long as he stays away from here, Tioja isn't our problem. It is a shame that Talgel could not pinpoint the identity of the Cursed One beforehand. Or else I would have forbidden him from smoking the potion in Soremin's temple. For that, I offer a heartfelt apology. A life of mediocrity would be better than being a dangerous living weapon. If he had lived in the kingdom, the Äimite guard would have recruited him and attempted to salvage any lingering benefits of his sorcery. As things are, I hope Tioja dies from exposure in the desert to finish with his suffering."

"How could you say that?! Dammit with you! He was just a child!" Desperate to appease his guilt, Jarahad rushed outside. He reached his bedroom and stared at his window, hoping to glimpse the elf. Much to his chagrin, Tioja was gone.

"It is useless." Henrietta entered his room while dressed in a somber black travel robe. "In case you are wondering, Talgel told me he will be safe for the time being."

Jarahad sighed in anxious relief. "I failed him. I was very close to helping him overcome his mental block. It's just so frustrating!"

Henrietta shook her head and smiled even further. "You are a kind leader. I am certain Tioja will always be thankful for your friendship. Stop taking everything seriously and continue working hard to bring wealth to our clan."

"Our clan. It feels strange when you say it. Aren't you ready to leave this place and return home?"

Henrietta sighed as she watched the first traces of sunlight clamoring to bathe the landscape. "Talgel told me to stay for a while longer."

"Foolish harlequin! There is no reason for you to stay. Why waste your youth in these lands? Someone as special as you… I…"

It was Henrietta's turn to be headstrong during these moments of despair. The softness of her hands embracing Jarahad was reminiscent of the moments Chandrice held him as an infant. He almost wanted to return her affection until he shook his head with terse stoicism. "Has Talgel discovered your presence is pivotal to a future event?"

"She told me my presence was unneeded, but I was welcome to make a choice. And I wish to stay here. Talgel tries to deny her feelings of gratitude for my company. We all know those are lies. I think I will remain until she accepts her handicap and corresponds to your love, which is what we all wanted from the start."

Jarahad stepped away with a sigh. "Perhaps I have to stop trying to control everything. Soremin and Talgel always enjoy berating me. I hope Tioja finds inner peace. If he could master his sorcery with a talented teacher, even better. You go back to Talgel and ensure she stays out of trouble. It is frightening to see Talgel and my father teaming up for once. I am unsure I could get used to seeing them plotting against me."

Henrietta chuckled with a jovialness that could warm even the coldest hearts. "Try to rest and let Jamarnid rule the clan for a day. Don't let Tioja's failure weigh on you. Maybe you should visit Jamad."

Jarahad lifted an eyebrow in disbelief. "You truly think Jamad would run off to join his son?"

"I sincerely doubt it. However, Jamad is still your friend. Be kind to him. You may never know when it will be the last time you see someone. Make every single day matter."

As Jarahad watched the kind and sagacious woman strut away, he wondered if Talgel was pulling the strings to her benefit. Whatever the purpose, he would follow his friend's suggestion. Jarahad then realized he hadn't slept and plopped on his bed. There would be plenty of time to inform the citizens regarding Tioja's unexpected departure. Whether anyone cared about his absence, at least he attempted to show concern for his wellbeing. Hopefully, Tioja will forgive everyone and come back.

CHAPTER 30 ♦ JAMARNID

It was strange to reach a common ground with Talgel. If anyone had told Jamarnid that he considered her to be a valuable confidant in the internal affairs of the clan, he would have accused the whistleblower of malice or hearsay. Soremin would have promptly punished the culprit under his command with a series of canings, or worse, for suggesting such a disparate lie.

And here he was, drinking tea late at night with one of the most significant sources of annoyances in his honorless life in exile. Worse, Talgel exerted an impressive amount of self-control over her blindness by feeding him tea with such a commanding precision. He soon realized something was up. "You saw this happen, didn't you?"

Talgel seemed rather indifferent as she sat in her chair. "You are correct. I still think we should celebrate the occasion. The Cursed One is gone with no bloodshed."

Jamarnid seemed reasonably convinced as he stretched his arms. "Will he ever return and cause havoc?"

"Only Tioja can know. He has the freedom to choose."

"Forbid his return if that ever happens. As your clan leader, you must obey my commands."

Talgel seemed even more aloof than usual as a rogue tear fell from the ceramic mask she pitifully tried to cleanse with a napkin. "I will try within my capabilities."

"You know where he is going."

"In case you are wondering, Tioja's safety will be guaranteed for the time being. He will live in a place where his sorcery will not pose a threat to anyone."

"You didn't answer my question."

"Give the child the chance to live the future for himself. He might even feel happy he fled after the scorn I caused."

"I couldn't care less if he lived or not, as long as he doesn't take vengeance on us with his dangerous sorcery."

A vicious grin etched on Talgel's mouth as she sipped some tea. "You will regret saying that someday."

"What do you mean?"

"Nevermind. I sent Henrietta to speak to your son. You must cover for him tomorrow while he speaks to Jamad privately."

"That sounds reasonable. Jamad has only suffered ongoing tragedies ever since I met him. His loved ones have constantly betrayed him, and I don't have any high hopes he will overcome Hamara's vile act of treason."

"We can both agree they will not reconcile. At least Jamad can still rely on Jarahad and the other pureblood elves."

"I doubt he will ever forgive Jamen after this."

"For now. Give Jamad time to heal from the loss of his wife and son. Perhaps even invite him for tea sometime."

"We have reached a sort of impasse in our strained relationship. Talgel, please tell me: what is your ulterior motive for organizing all of this?"

"What do you mean?"

In that instant, Jamarnid pressed Talgel's wrist as best as his hands could, causing her to yelp. Despite being unable to move his fingers, Jamarnid's wrists were still strong from constant rehabilitation exercises. "Don't act surprised. You already told me you saw this conversation some time ago. Therefore, you know I will not kill or incarcerate you. One thing is certain: you always inform us about future events for a reason."

Seeing the anguish invading the woman's mouth that the vacant expression of her mask couldn't hide filled Jamarnid's cruel heart with a sense of pleasure he seldom felt. Not even when he tortured prisoners as a guard felt so satisfying. "You try to hide the truth of your monstrous true nature with that stupid mask, and my son is too good-natured to realize something is wrong. As an Äimite guard, my superiors have trained me to identify signs of deceit. I always knew you became close to my dear Jarahad so that you could discard him once you became bored. Tell me, why did you reject his hand in marriage? Was it a harlequin lover?" Talgel's feeble attempts to release herself from his increasingly firm grasp only pleased him even more. "No, a creature like you could never love someone. For a while, I assumed you wanted to marry Hurrujat for power until you pulled your strings and broke the clan in half. I feel like there is a reason you do these things. Now that I think of it, the plan is too ridiculously sinister for a simple mind like Jarahad to understand. You just want to see the world burn for your pleasure. Do you enjoy causing misery? Does it compensate for the eyes you lost?"

"You will not die by Salman's hand but by your own!"

In that instant, the vertical elliptical pupils adorning Jamarnid's dark green eyes constricted, and his grip loosened enough for Talgel to pull her hand away. "What did you say, you ungrateful twerp? Do you truly believe someone as proud as me would dare stoop to the lowest dishonor by committing suicide? When the clan is finally attaining self-sufficiency? No, I will not fall into your mind games."

"You're wrong! Salman will never give you the beheading you always yearned for. Knowing this will only fill your miserable life with suffering in self-hatred until the last thing tying you to this world vanishes forever. I have seen your future, and it makes me laugh!"

"You bitch!" In the heat of the moment, Jamarnid pounced on the woman, who cleverly dodged the attack. A cumbersome fall hampered the moment of weightlessness while the stumps of his legs soon hit the ground. Under a feeble attempt to hold on to the chair with his forearms, Jamarnid's short stature couldn't hold on to the added weight, and he collapsed to the stone ground while the chair fell on top. After rolling to the side and shoving the chair away with his stumps, he spotted Talgel strutting off. "Come back here! We haven't finished yet!"

But Talgel didn't stop as she paced outside. Expecting a snide remark, the confounding sense of doubt met Jamarnid when Talgel left him alone.

***

The following morning, Jamarnid remained so confused by his puzzling argument with Talgel that he canceled all official meetings. Rumors had already spread like wildfire the Cursed One had finally left the city. It wasn't in Jamarnid's interests to let gossip continue because it could affect Jarahad's position as the interim ruler. However, his mind was too busy thinking about Talgel's haunting warning. This matter was necessary, and he needed to vent his frustration on someone.

Like always, Soremin entered his room with a carefree attitude and sat down. He opted to cut his chestnut wavy hair, which made him look so different that Jamarnid doubted he was seeing his friend for a brief instant. "Why did you cut your hair? Are you a ghost?"

Soremin shook his head rather nonchalantly. "Talgel told me to cut my hair the day after she warned you about the Cursed One."

"Why would you obey that useless witch?"

"As proof of my loyalty to her. She told me things, Jamarnid. Personal things about my future I would tell no one unless I had no other choice. Her sorcery is powerful, absurdly so. It is evil, and it causes me great concern. I just feel glad she has the common sense of retaining things and only confesses events that will not be altered. She gave me a test that day: when the Cursed One left, I had to choose to either believe her stories or denounce her predictions depending on what I did to my hair. She hasn't told me why this was important. If I cut my hair, it meant I believed in her and knew she had the best intentions of the clan."

"I couldn't care less what you choose to do to your hair, but she lies! She says that I will die by suicide! You can't believe her!"

In that instant, Soremin's sea-green eyes became cold as he stared at his friend's angry face with a sense of chilling tranquility; it made even an elf as hardened as Jamarnid pause in the last instant. "Talgel told me you would react this exact way several years ago, along with some vague remarks regarding my death. I will die in exile, executed by an Äimite guard during a surprise siege."

"Impossible!"

"I found it amusing more than anything else. How is it possible that a person could see such grim details about the fates of others without going insane? If my fate is to die in exile, I shall work within every extent of my being towards the clan's salvation. You don't have to love her as a person. All you need to do is believe in her predictions. She is never wrong."

Hearing the strange warning from his most trustworthy ally felt concerning. How could it be possible Talgel won Soremin's loyalty by telling him a few grim details that were likely false? Jamarnid shook his head in disbelief. "How did she do it? Win you over?"

Soremin sighed as his hands caressed his short hair. "Talgel told me to remain silent for now. Something is going to happen to the clan soon. She needs to continue using her beast to pinpoint the puzzle together. I just know my future prediction is true, and it fills me with great shame."

"Greater shame than killing Äimite guards and running off to exile to ally with harlequins?"

"I understand why you have a poor opinion of their kind, and I respect your decision because Chandrice lied to you. My students have proven there is still hope the harlequins will come to our aid, and we should keep our options open. Talgel caused a series of events that split the clans apart for an ulterior motive. Tioja is going to live with them, you know."

"What?! The cursed child is going to live with those demons?! Why?!"

"This was his fate. Perhaps living underground will be good for him. I was getting increasingly concerned he would end up insane if he continued to hide in my temple when it was the middle of the day. I hope he finds the salvation we couldn't give him."

Jamarnid had little choice but to accept Soremin's point of view. Despite being unable to tolerate Talgel's behavior, the certainty in Soremin's behavior meant there must have been some truth to her warning. Was he going to commit suicide someday?

Darkness. This was her realm. Spacious and welcoming of her deepest thoughts, Talgel wished she could stay in this place as she remembered Tioja's leyline stretching into endless infinity. Tioja was bound to feel the magnetic pull of the Great One that would smother him with warmth and later drive him away.

Like the planet that could always rely on the moon for its only company, Tioja would feel the attraction of the Great One's tides. More than a harbinger of destruction, it was an ever-changing source of change. Talgel's bare feet were long ago covered by the rising tide as the waves battered back and forth. She didn't quite know why she was standing alone on the beach this evening. Her mind must have entered a daze after she left Jamarnid to whimper in self-defeat a while ago.

Yes, the seed of self-doubt she planted into Jamarnid's mind would need watering. As an immortal, Jamarnid had plenty of centuries to wait for Salman's punishment until weariness claimed his last inch of sanity. Denial would soon wither into acceptance, followed by his demise. Knowing she would no longer be around to witness his death was her only regret.

As her feet sunk even deeper into the soft sand, Talgel felt the presence that became her closest accomplice and worst enemy at the same time. She was not using enough mana to summon her visions, but the being was there.

The crashing of the waves hitting against the dock seemed like an afterthought compared to the demon's voice. "You can feel him too."

"The Great One? He is just a child."

"For now. Ever since you saw him lurking in Hurrujat's future, you could feel the intensity of his power. Both of you are drawn to each other, whether you like it or not."

"You want me to marry him, so that our son Elias can kill the Elf King."

"Contrary to your suspicions, I couldn't care less if you do. I only want the Great One to awaken his beast."

"What do you care whether that halfling learns magic?"

An icy hand caressed Talgel's hair, covering her skin with goosebumps. "Did you know the demonic beast your kind summons is a manifestation of your innermost unfulfilled desires?"

"Huh? Why would I want to become blind and tolerate your relentless company?"

Now Talgel could feel the sharp claws tickling her skin. Not enough to cause pain, just to serve as a reminder of the bearer's warning. "Your blindness is a secondary defect. Every beast takes something away from the summoner; it's the price you must pay to forge a soul bond."

"So?"

"In your case, you wanted to know what would happen if you married Jarahad. Think about it. Remember the day you kissed him for the first time, you wanted to confirm your Happily Ever After. And I gave you a source of absolute truth. In Tioja's case, he strives for the power of absolute destruction. The elves don't understand his gift, but you know the harlequins will welcome him with open arms. His desire to be accepted for the monster he truly is will be what forever bonds him to the Great One."

"The Great One… his power…."

"Yes, his charisma can pull you in with a relentless force and never let go. I found it touching you told Tioja to make you a promise before he left."

"Harrumph! The wallop departed without asking what I wanted from him."

"Give him time. It may take a year or twenty, but Tioja will feel the primal urge to return to your side. I can't wait to see his expression when he meets me."

Surprised by the demon's foresight, Talgel was about to inquire about its sinister plans when she heard Henrietta's voice in the distance.

"Your ladyship! Why are you standing there all alone? Get out before you end up sucked into the sea!"

With a heavy heart, Talgel's hands folded her soaked dress and walked toward Henrietta's voice. For the first time in her life, Talgel felt glad to be bonded to the demon. No matter what happened, she would wait for Tioja's return and deliver her message.

AN OMINOUS BOOK SERIES

1. An Ominous Book
2. Separation
3. Exile
4. Diaspora
5. A Calamity
6. Quandary
7. Harlequins
8. Mortality (coming soon!)

FRAGMENTED FATES DUOLOGY

1. Fragmented Fates
2. Savior on the zenith